SHADOW
IN THE
MIRROR

To Bill
God Bless

[signature]

SHADOW
IN THE
MIRROR

A DELE H EWETT V EAL

SHADOW IN THE MIRROR

iUniverse books may be ordered through booksellers or by contacting:

iUniverse
1663 Liberty Drive
Bloomington, IN 47403
www.iuniverse.com
1-800-Authors (1-800-288-4677)

Because of the dynamic nature of the Internet, any web addresses or links contained in this book may have changed since publication and may no longer be valid. The views expressed in this work are solely those of the author and do not necessarily reflect the views of the publisher, and the publisher hereby disclaims any responsibility for them.

Any people depicted in stock imagery provided by Thinkstock are models, and such images are being used for illustrative purposes only.
Certain stock imagery © Thinkstock.

ISBN: 978-1-4917-6487-9 (sc)
ISBN: 978-1-4917-6486-2 (e)

Library of Congress Control Number: 2015905278

Print information available on the last page.

iUniverse rev. date: 05/13/2015

Acknowledgements

First I want to thank God. He is the reason I wake up in the morning and he guides me through all of my ventures. He encourages me to move beyond my comfort zone and rise above my present accomplishments to reach my untapped potential. Thank you, my dear Lord, for the talent that I refuse to hide under a bushel, but continue to let it shine for the world to see because through it, you receive glory.

Thank you, John. My wonderful husband, who has never complained about the late nights or early mornings, I spent writing instead of sleeping Thank you for being the first reader of my manuscript and listening to new paragraphs written and re-written. Thank you for your honesty and patience, but most of all thank you for a love beyond what I could have ever imagined for myself. In everything I have accomplished in life, I believe, marrying you, John Veal, was one of my grandest accomplishments of all.

Thank you to my children who I have watched grow into amazing role models for their own children. Dwight Jr., Treshele, and Yvonne, you were the first ones, for the lack of better words; you were the Guinea pigs for my writing and storytelling. You listened to every piece of poetry, every story, and every song I sang and even shared them with your individual children. A mother knows she's done something right when she hears her own words come back to her through her offspring. It's amazing to watch you live successful lives and become the footprints in the sand for the next generation. I'm proud of you all and your accomplishments, which includes raising my amazing grandchildren; Taylor, Moriah, Zion, Titus, Tyson, and Quinton. This list would be incomplete if I didn't include my spiritual daughter, Angela, who allows me the privilege of being "Nana" to her son, Tynan.

Thank you to each one of my siblings. You may not know it, but each of you has helped and supported me in one way or another. Carol, who has written and published two novels of her own, "Watch out for the Wind," and "Swift & Silent," took time out of her busy day to help edit my work. Anita, read the manuscript every time I made changes, and JoAnne sat with me for hours, brainstorming my 'what if' scenarios. Both of my brothers encouraged me in different ways also; Howard encouraged me with nudges to finish writing the book, and Jeff's encouragement came through teaching the importance of standing in faith for the success of it.

Lori Roane, my sister-friend and one of my biggest fans from the beginning. Your daily phone calls kept me writing so I could fill you in on what happened next all because I didn't want to face your disappointment by having to say, "I don't know." I love you, Sis. Thank you (Big grin).

Mary Ross Smith, my big sister and fellow author, whose books, "Soul Survivor," and "SOS" have become staples of encouragement to me, and I'm sure, many others. We have so much in common, and I never tire of our long conversations. I can't believe I know someone like you and your loving husband, Vern. It's such a privilege to call you friends.

Marcella Jackson and Sharon Visor, thank you so much! When I needed someone to read the entire manuscript and give unbiased, honest feedback, I knew I could count on you. Love you, girlfriends.

Adele Hewett Veal

Foreword

Ms. Adele Hewett Veal has used very well rounded creative license in exploring the world of those who suffer from Dissociative Identity Disorder (DID), often referred to as Multiple Personalities. While this is a very rare disorder that has been romanticized in the media, it is a very real psychological illness. Through very colorful and artistic writing, Ms. Veal takes us on a journey and provides a glimpse of what life may be like for those whose lives have been touched by DID. She allows us to see the whole person; the struggles, the laughs, the loves, the hurts, the disappointments and the victories.

I am a Doctor of Clinical Psychology. I have worked in a State Hospital and a State Prison- where the most psychologically ill reside. I have yet and likely will never have a patient who suffers from DID. During the 1970s and 1980s there were an overabundance of people erroneously diagnosed with this disorder. We must remember that although people suffered from this type of dissociative amnesia throughout time, it was not until 1980 that Multiple Personality Disorder was recognized as a condition separate from other types of Neurosis. According to the Diagnostic and Statistical Manual of Mental Disorders V, a person must have a disruption of identity characterized by two or more distinct personality parts. This disruption may be observed by others, or reported by the patient. As you read the melodic writing of Ms. Veal, you may wonder how she eloquently enters a world in which she has never known. What is it that led Les to split? What happened that is so horrible she cannot be one united personality? The mystery is in the story!

It is beautiful writing and a lovely read!

Angela Karolyn Kenzslowe Scott, PsyD, MBA

Sibling rivalry drove a wedge between them at an early age. At five years old, Lee knew her father liked her best. She could hear his footsteps heavy on the linoleum floor echoing louder as he got closer to the door of their bedroom. Les immediately curled into a ball and almost disappeared, which left Lee exposed and alone. Her Father stumbled through the dark to her bed, leaned down, and scooped her up into his arms, and then carried her to his bed. Lee knew what he wanted. This became the norm for them. Talk around town was what people 'thought' happened in the Cramer household. What everyone knew for sure was that Mr. Cramer was taken away the day he threw Les through the living room window during one of his drunken bouts. He was furious with Les because she wouldn't let him get to Lee. Everything was Les's fault! Lee was embarrassed, and it was almost unbearable standing there alone with the neighbors gawking at her. The paramedics were comforting Les, speaking softly as they worked on her, bandaging every minor cut just because of a little blood ---- most of it was on the ground. They lifted Les onto a stretcher then into the ambulance; Lee rode along and, although tears coursed down her face, no one cared about her . . . only Les! Lee felt her rage for Les build. She hated her!

1

Lee slowed her pace as she approached the doorway of the living room. A shiver started at the base of her spine and etched its way up, causing a bitter sickness in her stomach. She ignored the queasiness, pressed through the fog of blurred memories, and stepped into the room one last time. This room had been her favorite for eight years. She strolled to the fireplace.

What would she miss about being here?

She ran her hand across the mantel and stopped at a crystal frame holding her husband's picture.

Would she miss her darling Kevin?

She picked up the photograph and focused on Kevin's image. He was resting on a boulder, facing the photographer, an off-white sweater tied around his neck. His smile didn't seem to reach his eyes, but the vibrant amber color of them against his skin still boasted of their beauty. His expression and stylish appearance came across as surreal and captivating, seeing as the photograph was snapped at the precise moment the ocean sprayed in the background.

"He is outright oblivious of how handsome he is," she whispered returning the photograph to its place. During these last years, he'd become distant and aloof, and open about his dislike for her.

Looking past the pictures to the mirror on the wall; Lee studied the meticulous image staring back at her. She traced the outside of her face and moved her hand past her jaw line to her chin. She leaned in to examine her reflection closer, always amazed at the natural glow of her skin accented by her vibrant ruby red lips. "Tsk, tsk, tsk, what a disappointment." She whispered, and shook her head. She patted the bouffant hairstyle that had been ratted to give the style a fuller appearance, scooped up, and pinned on top of her head. With a flick of her hand, she smoothed a wayward strand into place and examined her reflection again before allowing her eyes to drift back to her husband's photograph.

Sighing deeply she waved a dismissive hand at it. "Who cares? He's an idiot anyway." He was nothing like she expected. *He was weak;* she thought, *and his ideas about life, marriage, and family were immature, especially since . . .*

May 23, 2008, was when all the proverbial crap hit the fan. Until then, everything seemed fine. They socialized together and even slept together. Okay, okay, there might have been a few incidents -- minor eruptions -- times she lost her temper a bit, threw things. So what, she made up for those little blowups, and he never complained about how she did that. She gave him everything he wanted. He wanted children; she gave him two. Lee rolled her eyes toward the ceiling as she remembered the dreaded children; Keith and Kelly. She certainly wouldn't miss them. Always underfoot and in the way -- too needy. God! You would think, after three or four years, they'd be able to do some things on their own instead she had to listen to, Mommy this and Mommy that . . . *wahhh, wahhh, wahhh'. My God.* However, *he* seemed happy with *them*, devoted to *them*, in love with *them*.

And what about the dog? Did she say anything when he came home with that flea-bitten animal? No! Well, not initially, Lee remembered the heated discussion.

***

Kevin walked into the bedroom and closed the door quietly, "Can't stand all the excitement, huh?"

"What do you mean?"

"Come on, Lee. The whole house shook when you slammed the door. Who missed the way you stormed out of the room? Why didn't you, at least put on one of the Oscar winning performances you're so good at? The children were watching, for Christ's sake. They've decided to call him Riley, by the way, I mean, so you know, the puppy's name is Riley."

"And who's going to take care of 'Riley,' clean up after 'Riley'? You? You know as well as I do, you're going to expect me to give up more time out of my day for that . . . that. . . DOG. You're not thinking about me and what I want. Why should I think about the likes of you and what you want? You're not being fair to me, but as long as you and the children are happy, that's all that matters; Right? A DOG? Why, in God's name, would you bring home a dog?"

*"Keep your voice down, will ya. This is between you and me. All I'm saying is; why not allow them the chance to be children for a change? My God, Lee, haven't you made their lives miserable enough? I'll take care of the damn dog. I just thought the children needed something more. Something to enjoy. I couldn't resist the puppy. He was sitting there wagging his tail as if he knew I was there to get him and the first thing I thought about was how the children would react when they realized he belonged to them. I believe he needed someone to love him as much as they do. Did you see how their faces lit up? They need this, Lee. With all the craziness going on in their lives lately, they need this. What's wrong with you? It's as though you're inhumane, like you can't feel. There's more to life than what **you** want, Lee. What about what the children want? What the children need? They need to be able to enjoy some parts of their childhood. They need you, and they need me. They need a mom AND a dad. Why can't you see that?"*

She didn't say anything. She stood watching as defeat began in Kevin's shoulders and worked its way to his eyes. Yep, that's what it was-- defeat. She smiled. If nothing else, she recognized defeat when she saw it, and she loved it! She loved knowing, once again, she'd won.

Kevin stood waiting for the answer that never came. After a while, he turned, opened the bedroom door, and stepped into the hall, closing the door behind him. Lee walked across the room to her vanity and sat facing herself in the mirror. She picked up a small tube of lipstick from her makeup tray, removed the lid and applied the deep red color evenly over her top and bottom lip. She slowly pressed her lips together; never taking her eyes off of her reflection. Finally, she sighed deeply and whispered "Wahhh, wahhh, wahhh, wahhh, wahhh."

✳✳✳

She turned her attention back to the mantel and picked up another photograph. This picture was a snapshot of the family. *Oh, how sweet*, one child on his lap, the other trying to climb up and Kevin's smile displaying the proud father image. She laid the picture face down on the mantel and walked to the window. No, there was absolutely nothing she would miss. She was looking forward to the rest and relaxation. She needed to sleep, and she needed to sleep for a long time. Lee turned and walked out of the room and up the stairs. She would welcome sleep tonight.

2

Leslee felt her head spinning out of control –throbbing. How long had she been asleep? The darkness seemed overwhelming, haunting and –and almost unendurable, but she had to stay strong and keep going. She had to push through the darkness.

I can't stop now, she repeated to herself. *I can't. I can't. I'm so close.* She could feel the tension in her muscles screaming in agony. She kept her eyes closed tightly, somehow she felt stronger with her eyes closed. She had more strength to push.

Where's the air? I can't breathe. Why can't I breathe? With every ounce of strength she could muster, she pushed.

"Uhhhh!" *Harder...!* "Uhhhhhhh!" SHE DID IT! She finally pushed through-- the first layer. "Uhhh," . . . another release. Another layer.

I'm at the top! I'm finally at the top.

Her head swirled faster and faster.

Breathe, Les, calm yourself and breathe, for Christ's sake. Don't pass out now. Stay strong, just stay strong. Pushing again. "Uhhhhhhh, *what* —*what's that?* Something cool brushed across her face. *A breeze. Yes -- a breeze. She didn't know how long* it had been since she'd felt one, but she remembered breezes. She lay still with her eyes closed, enjoying another; this time the breeze seemed to linger and caress. It was cool and familiar -- delicious.

She breathed deeply and exhaled long. So engulfed in her awakening, Les was unaware of the single tear that left her eyes and trailed passed her temples.

Open your eyes, Leslee, She instructed herself.

She took another deep breath and in what seemed to be slow motion, she opened her eyes and squinted against the brightness of the daylight.

Where am I?

She lay still, blinking and staring at the ceiling. She allowed her eyes to adjust to the light. She blinked and closed them again and this time, when she opened them, she slowly turned and focused on the figure beside her.

"Well, good morning." The man's voice was low and steady. He was propped up on his elbow looking down at her. "You had a pretty rough night. What's this?" He asked sarcastically, wiping his finger across what was left of a tear. "Melted ice from the ice queen?"

Les could not pull away from the eyes that kept her spellbound. They were hazel and seemed brighter against his almond complexion.

"Must have been some dream; you tossed and turned most the night." He rolled over, pulled the covers back and sat up on the side of the bed. "At one point, I thought you were going to fall right out of the bed." He chuckled as he stood and reached for the bathrobe he tossed on a chair the night before. She watched the muscles on his nude back contract when he threw the bathrobe around his shoulders and shoved his arms into each sleeve in one solid motion, then walk across the room.

Les watched him pick up a newspaper and read the headlines. He tucked the paper under his arm and moved slowly to her side of the bed. She closed her eyes and slid the covers up closer to her chin.

What was he going to do? She opened one eye; he was still there--looking down at her. *Wait a minute, she knew him.* She opened the other eye. *This man was Kevin. Kevin Jenison! High School, Kevin Jenison! What was he doing here?*

"Don't freak out." She whispered.

She forced herself to meet his stare as uncomfortable as it was, she didn't move her eyes from his, and the awkwardness made her blush.

She wondered why he was there.

He finally turned away and walked to the other side of the room.

Kevin Jenison was the star football player at Lexington High School and was recruited to Ohio State University on full scholarship. The question was, *what was he doing standing in -- she flashed her eyes around the room. Was this her bedroom or his?*

He turned and caught her looking at him. Yes, it was Kevin all right; the same hazel eyes and dimples that made every girl at Lexington melt with desire, even some girls at Les's school were infatuated with him. He seemed older though. His thick dark hair was sprinkled with a hint of gray, staining the crown of his head and around his temples. She could even see a little gray in his mustache, but there was no doubt in her mind, this was the same Kevin.

Les finally spoke, "What – what day is it?" She asked.

"What?"

She cleared her throat and spoke louder, "What day is it?"

"It's Friday. Why?" He turned and cocked his head to the side, waiting for an answer. "Oh, Come on, Lee, we agreed; no more excuses! We've got the appointment with the attorney this afternoon at 1:00. Remember? 1:00! All you need to do is show up, sign your name, and we'll be done. You promised, Lee. Don't make me pull my trump card." He pinched the bridge of his nose and shook his head. "I'm telling you, lady, you don't want to mess with me."

Les shrugged and sat up in the bed. "Attorney?" She asked, wrapping the sheet around her body several times before standing. Realizing the feat had taken much longer than it should have, she stopped and flashed a glance in Kevin's direction. His expression told her he was thinking the same thing.

"What are you doing?" He asked.

"I'm – Uh – I'm going to the bathroom." She said, studying the three doors in front of her. One she knew had to lead to the hallway, and one of the other two must be the bathroom, but which. With the sheet clinging to her body, she walked over and opened the door she thought might be the bathroom, she was wrong. She quickly closed the closet door and whipped around hoping Kevin hadn't witnessed her mistake; he hadn't. Fortunately, he had turned his attention back to his newspaper.

"Don't freak out," she told herself as she opened another door and rushed through it into the bathroom. She closed the door behind her, afraid the thumping of her heart would expose her nervousness. She couldn't slow it down.

She tried taking slower breaths and reminding herself to *inhale - exhale - inhale - exhale.* Her heart continued to race, she clutched the sink with one hand trying to steady herself.

"Calm down, Les, calm down," She said.

She glanced at the reflection in the mirror and without thought turned away. She stopped. Something was different. She slowly turned back to the mirror.

"What the --?"

She first touched the mirror then, as she stared at her reflection, turned the same hand to her face.

"Wha--?"

She leaned in closer, touched her cheek right under the eye, "Oh my God! It's me!" She gasped. She touched her other cheek, and ran her hand through her hair. Confusion mixed with anxiety gripped her senses, and she reeled backward.

"No, Les, get it together girl. Get it together. Breathe -- just breathe.

"Oh My God, how long have I - -? I look so - -"

She peered into the mirror again. Her sun-kissed almond complexion was still flawless only a few crow's feet around the eyes.

How much time had passed?

She knew she couldn't ask Kevin what year it was. The way he was looking at her, he already thought she was nuts. No, there had to be another way. *The newspaper!* She saw a newspaper under Kevin's arm.

Kevin rapped at the bathroom door. "Um, let's try to get out of here on time. I don't want to hold Dave up today; he's already doing us a favor by squeezing us in. All we need to do, Lee, is meet him at his office, get the paperwork out of the way, and we're divorced. He took care of everything."

Divorced?? The word echoed in her mind. "You mean, the divorce will be *final* today?"

"That's what we said we wanted! We said we wanted a quick and simple divorce. It can't get any quicker than this. And now that I know what I know, it's still not quick enough for me." Kevin leaned closer to the door. "You're not having second thoughts *again*, are you?" He waited for an answer, and when none came, his anger escalated, "Oh, God. Come on; don't tell me ---"

"No. No second thoughts." She said, "But after the divorce, then what?"

"What do you mean 'then what'? We go our separate ways. The children stay with me, and you go away. That's what you wanted, that's what you got." Kevin turned and walked away from the door mumbling his frustration under his breath.

"Children? I have children?" she whispered, shaking her head in disbelief. "What did I do so terrible you want me gone?" She asked through the door. Why . . .?"

Before she could finish, Kevin interrupted, "What have you done? Lady!" He lowered his voice, remembering the children were right down the hall. "This whole marriage thing has been a farce from the beginning, and you know it." He rushed across the room and whispered loudly through the closed bathroom door. "You've established you don't want anything to do with us. We got it, Lee." He emphasized with his fingers pointing to his head, "it finally sunk in! So we're gonna make this as painless as possible for everybody. Let's just sign the damn papers!" I can't keep dragging Keith and Kelly through this shit. They don't deserve it, and neither do I. I knew this was going to happen. Can you, for once in your life, follow through on what you say you're gonna *do*?" He punched the door hard. The punch startled Les, and she jumped backward toward the tub. She took a deep breath, and then moved slowly to the mirror again. She stared at her reflection and raised her hand to her face to examine one side then the other, her hand gently smoothed around her eyes, and then under her chin.

Finally, she asked the questions she had wanted to ask since she opened her eyes that morning, "What have you done now, Lee? What mess did you leave for me to clean up this time?" Les moved backward and eased herself onto the edge of the tub, exasperated and too tired to argue any longer. She put her head in her hands,

"All right, Kevin," she finally answered, "give me a minute, and I'll be right out. Okay? Just give me one minute."

"Fine. I'd like to talk before I go downstairs. I don't want the children in the middle of this." His voice was quieter now. "I'm tired of arguing. Let's agree to sign the papers and be done, and then you can do whatever you want."

"Yes," Les agreed, "I think we need to talk too."

Kevin stepped away from the door and walked to the chair to wait for Lee to come out of the bathroom. He opened the newspaper and tried to read, but his attention kept being drawn to the closed bathroom door.

When Les thought enough time had passed, she stepped out of the bathroom still wrapped in the sheet. She sat on the edge of the bed, cleared her throat and whispered, "The point is, I don't have anywhere to go. All I'm asking is that you call the attorney and ask for an extension or something." She swallowed hard, "that's all."

"Extension! Are you kidding me?" He slammed the newspaper down. It's been eight years. Eight miserable years! And you keep doing this, Lee. You agree to a divorce then you back out. Why?" His eyes seemed to plead for an answer she couldn't give. "I assured Dave we'd be in today. You don't want to be with me any more than I want you. Don't make me do something you'll regret.

Les, was taken aback by Kevin's threat, wondering what he meant by it, but too afraid to ask.

"There's nowhere for me to go! What am I supposed to do?"

Kevin shook his head, "That's not what you told me last week. What happened to the condo over on Sixteenth Avenue?"

Their conversation was interrupted by a little knock at the door, followed by a little girl's voice, "Daddy. Me and Keith are hungry. Can we fix our own cereal?"

"No, Kelly, I'll be downstairs in a minute. I'll fix it for you."

"But Dad, yesterday I fixed my own cereal and didn't even spill the sugar or anything, and you said I did good."

"You did do good, Sweetheart, but I was there to make sure you didn't spill anything. If you wait awhile, I'll watch you again. Let me finish talking to Mommy, and I'll be right down. Okay?"

"Okay!" Kelly left the door, yelling downstairs to her brother. "Keith, Daddy said I can make my own cereal when he comes downstairs, I get to make my own again, just like yesterday!"

Hearing the little voice, tugged at Les's heart. Her hand went to her mouth to suppress the sound that tried to escape her lips. A sound that would have given away her desire to run to the door, open it wide and scoop the little girl into her arms. She had always wanted children. So engrossed in her thoughts, she missed Kevin's reaction to the way she responded to hearing Kelly's voice.

Not wanting to get sidetracked from the point, he rushed on, "I'm sure you can think of a friend you can call."

Kevin's voice brought Les's attention back to their conversation. *A friend?* A glimmer of hope tapped Les's remembrance and triggered a memory. Something she was to memorize... *A number? Yes, a number.* She closed her eyes trying to visualize a telephone number . . . *4-9; No, 480 . . . 5 . . . 55 . . . 3325. That's it 480-555-3325!* She repeated the numbers to herself over and over again. Now all she needed was a phone. "Tell you what, Kevin. You go ahead down and help Kelly while I get dressed. No more arguing. I'll be down soon to help."

Kevin laughed, "You're coming down to help with the children? This I've got to see." He laughed again. She watched him carefully as he put on a pair of pajama bottoms, adjusted his bathrobe, and left the room.

***

Once out of the room, Kevin breathed deeply and turned back to the bedroom door.

What the hell was that about?

He leaned against the wall and raked his hand through his hair.

His mind went over the argument that transpired between them. In the years they've been married, Kevin could not recall a time their conversations didn't end in some type of screaming match. But today, Lee was quick to concede. She understood? *Unusual.* She seemed shaken when Kelly came to the door and, if he wasn't mistaken, he could swear she was showing signs of affection. *Affection, from someone who has never been affectionate? Bizarre!*

He recalled how violently she tossed and turned that morning.

He propped himself up on his elbow and toyed with the thought of shaking her awake, but suppressed it and watched. If he were to describe that moment to anyone he would say, it seemed she was pulling herself out of a deep cavernous well. When she finally pulled herself free; she began to gasp for air. And then he saw something unbelievable, something he knew Lee would never want him to see. A lone tear ran from the corner of her eye, streamed the side of her head, and got lost in her hairline. It was at that moment she opened her eyes, turned and looked at him.

He thought about how awkward she seemed, wrapping herself in the sheet to go to the bathroom and her desperate attempt to select the right door. It took everything he had to act as though he was reading his newspaper when the truth was, he had seen her select and open the wrong one.

Kevin laughed and shook his head. He pulled himself away from the wall and shoved his hands into the pockets of his bathrobe still baffled, but not surprised. It was just like Lee to pull one of her deceptive pranks today. In the past, she'd be known to deceive him into thinking she'd changed, professing the desire to go to counseling and save their marriage. Giving them the chance of becoming a *real* family. How many times had he fallen for that trick only to have her laugh in his face, call him weak, and boast about how easy it was to get over on him?

"Not this time, Lee," He chuckled, and then he turned and went down the stairs.

***

Les took a quick shower and brushed her teeth with a new toothbrush she found in the drawer; because she couldn't figure out which toothbrush hanging in the cabinet was hers. Kevin's words kept swirling around in her head, *'Don't make me do something you'll regret'*?

What could he have meant by that? She wondered. She decided to ask him about it the first chance she got, but right now she needed to focus on getting dressed.

She opened the closet door and was taken aback by the array of colors. So many colors and suits. Summer suits on the right, winter suits on the left.

"Jeans, Lee; A simple pair of Jeans. Where – would – you . . .? She moved to the back of the closet.

"Ah huh," she said, pulling out two pairs of jeans, a few sweaters, and some old shirts she had found. She returned to the back of the closet and found a pair of sneakers on the floor in the corner.

She stepped into the jeans and slipped on a blue shirt. Then she raked her fingers through her hair and swept it into a ponytail. Holding her hair in place, she rushed around the room looking for a ponytail holder.

"Come on, Lee, you've got to have ponytail holders." She settled on the rubber band Kevin discarded from the newspaper and twisted it around her hair.

She opened a drawer. Kevin's underwear. Another drawer, his socks. She grabbed a pair of his socks and put them on, and then slipped her feet into the sneakers.

She was pleased with the reflection in the mirror, although, she seemed older, she had to admit she still looked good.

How old was she anyway? How long had she . . .? Kevin mentioned they had been married for eight years. She looked around the room for the newspaper he left behind. When she spotted it, she took a few quick steps toward it, and then slowed her pace. Was she ready to face the truth? She *needed* to face it but was she ready? She picked the paper up, opened it, and skimmed the top of the page for the date. When she found it, she gasped. The date stood, screaming back at her as she glared at it in unbelief. "Oh, My God, ten years? I lost ten years of my life?" She slowly lifted her gaze to her reflection in the dresser mirror and tears stung her eyes. "Ten years." She whispered.

She pulled her gaze away from the reflection, and her eyes swept around the room. *There has to be a phone here!*

When she found the phone, Les ran around to the other side of the bed, picked it up and tried to stop shaking long enough to make the call. "Let's see," she studied the contraption -- much more complicated than she remembered.

"Uh, I want to talk." She pressed the 'talk' button and listened for a dial tone, and then she pressed the numbers, 480-555-3325. While the phone rang, Les closed her eyes and prayed, "Please be there. Please … please."

The phone continued to ring longer than she thought it should, and her shoulders sank. Realizing no one was going to answer, she lowered it from her ear.

What did she expect? It had been ten years. Anyone would have given up by now.

And then she heard a familiar voice,

"Les! Les! Is this you?"

3

Mornings were Veronica's favorite time of the day, especially in Arizona. She tucked the newspaper under her arm and poured herself another cup of coffee. By opening the screen door, she was given a clear view of her backyard. She stepped onto the patio and looked around at the small retreat she had created for herself. In eight short years, the yard seemed to take on a personality all its own. Rushing water spilled from the rocks of a man-made waterfall into a kidney-shaped pool. "Euphoria," she whispered. The breeze was cooler than usual but pleasant for a March afternoon. Two palms stood tall and loomed over the pool and patio providing a shade of protection from the morning sun. Veronica adjusted her chaise longue and sat in the direction that allowed her the pleasure of a panorama view the whole yard. She placed her coffee on the table next to her. Settling herself comfortably, she extended her legs, closed her eyes and allowed the warmth of the morning sun to bathe her. She whispered, "Ahh, this is the life."

She picked up the newspaper, reached for her coffee and took a long sip. The hot liquid filled her mouth. The sweet burst of Vanilla crème mingled with the taste of freshly brewed Columbian bean and danced across her tongue then traveled down the back of her throat. She closed her eyes again enjoying her piece of heaven. Finally ready, she sat the coffee cup down and opened the newspaper.

If Veronica hadn't been so immersed in her reading and in tune to familiar sounds around her, the distinct ringing of the telephone may have been detected sooner. However, the faint ringing was considered more of an intrusion and would've gone unanswered had it not been for its annoying tone that caught Veronica off guard. She sat up and leaned into the direction of the ringing. "It couldn't be!" She bolted from the chaise lounge and moved to the patio door. She listened. Another ring.

"Oh, My God!" She snatched the door open and rushed inside.

It wasn't just 'a' phone ringing, it was *'the'* phone ringing. Veronica opened the cabinet door and pulled out the ringing cell phone.

"Oh my God, she actually did it!" She tapped the 'answer' button on the phone and placed it to her ear. "Les! Les. Is this you?"

"Veronica? Ronnie?" Oh My God, it worked!" Tears of joy spilled over onto Les's cheeks. "When I saw the date, and the phone rang for so long, I was afraid you had given up. The newspaper said it's been ten years. I just got here this morning, but I don't even know where 'here' is, Ronnie."

"I told you I wouldn't give up. I promised! Didn't I promise?" Veronica cried. "I can't believe I'm talking to you right now. Wait a minute, let me calm down. Oh my God, oh my God, oh my God!"

"I need to find a way to get to you. Do you still live in Chandler?" Les asked.

"Yes, but how are you gonna find me when you don't even know where you are? I'll come to you. I know where you live, and I'm only ten minutes away," Veronica took a long pause. "I still need to get showered and changed. There's a little park on the corner from your house. If you go out your front door, and turn left. You can't miss it." She checked her watch, "It's 10:00 now; meet me there at 11:30. Do you think you can get away?"

"I'll try. Keep the cell with you, and if I encounter any problems, I'll call you. Okay?

"Okay, girlfriend, it's good to hear your voice. I'll see you soon." The phone hung up but Veronica didn't move. She stood in the middle of her kitchen still holding the phone to her ear after the conversation had ended.

Les wrapped a tan sweater around her shoulders and tied the sleeves of the sweater across her neck. She studied her reflection one last time, turned sideways and to the back. "Okay, Les, how are you gonna pull this off?" She said under her breath. She breathed deeply, opened the bedroom door, and headed for the stairs. She rubbed her hands together and leaned over the top of the stairs to listen. The sound of her children's laughter gave her the courage she needed to put aside her apprehensions and proceed down the steps. She couldn't wait to see them-- to hold them. She walked through a contemporary living room until she found herself standing in the doorway of a large kitchen. She stood as quiet as possible watching and enjoying the picture of a happy family – *her family*. Kevin teased the children, and they loved it. She ached to be a part of the fun, but her place, for now, was there on the side--watching.

"No – no, Daddy's helping me first, Kelly, he helped you first yesterday. It's my turn to be first, huh, Daddy? Tell her it's my turn to be first."

"Okay, Keith, you can be first today." Kevin chimed, "You ready? Now, pour your milk. That's it. Steady. You've got it, son."

The barking from the dog went unnoticed as the children continued their bantering back and forth.

"He can watch me. He's my dad too." Kelly exclaimed

"No, he's not!" Keith teased.

"Uh-huh, aren't you, Dad? Aren't you my dad too, Dad?

"No, he's nooo--." Keith's sing-song voice trailed off as he turned to the figure standing in the doorway. He could not pull his eyes away from the familiar stranger.

Unaware of the change in Keith's voice, Kevin continued. "I am the luckiest dad ever. I get to be the daddy of two of the most wonderful children in the world." He held the milk in one hand and turned Kelly's cereal bowl toward him, "Here we go, Kelly."

"Daddy, I want to - pour - my -" Kelly's voice trailed off as her eyes followed Keith's wide-eyed stare. Her mouth dropped open in shock when she saw who it was that held her brother's attention.

"I know Kelly. You want to pour your own milk. Lay your hand on top of mine, and it will be like you're pouring, but I have to help." Kelly didn't move. "Kel?" The silence from one of the children was unusual, but silence

17

from both children never happened. Kevin glanced up, looking from one child to the other and finally followed their eyes to the doorway. He froze.

"What?" Les asked, checking herself, "What's wrong?"

Kevin suddenly became aware of the sound of liquid, hitting the floor and realized he had missed Kelly's cereal bowl altogether. Milk puddled across the table and dripped over the side. He rushed to the sink and grabbed a handful of paper towels, then hurried back to the spill while Riley continued to bark at the intruder despite the treat he could be lapping up.

"Good morning. Can someone please tell me what's wrong?" Les asked, examining her clothes and trying to find the problem.

Keith gestured with his hands, "You're – wearing – pants. And your –" pointing to her hair, "your –"

Kelly interrupted, also pointing to her hair, "Your hair's not poofy."

"Poofy?" Les asked, smoothing her ponytail.

Kevin continued to wipe up the spill, but when he cursed under his breath, it brought both children's attention back to him.

"Uh, Riley, go sit, boy!" The dog grumbled as he ambled toward the milk and drank with loud slurps still keeping an eye trained on Les.

"Okay," Les responded. She clapped her hands together and began moving about the kitchen, "where were we?" Les walked to the table and picked up the carton of milk to pour over Kelly's cereal. Kelly turned around in her chair and sat down hard never once taking her eyes off the woman coming toward her with the milk.

"Daddy?" Kelly shrank into her chair as Les continued to lean over her to finish her task.

Keith's movements became snail-like as he picked his spoon up and began to eat. His eyes went from his mother to his father and to his mother again. Finally, he turned to his sister who exchanged a wary glance with him.

Meanwhile, Kevin took giant steps from the table to the sink with his hand cupped under the milk sopped paper towel. He squeezed the paper towel and stood watching the milk run down the drain. Unaware that Les was on her way with another soaked towel, he almost collided with her on his way back to the spill. Frustrated and confused he murmured,

"What the hell are you trying to pull now?" The quick movement alerted Riley, and he began to bark again.

"Pull? What are you talking about?"

"You know perfectly well what I'm talking about. How long has it been since you've wanted to be included as a part of this family? I don't recall you ever coming down to help with breakfast for the children. Why now?" He turned to the barking dog, "Riley, hush!" and then back to his wife, "You've got something up your sleeve but it's not going to work."

Riley continued to bark.

"I have every right to be here,"

"Do you think everything you put this family through is going away because you decide to change your clothes and come down to breakfast? You're crazy, lady. Riley, Hush, boy!" Kevin snapped his finger at Riley and gesture toward his pillow, expecting him to obey his command; he didn't. Riley was unmanageable and continued to bark.

"I don't understand what's been going on or - or why you're so angry with me, but if you'll give me some time, I'll be able to explain everything. Just give me some time!" Les pleaded.

"Time?" Kevin's voice elevated, "I've given you plenty of time." His loud whisper strained against his anger, and he could feel himself wanting to explode. "He thought about how many years he spent trying to make his wife happy and the abuse he encountered because he couldn't. He thought about the nights he lay awake, waiting for her to come home. Listening to the night's silence. Hoping for the sound of a closing car door or her footsteps coming down the hall, any sign to show him she cared enough to at least come home. All the while, he carried the full weight of a bruised ego that reminded him he simply wasn't enough for her. She needed more than he could give her, *and now she needed 'time'.* He closed his eyes to calm himself before he spoke, and when his words finally came, his voice was low and steady – haunting. "We have – an appointment – this afternoon at 1:00. Take as much *'time'* as you need, but," his eyes narrowed ominously, "you'd better be there."

"Listen." Les leaned in closer, trying to rationalize the situation. "I'm not trying to cause a problem for God's sake."

"Not trying to cause a problem?! He exploded, "Lady; you *are* the problem!"

19

The sudden explosion of Kevin's voice brought Riley closer to the couple, and he barked louder, but this time Kevin turned to the dog and shouted, "*Riley*, shut up and go *sit!*"

"Dad, Kelly's crying," Keith yelled over Riley's wild barking.

Kevin turned to Kelly, and then rolled accusing eyes toward Les.

"Oh, you're–" she couldn't believe he was blaming her for Kelly's tears. Immediately Les, picked Riley up and walked with him to his pillow. Once there, she sat the dog down and patted the top of his head then walked back to Kevin.

"You know," she argued, "you don't even know me, but if you want me gone so badly – fine; I'm gone!" Her eyes filled with tears. "I'll be back before your *meeting.*" She spat, "I'll sign the damn papers if that's what you want." Les stormed out of the kitchen. She couldn't let him see her cry. She hurried toward the front door, unaware of Kevin at her heels, opened the door and stormed out of the house.

When the door didn't slam as expected, she whipped around and came face-to-face with Kevin holding it wide. The sneer on his face evidenced the mini victory he claimed. He was not going to give her the satisfaction to even slam the door.

"Dave's office is on the third floor of the Marshall Building, Suite 310. Either be back here at 12:30, so we can ride together or meet me there at 1:00. Don't mess this up, Lee!" Kevin shouted and shut the door.

He's so angry. She thought, untying the sweater from around her shoulders and pulling it over her head. The chill in the air was unexpected. March was usually warmer than this in Arizona. She walked in the direction Veronica had given her. It would be good to be around someone who understood what was going on. She hoped Veronica would be waiting for her. To stand around and wait would make her overly anxious about solving the many unanswered questions going around in her head.

"Please, be there, Ronnie."

4

The sounds of children playing in the distance made it evident Les was near the park where she and Veronica were to meet. She shoved her hands deeper into the pockets of her jeans. She welcomed the coolness in the air and the unexpected breezes. The park was occupied with children scattered; running and playing—laughing. She smiled at a little boy who ran past her to retrieve a ball that he had overthrown. *Not a care in the world; Oh to be a child again.*

She searched for Veronica and was disappointed she hadn't arrived. Parents sat on the benches to watch over their children, keeping a protective eye peeled for strangers. Two of the mothers whispered to each other, then turned their attention to her. She was the stranger to them. She nodded a friendly hello and gave a slight smile as she moved to sit on an empty bench out of the way. And just as she feared, the thoughts came – the questions came and, although she had no answers for them, she sensed somehow her situation was not half as complicated as it was going to get.

She studied the children again, and her childhood flashed through her mind. Her childhood had been different from most children she knew. By the time she was five, her father had 'gone away' and there was no one who cared about her until she met and made friends with Veronica. She

21

remembered being afraid to fall asleep at night, not because of monsters under the bed or in the closet, but because of a reoccurring dream that haunted her during her subconscious state. While she waited for Veronica, she remembered the dream:

She saw the little girl in a tattered dress, standing at the edge of the yard watching her play.

Did she want to play with her?

Les walked to where the little girl stood, but as she got closer, the girl retreated. And then she was gone. Les, shrugged and turned back to play with her dolls. It wasn't until the following year the little girl came to play again.

"My name's Les, what's your name?

The little girl was afraid to speak at first, but finally, in a low voice she told Les her name, "It's Lee," she whispered.

She never stayed long. Just long enough to play with the dolls and attend an occasional tea party. Always nervous. Watching for someone to come get her.

"Is somebody coming for you? Les asked, looking in the direction Lee kept turning.

She didn't say anything.

"Who's coming for you?" Les asked again.

"Shhhhh," Lee put her finger across her lips. "I could be in trouble for this. I'm not supposed to be out, "shhh shhh," she put the same finger across Les's lips. "It's a secret."

Les giggled and then nodded her head in agreement. "I won't tell." She agreed

Lee smiled and then turned and skipped away. As she twirled around to give one last wave, her face became vile and distorted as she laid her finger on her lips to remind Les of their secret. The sudden change in the little girl's face frightened Les so badly she jerked herself awake and cried.

"Les! Les!"

Veronica was standing outside her car waving her arms and calling to Les.

"Les!" She called again.

Les sprang from the bench and ran to the car. "Ronnie! Oh, my God; Thank you, it's so good to see you." The two women embraced.

Veronica stepped back and regarded Les.

"Girlfriend, you are a sight for sore eyes. Come on, get in the car. Let's go someplace where we can talk. There's a little coffee house on the corner. We'll stop there; how's that sound?" They got in the car and drove off.

"I knew I could depend on you, Ronnie. It worked! You actually kept the cell phone, after all these years. You never gave up on me! When I called that number, I can't tell you how the sound of your voice made me feel, I was so relieved. Thank you," Les whispered and laid her head on the headrest, "Thank you!" She whispered again, wiping a tear from her cheek. She turned her head in Veronica's direction. "You never gave up on me."

"Of course, I'm not going to give up on you. We're sister-friends. There were times I wondered if you were going to be able to get back, but no, I couldn't give up on you. The cell phone had to be upgraded often enough, but they let me keep the same number. Technology changes so quickly nowadays. As soon as a new phone comes out, somebody comes along with a better one to top it. But the important thing is we pulled it off. Veronica turned to her friend. She laid her hand on Les's shoulder, "Don't cry, Les." She comforted. "It's going to be okay. I know this is hard, but you're back now. We'll figure it out. Don't cry."

"God, Ronnie, what is going on? I wake up, and ten years of my life is gone, like that." Les snapped her fingers. "Eight of those years I spent married to Kevin Jenison. Today I find out I'm in the middle of a divorce, and there are two children to consider, who I just met at breakfast. It's too much, Ronnie. I would at least like to know more about my children. All I know are their names; Kelly and Keith. I wish I knew why he dislikes me so much?"

"Who dislikes you?" Veronica asked.

"Kevin – my husband, I mean, *Lee's* husband; he *hates* me. Apparently there's an appointment to sign divorce papers today; how convenient for Lee to leave now and expect me to clean up her mess. And where am I supposed to go?"

Veronica pulled into a parking space, turned off the engine and faced Les.

"First of all, he doesn't hate you; he hates Lee. And second of all, there's always a place for you to stay as long as I'm around; that's the least of your concerns right now." She reached into the glove compartment and pulled out a small package of tissues. She drew one out and handed it to Les. "There's a lot you don't know about '*Miss Lee,*' I've been keeping up with her. I stayed out of her way like I promised, but I watched her, and you need to know some things. Come on, girlfriend, let's go inside."

There was no question about the friendship between Veronica Moore and Les Cramer. They were inseparable and best friends since elementary school, and they knew the *secrets.* Veronica was there the first time Lee showed up on the playground.

It happened during recess. The two girls ran past everyone else and headed straight for the swings. All the other kids wanted to play on the slide or the monkey bars, but not Veronica and Les, today they were going to be birds; flying high in the sky." They laughed as they sat side by side on the swings. They laughed louder as the swings soared higher and higher.

"I can go higher than you," Les laughed.

"Huh-uh, I'm this high already. You can't catch up. Don't even try."
Veronica teased.

Suddenly, Les began to drag her feet on the ground to slow her swing. Her face changed from excited and playful to hard and uninterested.

"Hey, whatcha' doin'?" Veronica yelled, still laughing.

Les jumped off the swing and moved to sit on a nearby bench.

"What's wrong, Les?" Veronica slowed her swing and hopped off too. She ran to her friend's side and began examining her arms and knees. "Did you get hurt?"

The girl said nothing.

Veronica stepped in front of Les trying to force her to look at her.

"Helloooo," She waved her hand in front of Les's face, "Les, what's wrong with you?" Still no reaction. "Look at me. Are you okay? Hello. What's my

name? Tell me what my name is?" Veronica continued to try to force Les to look at her.

"Mrs. Thomas," Veronica yelled across the playground. "There's something wrong with Les! There's something wrong!" She screamed.

Mrs. Thomas came running, along with some of the other students who heard Veronica's frantic call.

"You're scaring me, Les!" Veronica screamed, "Tell me my name. Who am I? Who are you?!" Veronica staggered back as Les finally responded.

Slowly, she turned to face the screaming girl in front of her. She opened her mouth and just above a whisper she said, "My name is Lee." Her eyes rolled up, and the little girl fell in a heap onto the ground.

Veronica stepped away and gave Miss Thomas room to get to Les. "Run to the office and get Nurse Flemings." She yelled. A couple of the children took off running.

Veronica stood watching, not able to move; frozen in one spot. "Lee?!"

When Les opened her eyes, a blurred figure towered over her, and as she focused, she realized the figure belonged to Nurse Flemings.

"Well, there you are," Nurse Flemings said in a sing-song voice. Anyone who spent time in the nurse's office at Coball Elementary knew Nurse Flemings used her sing-song voice anytime something serious happened. Les's eyes flashed around the office.

Why am I in the office? She wondered.

Nurse Flemings turned to someone sitting on the opposite side of the room and again, in her sing-song voice she said, "I told you she'd be fine."

Les sat up on her elbow and turned in the direction Nurse Flemings spoke and there, sitting by the office door, with her hands wiping away fresh tears was Veronica. Veronica ran to her friend's side.

"What happened?" She cried. "I thought you were dead."

"I'm okay, Ronnie." She leaned closer and whispered, "I pushed back."

Before Les could tell her what she meant, Nurse Flemings scooted Veronica away from the cot and outside the office door.

"I called the number for Les's Aunt Marie and left a message. She should be on her way to pick her up. I'm sure she'll let you visit after school, dear. Now, back to class with you."

Veronica looked past Nurse Flemings at Les still sitting up on her elbow. She shrugged.

"What?" Veronica asked.

Les and Veronica entered the café' and sat in a booth close to the door.

Veronica took a deep breath and let it out. "Okay, how much do you remember?"

She asked.

"Honestly, not much. I remember we were supposed to go somewhere together. I was waiting for you to pick me up, and the next thing I know, I wake up this morning in bed with Kevin – Oh my God. I'm married to Kevin Jenison, who, by the way, loathes me," she said sarcastically. "Try waking up to that problem."

Veronica put her finger up to draw the attention of the waitress and ordered two cups of coffee. It didn't take long; the waitress returned and placed the coffee cups on the table along with a pot of freshly brewed coffee. Veronica sat back and watched her friend take a sip. With her eyes closed, Les leaned her back against the booth's cushion and savored the taste of her coffee.

"Now this is good coffee," she sighed.

Veronica smiled, "I knew you'd like it. Coffee has always been one of your favorite things. When they first built this place, I would come in and sit right over there." She pointed to the table near the window, "I told one of the waitresses about my best friend who loved coffee. I said 'she'd love this place.' She asked me if my friend was here, and I'd tell her everyday how you were trying to get home. I knew you were going to fight, girlfriend. I just didn't know it was going to take you ten years. It's good to see you, though." Veronica reached over and covered Les's hand with hers, then raised her hands to fan her eyes so the tears wouldn't come. "Ten years, girlfriend, *ten years!*" I said, 'the first thing I'm going to do is take Les to get a good cup of coffee', and here we are." Veronica glanced around the café, "The ambiance in here is warm and cozy; don't you think?"

Les considered the room, smiled and nodded. "Yeah, I like it here. Ya done good." Les teased.

Veronica regarded her friend across the table. "This must be so hard on you, Les."

She watched Les shake her head slow.

"I - I honestly don't know what to do, Ronnie. This time there are others involved. That's never happened before. It kind of changes the dynamics of the problem. You know what I mean? It has always been, I'd wake up, and you'd be there along with Dr. Whitfield, and we'd try another treatment, but we'd move on. I've been gone for so long, Ronnie. A whole decade! So much has changed - - - styles - - -places - - -*my life*. How did I get here?" Les laughed. "Honestly, it's not that I care about the divorce, My Lord; I don't even know Kevin that well, but I have two children. They're mine. Well, *ours,* but I'd like to get to know them; it's only fair; isn't it? You know I've always wanted children!"

"Yeah, but Lee didn't. Rumor has it; she treated those kids real bad. She didn't want to be around them; she treated Kevin bad too. The only time I saw them out together was when Kevin's office gave some sort of event, when they first got married.

There was talk after that about Kevin leaving the firm. He's an attorney with "Jackson, Hinkle & Smithe," and he's good too. Anyway, his leaving the firm had something to do with Lee having an affair or planning to have an affair with his boss. I'm not sure if the affair actually happened."

"His boss?!" Les shouted, "What?"

"Here's what we know about the situation. We know the relationship is complicated and in trouble, and we also know Kevin is entangled up to his neck. I heard he filed for divorce a couple of times, but decided to reconcile, for some reason or another. Apparently, Lee changed his mind.

Kevin tried to give her everything she needed and wanted. But Kevin wanted something too, he wanted love, Lee couldn't love him. It was obvious Kevin tried to make the marriage work, but Lee did anything and everything to tear it down. Everyone knew it! She humiliated him every chance she got, most times in public and nasty.

I remember once, at a Gala event downtown. I don't know how, but Kevin convinced Lee to go with him. I was there that night and watched from across the room. The evening was magical until it was time to go home. I waited for my date on the stairs of the Civic Center. I saw Kevin standing at the top step looking around. I knew he was trying to find Lee and, when he spotted her, Girl, you should have seen his face. He turned angry in a split second and almost fell down the steps trying to get to her. When he reached her, he whispered something in her ear that set her off.

Lee shouted, 'You don't tell me who I can talk to!' He made the mistake of telling her they'd talk about it later. Now, why he said that I don't know, because she came back at him with a vengeance. Girl, if words were slaps, I'd have to say, Lee slapped Kevin silly that night."

Veronica continued. "She told him to go home to his children and to remember she wasn't one of them. She said she would be home when she got good and ready to go home. Then she turned and got into the car with someone, a man of course, and left.

Kevin looked beaten, and I felt so bad for him. He stood there in front of all those people, looking foolish. That was the last time I saw the two together in public. There were times, before that night, I witnessed more than I should have but after the night of the Gala, I guess Kevin gave up on Lee. She's just a nasty person!

It was always a pleasant surprise to see Kevin out with the children though. He's good with them, but I never saw him with Lee again."

"I know what you're saying. I saw him this morning with the children. He seems to be a great father." Les said.

"Oh, he is Les. I was at a restaurant one day and he came strolling in with Keith and Kelly. He didn't know anyone was watching, but I got such a kick out of what I saw."

"Tell me?"

"He bought the kids milkshakes and hamburgers with fries. But, Les, it was taking them so long to eat. Kevin kept looking at his watch and trying to encourage them to eat their food but they wouldn't. So Kevin came up with this idea. He said," Veronica laughed, cleared her throat, and deepened her voice, 'Kids, tell you what.'

'What, Daddy?'

'We're going to have a hamburger race. The first one finished with their hamburger is the winner. Okay?'

'Okay, and Kelly started eating her hamburger right away, but Keith ate his fries and drank his milkshake— just really messing around.

Finally, Kelly shouted, 'I won. I won!'

Kevin was so supportive of her. He said, 'Good girl, Kel! YOU ARE THE WINNER OF THE JENISON HAMBURGER RACE.' He announced proudly. Kevin picked Kelly up and pranced with her around the table. Kelly giggled and squealed. She was so excited.

Well, Keith tried to reason with his dad.

'But Dad, I ate all of my fries.'

Kevin said, 'Yes I know, Keith, but Kelly ate all her hamburger, and since it was a hamburger race, she won -- she ate all of her hamburger.'

Keith said, 'But Dad, I even drank my milkshake and Kelly has all of her milkshake left.'

Kevin said, 'It was a hamburger race, Keith – a hamburger race! Come on, Kelly won. It's not the end of the world, son. She won a hamburger race.'

I laughed so hard, Les; he was really good with them, even when Keith started crying-- because when Keith started to cry, Kelly started to cry. She said she didn't want to be the winner if it was going to make Keith cry. The whole thing turned into a chaotic mess with both kids crying.

Kevin left out of the restaurant trying to console them both. It was hilarious, and anyone watching would have seen how awesome he was with them. He is such a good father, and you can tell he's determined to protect them."

Les listened intently as Veronica divulged one story after another. And the stories she told about Kevin and the children helped her realize, what she witnessed at breakfast, was not a rare occurrence, but it was Kevin in true form with his children.

Les thought how good it was to sit across from her friend, drinking a hassle-free cup of coffee, catching up, and putting aside the pressures of the morning

Finally, Veronica got quiet. She leaned back and smiled at Les.

"Let's get back to you, though." She said. "You say, you remembered we were supposed to go out? Do you also remember I was going to introduce you to Aaron's friend? I was dating Aaron at the time. Could that have been what triggered --?"

"I honestly don't know," Les said. She sat forward and put her cup down on the table, trying to think back and remember what she thought about the situation. "I remember saying I didn't think it was a good idea."

Veronica saw Les was getting irritated and decided to change the subject. She made light of the situation, "Is that why you clocked out

on me for ten years. You were trying to avoid meeting Aaron's friend?"
Veronica laughed.

Les laughed too, but the seriousness of everything brought her back to
reality and the two friends sat quietly for a while. Les finally lifted her eyes
to Veronica, "Ronnie, I don't know what to do. You should have seen me
this morning. I was fumbling all over myself. I wear jeans, but Lee doesn't.
I put my hair in a ponytail, but Lee wears her hair "poofy". It's getting
worse, Ronnie. I'm married to a man I don't know. Keith and Kelly adore
their father, but they're scared to death of me, I mean Lee. You can see the
fear in their eyes when I walk into the room."

'Honey, when I first met Lee, she scared the hell out of me too. You
have to admit, she's a bit scary, poor kids." She poured more coffee into
her cup. "Now's a good time to fill in some blanks for you; I'm just trying
to think of where to start."

"Start from the night I left," Les said. She took a sip of coffee and
waited.

"I've gone over that night in my head so many times." Veronica sat
forward and folded her arms in front of her. "I called your house at around
10:00 that night. Do you remember that?" Veronica paused long enough
to see Les shake her head. "I wanted to let you know we were on our
way, but you didn't answer. I called your cell, still no answer. When we
pulled up in front of your house, I told Aaron to wait for me in the car,
and I went to the door and knocked. You opened the door with the same
expression on your face I see every time Lee takes over. Your hair pinned
on top of your head, and that dreaded red lipstick smeared across your
lips. You didn't know who I was, as usual. I stepped back from the door
and said I was looking for Leslee Cramer. Lee said she had never heard
of you. She said she would ask 'Aunt Marie' if she had heard of you, but
she never came back to the door. I turned and walked away. I went home,
got the cell phone we bought, plugged it in like I promised, and waited."
Veronica shrugged.

"In March, a year later, Kevin came home from Ohio State. He had
thrown his arm out playing football, so his career was over. Aaron and
I were at Macy's Club over in Mesa when Kevin walked in; a few of his
buddies were playing pool and drinking,"

Veronica stopped talking long enough to take another sip of coffee. She acknowledged the waitress standing at the table with a fresh pot of coffee to replace the one at the table. Veronica shook her head then turned her attention to Les.

"Les, you want more coffee?"

"No, not yet. I'm good."

The waitress left the table, and Veronica leaned in to continue the story.

"Well, I was surprised when Lee stepped into the club at that point because, she was always careful about where she went and who she was around. She had on her usual red lipstick, and her hair was pinned up into some type of bee hive," Veronica made an up doo funny movement with her hands. "Kevin stopped playing pool and walked to her table to talk but Lee wasn't having it. I heard him at one point, trying to get her to remember something, and she turned and glared at him. I guess he won her over because, not too long after that night, I heard rumors about Kevin and Lee dating, and I was shocked."

Les cleared her throat and leaned across the table.

"Hold on --there's something you need to know, Ronnie." Les put her head in her hands and shook it slowly. "Remember the night you met Aaron? We were sitting at. . ."

Both women spoke at the same time, "Lenny's Pizza."

"Yeah, so?" Veronica asked.

"Well, when you left, Kevin came in. Eventually, he found his way to where I was sitting, and we began chatting almost immediately. Seemed like we had a lot in common, and we talked *for hours*. He was excited about going away to college, so we talked about it. Then he wanted to know about my plans for the future. We exchanged numbers, but--" She stopped.

"WHAT?!" Veronica asked.

"Well, we . . . we, Ohhhh," She covered her forehead with her hands then her cheeks. "You've got to understand, I never thought I'd have to speak about this, but we left Lenny's and ended up... you know--" She rolled her hand over and over until Veronica seemed to get the point.

Veronica's eyes widened, and she leaned across the table and whispered, "Shut. . . Up. No, you didn't!"

"Afraid so." Les nodded.

Veronica leaned further in and whispered again, "No way!"

"Way!" Les confirmed with another nod.

"You and Kevin Jenison were – together? Together?" She mimicked Les by rolling her hands.

"Yep,"

"So, that's why he wanted to talk to Lee. He thought Lee was *you*. You never even told me and I'm your best friend!"

"I never had the chance. Plus, he was leaving and I didn't want anyone to know about it. Imagine how I felt; another of Kevin Jenison's conquests -- another notch in his belt. Was I supposed to be proud of that?

To make matters worse, the morning after, I could hear Kevin on his cell phone talking to someone named Brenda. I figured it was Brenda Crenshaw. You remember her? He was whispering to keep from waking me. I watched him tip-toe into the bathroom and close the door. I got up and walked to the bathroom door and could hear him telling Brenda how he would see her later. He was sorry about their date. He said, 'something' came up, and he promised he was going to see her later that evening. Then they started to argue. I took the opportunity to get my clothes on and high-tail it the hell out of there."

"You didn't see him anymore? Did he ever try to contact you?"

"The next night, he came to my door wanting to talk. He kept knocking, and I didn't want my nosy neighbors to get curious, so I opened the door. . .

"What do you want, Kevin?"

"You ran away from me. When I went to get back in the bed, you were gone. I've been trying to call, but . . ." He cocked his head. "Why are you running from me, Leslee? His voice was deep and inquiring. Les tried to look everywhere to avoid Kevin's eyes.

Among everything that made Kevin desirable, his eyes were what women spoke about the most. They were soft but appeared more brilliant tonight against his caramel complexion. His dark lashes completely outlined them, and he seemed interested and ready to listen to anything she had to say. She noticed he angled his head to the left when he waited for her answers, and she paid close attention to the way he regarded her when she spoke. His eyes drifted from hers to her mouth, her neck, and then back again. He was seducing her in the subtlest way, and he didn't even realize it.

As Kevin spoke, his lips curled into a playful smile. But, his eyes seemed to penetrate her soul. So to keep from tumbling head first back into his seductive web, she wouldn't allow her eyes to connect with his.

"It's complicated." Was all she could think to say.

"Complicated?" he repeated. "Leslee, I'm leaving in two days, and I'll be gone for . . . for who knows how long. I've been ready to leave here since I got my acceptance letter. I couldn't wait to get the hell out of here. Then, I meet you. You come into my life, turn it upside down then disappear? That's not acceptable to me!" He slammed his hand against the side of the door, "Look at me, for God's sake! Don't give up on me, Leslee. Look at me!" Kevin demanded.

She jumped at Kevin's sudden burst of anger. Her eyes met his, and just as she thought, she was unable to pull them away. It was at that moment she realized he was reaching out to her. Not being arrogant or condescending. He was reaching out, and her heart tighten.

"I woke up while you were talking to Brenda, and I overheard some of the conversation."

Kevin took a deep breath and relaxed his shoulders. "Brenda? Baby, Brenda doesn't mean anything to me. She heard I was leaving and wanted to go out. I knew her plan was to talk about getting back together, but there was no way that was gonna to happen. I was going to meet with her to make sure she understood we were NOT getting back together. And then I saw you at Lenny's, and you changed all my plans." He chuckled. "I love what you're about. I'm captivated by your conversation, your plans for the future, and your feelings about family."

Kevin moved closer to Les, "I may have moved too fast, but it's not like I have the luxury of 'time' on my hands, Leslee. I've never met anyone like you, and I didn't want to let you go . . . I still don't." Kevin laid his hand on Les's cheek and tilted her head so he could easily search her eyes. With his other arm, he encircled her waist and pulled her against him. He kissed her on the cheek and allowed the kiss to linger, taking in the scent of her, and then his lips trailed from her cheek to her neck, and then to her mouth. She moaned and pressed herself against him. He moved his lips to her ear and whispered, "You can't tell me you don't know how I feel about you, Leslee. Don't run from me."

Leslee slowly moved her arms around the back of Kevin's neck and pulled back to look into his eyes. She took a step backward into the house bringing Kevin with her and closed the door. "Kevin," she whispered, "I . . . I thought---" Before she could finish, Kevin covered her mouth with his.

"Earth to Les, earth to Les," Veronica snapped her fingers to pull Les out of her daze. "Where'd you go, girlfriend? I feel like I've been sitting here by myself for the last ten minutes." She laughed.

"Sorry, Ronnie, I just remembered something. She told Veronica the details of what happened between her and Kevin. "So, the last time I saw Kevin was the same night you called and wanted me to meet Aaron's friend. My next memory is waking up in his bed this morning, *married*, with two kids." Les motioned to get the attention of the waitress and gestured for her to bring more coffee. "I need a drink."

Veronica's laugh was light and uneasy; her face turned serious, and she lifted her eyes to meet Les's.

"What?" Les asked.

"Something just dawned on me, Les. Kevin! When he married Lee, he must've thought he was marrying you." Her hands gestured wildly, "Don't you get it? That's why he's so angry. He was in love with *you* and wanted to be loved -- by *you*, Lee couldn't give him that. Can't you see it?"

Les sat stunned, allowing Veronica's words to sink in; then she began to slowly nod her head. "That's it, Ronnie." Les drew in a breath as she realized the truth about her situation. "Oh My God, Kevin was in love with me. He came back for me, but--"

Veronica finished the thought. "-- *Lee* was there and like I said, she couldn't give him what he wanted -- he wanted -- *you*." She pointed to Les across the table, and the two women sat frozen and amazed as reality sunk in. "Les, I'm going to ask you something and I want you to be honest with me. Don't give me any B.S about this -- be straight up. Did -- did you fall in love with Kevin Jenison?"

Les thought about the question before she answered. She met Veronica's gaze, and tears stung her eyes as she nodded, "Yeah, Ronnie. Honestly,

I knew I was falling in love with him, but I didn't think he loved me. I mean, he was leaving."

"But . . . he came back for you."

Les felt the warm tears slide down her cheek, and she quickly wiped them away. "What now?"

"I guess that's what we need to figure out. One thing for sure. You're going to have to tell Kevin the truth. If you want him, you're gonna have to fight for him. Don't let Lee rob you of that part of your life too. She's taken enough."

Les nodded, "You're right." She whispered.

The waitress filled their cups and walked away. Les sat quietly, watching Veronica pour the cream into her coffee and lay three packets of sugar down on the table. Veronica tore each packet at the corner and poured it into her coffee. Most people would take all three packets, put them together, tear them at the same time and pour them, but not Veronica. "I can't believe you still do that."

"What?" She looked down at her coffee. "What?"

"That!" Les motioned toward the empty sugar packets and laughed.

"Girl, please." She waved her hand, then picked the coffee cup up and lifted it to her lips. After blowing the steaming brew, she took a long sip. "Now that's good coffee." She teased, and they laughed.

"Ronnie, are you still working at Dr. Whitfield's office?"

Veronica shook her head, "No," she reached out and took both of Les's hands, "that's another thing I need to talk to you about. Some changes took place since you were last here, Les." She took another deep breath, wondering what impact her news would have on Les.

"Changes . . . like what?"

Veronica hesitated and then said, "Dr. Whitfield died a couple years ago, Les."

Les's hands went to her mouth, "Oh Ronnie, My God, can this get any worse? That's horrible. How?"

"It was cancer. I couldn't believe it either. The whole town was in shock, but guess who took over his practice?"

"Who?"

"Do you remember Alexander? We called him Little Alex?"

"The little boy who followed his dad around the office with a stethoscope around his neck?"

"Well, that's who took over the practice-- Little Alex."

"You've got to be kidding me. He's a kid! He's not old enough to be a doctor?"

"You've got to remember; when you last saw him, Alex was 16 and smart as a whip. We kept shooing him out of the office because all he would do was sit and read his dad's medical books. His dad wanted him to go play with his friends." Veronica shrugged. He skipped a few grades and got into college early. Shortly after, he went to medical school, did his residency at the hospital, got a license to practice and eventually took over when his dad passed away."

"How am I ever going to get used to all these changes?" Les covered her eyes and didn't speak for a while. Finally she said, "I'm so sorry to hear about Dr. Whitfield, but on a personal level, I have to ask, what am I going to do now?"

Dr. Paul Whitfield stood a little over 6 feet tall. He was a dark skinned, older gentleman with salt and pepper hair. Although his hair was thinning, he wore sideburns, mustache, and a beard to compensate for what he lacked on top; it lay well-groomed around his face. He dressed impeccably and could still draw the attention of the ladies even at the age of 63. Nurses smiled and whisper among themselves when he walked into their stations after making his rounds. They would compliment him on his choice of suits, ties, or the scent of his cologne then turn to each other to whisper and feign swooning when he finished his work and left the area. No doubt Dr. Whitfield was an attractive man.

At twenty-three, he met his wife, Loraine and knew he couldn't live without her. She had other plans-- she wanted to travel and visit far-away places, experiencing what the rest of the world had to offer. So he made her a promise, if she would marry him, he would honor her desire and take her where ever she wanted to go. She agreed and he kept his promise. Every year, he'd devise unique ways to surprise her with the trips and she loved it. And it continued like that for five out of their forty years together. On Fridays Paul would send his wife flowers - - - always eleven long-stemmed red roses. Loraine asked why he sent only eleven roses and not twelve. He took her face in his hands and said, "Because, my darling, you will always be the twelfth rose in my life."

One evening he set a table outside and hired a waiter who served them dinner under the stars. During the dinner, he surprised her with airline tickets for Europe that spring, but this was the first time since they were married that Loraine declined the trip. Loraine had a surprise for him, they were expecting their first child (Richard) and soon after Richard came a second (Alexander), and two years later, a third (Gwendolyn). Dr. Whitfield was a devoted husband and father and proud of his family.

Out of his three children, Little Alex was the one who took an interest in psychiatric medicine. On any given day, Alex could be found in his father's study reading anything about the science of the mind. Or he'd be in the medical library obtaining information on how visual perception relies on external stimulus or studying Ivan Pavlov, Sigmund Freud, and B. F. Skinner. It became the 'norm' to walk into Dr. Whitfield's office and be greeted by Little Alex who would hit you between the eyes with one question after another. He'd ask, 'Did you know that Ivan Pavlov was awarded a Nobel Prize for physiology and medicine?' And he would stand face-to-face with the clients, expecting, daring, and certainly waiting for them to comment, which gave him the opportunity to divulge everything he read about the subject.

At eighteen years old, Alex walked into his father's office and found him passed out on the floor. They rushed Paul Whitfield to the hospital, and Loraine remained at his side every day until he was released to go home. And even then Loraine cared for him with a few nurses who she allowed to come in from time to time. Paul tried to convince her to hire full-time nurses to take the strain off her, but Loraine wasn't having any of it. She was convinced, no one was capable of giving Paul care equal to hers. She would not leave his side nor would she relinquish her authority to anyone. 'A full-time nurse', Loraine said, 'would reduce your care to two pills, four times a day, a fluffed pillow, and an IV drip on wheels following you to the bathroom and back. No!' She said. And no one spoke about the matter again. Loraine was in charge, and she stayed in charge until the end. She was there for him as his hair turned whiter, and his frame became thinner and weaker. She watched the man she loved lose his grip on life and begin to fade away. Only when she looked into his eyes did she recognize the man who sent her flowers every Friday and took her to the faraway places she desired to visit. Loraine sat with him and caressed his face and spoke to him about her love for him. She guided and positioned his hand over her heart, hoping somehow the rhythm of hers would connect with his and keep him alive longer; she was wrong. Dr. Paul Whitfield passed away of Cancer soon after being diagnosed.

Without Paul, Loraine's life became blurred and uncertain. She began stumbling through life as if she were placed in a darkened room filled with foreign objects. She needed Paul to give her direction. The Friday, after his funeral, a package arrived doing exactly that. Inside the package she found eleven long-stemmed red roses with a letter from Paul telling her how much he cherished the time they spent together, he spoke of the priceless moments and unforgettable pleasures. But he also spoke of her strength and determination. And Loraine realized, within that gift box, Paul provided the delicate light she needed to make her way around the darkened room of foreign objects and move through life without him. Paul assured her of the foothold she would gain to stable herself and move on. He gave her the name of the travel agency and agent to contact for her traveling pleasure, all expenses paid for the next five years. Where ever she wanted to go. Loraine held the letter close to her heart and cried.

Before his dad passed away, Alex sat with him for hours listening to him rattle on about his filing system and where he could find information about his patients. He was impressed by his father's recollection of details, dates, and times. His father's feeble hands shook uncontrollably as he opened file after file. "The difference between being a good doctor and a remarkable one," his father would say, "is designed by the genuine attention you show your patients." He showed Alex the sticky notes sprawled on the inside of certain files. As Alex read them, he realized his father wrote what other doctors would consider insignificant information, little facts he wanted to remember about the patient, so he or she would appreciate his knowledge of them. For instance, in John Bland's folder he wrote; 'Wife loves oranges.' So, whenever he scheduled appointments with John Bland, he'd stop at the market and pick out four of the best oranges he could find for John to take to his wife. Whether John actually took the oranges to her, he didn't know and whether he told her the oranges came from his doctor didn't matter to him. The gesture, he thought, simply demonstrated to the patient he remembered and cared about something personal pertaining to him and his life.

Reading his father's file on Les Cramer had Alex's full attention. This was the field of medicine he was interested in the most. He read the file repeatedly, did research, took notes, and waited for the opportunity to meet Les or Lee Cramer. Alex took over his father's practice when he was twenty-eight.

It was Dr. Paul Whitfield, who made the decision for Veronica to stay clear of Lee until she went to 'sleep',' and Les returned. He said he felt it was best if Les knew she had an ally; someone she could trust. A person Lee didn't know anything about. But when the days turned to weeks then months and years, Veronica began to get discouraged thinking Les wasn't coming back at all. Dr. Whitfield was the one who encouraged her not to give up. When Veronica went to him again and said, she felt she was wasting her time. It was Dr. Whitfield, who reminded her that Les would eventually gain the strength to push back, and she would need her.

Veronica acknowledged he was right. After all, she had made a promise to Les, and she had to see the promise through. She was reminded of the comradery she and Les formed during their school years. Neither of them had siblings, so they attached to each other, and now the two were not only best friends they were like sisters. If anyone was going to be there for Les, it was going to be her. So, she did as Dr. Whitfield suggested, she stayed her distance, watched, and waited.

Now with Dr. Whitfield gone, Veronica felt she had no one to encourage her to stay strong and hopeful. She cried the day Loraine Whitfield asked her to remove Dr. Whitfield's degrees and certificates from the office wall and put them into a box for her to pick up. Little Alex walked in, dressed in a suit and tie that reminded her so much of his father. She smiled. They began to talk about Dr. Whitfield and all his accomplishments. His comments about Les let Veronica know he understood better than she gave him credit. He made her feel hopeful again, and on that day she realized Little Alex had grown up and was now ready to walk in his father's footsteps. And as time went by, she had to admit, Alex Whitfield no longer needed the footsteps of his father. He had bypassed Dr. Paul Whitfield's steps and began taking longer and bolder strides of his own, eventually developing his own pace; a pace that would have made his father proud.

"Would you feel awkward talking to Dr. *Alex* Whitfield?"

"*Dr. Alex Whitfield.* Wow, that sounds so strange." Les chuckled then shrugged. "I think I do remember Dr. Whitfield being sick, but I didn't think it was so serious. I don't know, Ronnie. I'd have to consult with Alex before I make a decision like that. In my mind, he's still a kid."

"I understand. It was just a thought."

"I'm not saying no. I—I'm not familiar with his work. We'll see."

"Are you hungry? I'm hungry."

"Maybe some toast or something? M-m-m covered with strawberry jam."

Veronica laughed and motioned for the waitress, "It's good to be sitting here with you, Les. I've missed you so much. You don't know how hard it was to stay away from Lee. There were days I needed to talk to you, but it wasn't you. Can you imagine the messes I got myself into since you've been gone? I wanted to strangle her. I remember one day I was in the same store with her, and it seemed she turned and looked right at me like you were trying to reach out. I walked toward her, and before I had the chance to say anything, she turned away."

"Oh, Ronnie, that must have been awful for you. What store was it?"

"Huh?"

"What store were you in?

"It was so long ago. Oh yeah, It was a - a sporting goods store. That was the summer I was invited to go on a camping trip," Veronica held her hand up and stopped Les before she could comment. "Don't you say anything, I was asked to bring the games." She finished, and they laughed.

"Sporting goods? Well, we both know Lee wasn't going camping. I wonder what she was doing in a sporting goods store."

Les's eyes darted around the restaurant. "What time is it?" She asked nervously.

Veronica looked at her watch, "It's 12:45. Why?"

"I'm supposed to meet Kevin downtown at 1:00. We've got to go, Ronnie!" Les was already scooting out of the booth. "I promised him I wouldn't be late."

Veronica was scooting out of her seat too. "You're not going to sign the papers are you? Where do you have to go?" She left money on the table to cover their bill and tip and motioned to the waitress that they had to go.

"The Marshall Building downtown. Can we make it in fifteen minutes?"

"Depends on who's driving," Veronica chuckled.

They ran to the car, swung open the car doors and hopped in. Securing their seatbelts, Veronica started the car and raced to the end of the parking lot. She checked both ways and pulled out, making a left turn. A screech of tires brought her attention to the opposite side of the car. She slammed on her breaks and swerved to get out of the driver's way, but it was too late. The sudden impact sent Veronica's car spinning out of control. Someone screamed. Another impact, and then silence.

Veronica could hear sirens in the distance; she opened her eyes and tried to move. She hurt all over.

"Be still. The paramedics are on their way" She looked in the direction of the voice. The figure was blurry.

"What happened?" Veronica asked.

"You've been in an accident, but the paramedics are coming."

"Les!" Veronica called. "Where's Les? My friend was here with me. Is she alright?" Veronica forced her body to turn. The pain in her leg was excruciating, but she was bent on finding Les.

The second impact she now knew was a tree. She struggled to call Les's name; there was no response.

"Please, let her just be unconscious." Veronica prayed.

"Les, Les," she cried, "open your eyes. Please, open your eyes." Veronica tried to move again, but the pain was excruciating. The airbags had left burning powder on her arms, and she couldn't move her leg. She finally saw a movement out of the corner of her eye; it was Les. She was trying to come around.

"Les, Les," Veronica called to her. Les turned slowly in her direction, and Veronica cringed when she saw blood oozing from Les's head and nose.

Les was confused, and her voice was weak. "What happened?"

"Ma'am, try not to move. We're going to get both of you out of here. Are you hurting anywhere?"

"My head hurts," Les said, lifting her hand to her head, "and my neck."

Another paramedic was on the other side with Veronica. "I can't move my leg," Veronica told him.

The paramedics carefully pulled the women from the wreckage, put them on stretchers and the next thing they knew; they were on their way to the hospital. The sirens were blaring as the ambulance sped through the streets.

Les knew she must have gone unconscious again because when she opened her eyes, she was at the hospital. Veronica was standing at her bedside. "Hey, girlfriend, how ya doin'?"

Les saw the crutches under Veronica's arms. "Oh No, Ronnie!" she whispered.

Veronica was relieved to know it was Les and not Lee, who opened her eyes in the hospital room.

"Yeah I know. Can you believe it?" Veronica hopped back to show Les her cast. "Broken. It doesn't hurt though. Not yet." She laughed. "How are you? Girl, you kept the doctor's here on their toes. They want to keep you overnight.

I'm going to call Dr. Alex. You've been complaining of a headache, and I think he needs to take a look at you." Veronica got close to her ear. "Les? Les, listen to me. *Push back!*" Veronica demanded. "Whatever you do, if you have to, Les, *push back*. Don't let her through"

"Okay. I'll try." Tears filled Les's eyes. "I'll try." She said again.

"Les, I had to call Kevin too. They're asking questions I can't answer. He needs to be here. I only had the number that came up on the cell phone, so I called and left a message."

"He won't come," the headache was making Les sick to her stomach. "He hates me. He'll probably consider this a blessing in disguise." She felt the room spinning, and before she knew it, darkness engulfed her. Les could hear Veronica's voice, in the distance, echoing. "Push, Les, *push back!*"

5

Kevin was furious sitting in the waiting room of 'Hinkle, Matthews, and Iron'. How long had it been? He glanced at his watch, 2:30. He specifically told her to be there at 1:00.

"I knew it!" He said. "I knew she'd pull something to mess this up."

Dave Hinkle popped his head out of his office door, "Is she here yet, Kev?"

"Nope. Not yet, Dave." Kevin looked at his watch again, and then at the door, hoping she'd burst in at any moment. He stood and walked out to the hall and stood in front of the elevator.

She's not coming. He told himself.

He called the house. No answer. Kevin walked back into the office and strolled to the receptionist's desk.

"Can you reschedule my appointment?" He asked.

"Sure," she said. "Let's see here. Attorney Hinkle will be leaving town tonight. He'll be gone for a week and the week after that, is full. He'll be in court too, so the soonest I can get you in is - Ahh - how about three weeks, April 20th?"

"Three weeks! Can't I get in before then? All we have to do is sign papers."

"I can put you on the list to call if we get any cancelations. Do you want to do that?"

"Yes. Please. Can you get a message to Dave? Tell him I'll be in touch."

"I'll give him the message, Mr. Jenison."

Kevin stormed out of the office.

"When I see that lyin' . . ." The elevator doors opened, and he stepped in. The intensity of his anger made it seem like he would explode if one more thought entered his mind about that woman. He rode the elevator to the first floor. When the doors opened again, Kevin all but sprinted from the elevator and hurried across the lobby, causing people to move cautiously out of his way as he made his way to the front doors. His long strides turned into a jog when he burst through the doors and he found himself almost running to his car. All along, mumbling under his breath.

"Lord, please don't have that woman anywhere I can get my hands on her."

When he got home, he walked in and listened at the bottom of the stairs.

"Lee!" He called. "Lee!" He yelled louder as he entered the kitchen.

The message machine near the phone was blinking to indicate someone had called. He'd get it later. Right now, he was on a mission. He took the stairs two at a time, changed from his suit into a pair of jeans and a shirt, then went in search of his wife.

He had no idea where to start looking or even what he would say or do to her when he found her. It was 3:15 and still no word. He checked his rear-view mirror and was backing out of the driveway when his cell phone rang. He unleashed the phone from his belt and read the caller ID; it was Dave.

"Hi, Dave."

"So, what happened?"

"I don't know, but I'm going to find out. Let me call you back, man. I'm sitting here in the car trying to figure out which way to go to search for her."

"Why do you feel like you need to find her?" Dave asked.

"I don't know. Partly because I'm so angry, and I want answers, I guess. I mean, she wanted this divorce as much as I did. Here we are, at the final stages, and then this happens! You should have seen her this morning.

She was a completely different person; I'm talkin,' ponytail and jeans --
wanting to help the children fix their cereal -- picking up the dog to *comfort*
him, and then laying him on his cushion. Now, if that ain't strange, I don't
know what is. It was like she was seeing us for the first time. And then she
left to meet someone." Kevin realized his rambling probably made no sense
to Dave. "Dave, I don't have a clue where she might be."

"You say, she went to meet someone? Who?"

"I'm not sure."

"Do you think she's seeing someone? Another man?"

"I don't know. I wouldn't doubt it."

"Well, that's a good place to start, Kev. Go inside and check the call
log on the phone. See if she made any calls before she left. Come on, man,
you're an investigative attorney. You know what to do. This is stuff you'd
tell your clients."

Dave was right, he was allowing his anger to get in the way. He had
to take a deep breath, slow down, and think clearer.

"Dave," he said into the phone, "I'll call you back when I find out
what's going on."

He pulled back into the driveway, hopped out of the car, and went into
the house. He walked to the phone and realized the phone would only give
him the calls that came in. But, since no one was there to use the phone,
if a call had been made, all he needed to do is press redial. It was worth a
try; he picked up the phone and pressed the redial button.

✳✳✳

Veronica was surprised when the cell phone inside her purse started to
ring. *Who would be calling that number?* She pulled it out and answered.

"Hello?"

"Ah, yes, hello. My name is Kevin Jenison. Your number was on my
home phone. Who is this?"

"Hi Kevin, this is Veronica. Veronica Moore. I'm a friend of your -
umm - your wife. Did you get my message?"

"Message? No. What message?"

"I left a message on your telephone."

45

Kevin turned looking at the red beeping light on the phone. "You left a message on my phone? About what?" He asked.

"It's about Les, I mean Lee."

"What about her?" He asked coldly.

"There's been an accident. She's at the hospital."

"The hospital. What happened?"

"We were having coffee at the new coffee shop around the corner from you. She said she had to get to an appointment at 1:00, so I was taking her, but when we pulled out of the parking lot, a car went through a red light, and it hit us. The hospital needs information for L---Lee. Can you come?"

"What hospital?"

"Gilbert Mercy on Val Vista. They brought us here by ambulance. My car was totaled."

"Okay, I'm on my way. Is she alright?" He asked dryly.

"I don't know too much of anything yet. I'm still waiting for the doctor to come in. But, like I said, they need information I don't have."

"Is she conscious?"

"Sometimes. She's in and out."

"What information do they need that she can't give them?"

Veronica thought for a minute. *What should I say?*

"She left her purse at home, and they need her insurance card and driver's license."

"Okay, I'll be there in 15 minutes."

"I'll tell her you're on your way."

Kevin didn't care whether she told her he was on his way or not; the point was; he *had* to be there. The sad thing about it, is at least now, there was a reasonable explanation as to why she missed the appointment. During most of their marriage, the problems that came up stemmed from the fact that she could care less. This was a welcomed change, as morbid as it sounded.

On the way to the hospital, Kevin called Dave to inform him about Lee. He got his voice mail and left the message. "I'll call you when I get more details." He said and hung up.

It only took Kevin ten minutes to get to the hospital. He found a parking space and walked toward the emergency doors. The receptionist sitting behind the glass sat up and smiled when he walked through the doors and approached the window.

"Can I help you?" She asked.

"I'm looking for my - - wife."

Immediately the receptionist's smile disappeared.

"Her name is Lee Jenison. She was brought in this afternoon by ambulance after a car accident."

"Lee Jenison? No, we don't have a Lee Jenison."

Kevin closed his eyes and sighed, "How about a Lee Cramer?" He asked.

"No, no 'Lee' Cramer either, but there's a 'Les Cramer. Please wait here." She disappeared for a while and when she came back to the window, she was smiling again.

"I'm sorry, I must have written the name wrong. The doctor wants to admit her for observation. She'll be going to the third floor."

"I was told you needed some information to treat her properly." Kevin reached into his back pocket for his wallet and removed a plastic card and handed it to her. "Here's my insurance card, she should have one too."

"Fantastic, thank you." She said, taking the insurance card. She turned to make a copy. "I also need her social. She couldn't seem to remember that either, or her telephone number."

"She couldn't remember her social or telephone number?"

The receptionist chuckled and shook her head, "Her address either. She's had a pretty bad blow to her head. That could be the reason. She said she usually carries everything in her purse, but she didn't have a purse when she came in."

Kevin thought about what the receptionist said.

Strange, she couldn't remember? Lee never forgot anything, her purse, her social, or anything. What was going on?

"There was someone with my wife. Her name's Veronica. Where can I find her?"

"Oh yes, Ms. Moore is in the room with your wife. They're in room six. If you go to the door, I'll buzz you in."

"Thanks." Kevin walked to the door and waited for the sound of the buzzer before pulling it open. He searched for room six. The door was closed so Kevin knocked.

The voice inviting him into the room did not belong to his wife. He stepped inside and saw Lee on the hospital bed. "Is she sl- - - sleep?" He whispered.

"Unconscious." Veronica replied, "She opened her eyes for couple of minutes, and then she was gone again." Veronica pulled herself up on her crutches then stood and offered her hand, "My name's Veronica. Veronica Moore."

Kevin shook her hand and gestured toward the crutches. "You okay?" He asked.

"Yeah," Veronica nodded, lowering her eyes to the cast on her leg. "It's broken. I'll be in this thing for six to eight weeks." She gestured at the crutches." If I don't kill myself first." She tried to chuckle.

Kevin ignored her humorous attempt, "Can you tell me what happened, Ms. Moore?"

"Someone ran a red light and smashed into my car when we left the coffee shop. He hit us pretty hard and sent us spinning into a tree. Les has been in and out of consciousness since we got here. Drunk driver."

"Les?" Kevin asked.

"Pardon me?"

"You called my wife Les. Her name's Lee."

"I've only known her as Les. I'm sorry; that's the name I gave the receptionist too. She came back and told me you were out there inquiring about a 'Lee Cramer'. I told her about the mix up. We went to school together."

"Tell me something - uhh - Veronica. Are you here for a short time? Just visiting Arizona or something?"

"No, I live close by. Why?"

"I don't understand why I've never heard of you? Suddenly, you and my wife are best friends - - - School chums - - - having coffee?" He tilted his head and waited for her answer.

"Well." Veronica turned and looked at Les then back to Kevin. Uh, well now, that's a *very* good question and I - - - I've, I mean." She pointed back and forth between her and Les, "We've got a good answer for you too. As soon as Les wakes up, I'm sure she's going to want to tell you everything herself."

Kevin looked suspiciously at Veronica, and then to his wife. "Are you two, you know?"

Veronica didn't understand at first, but soon realized what he was implying, "NO! God, No. Nothing like that."

"Because if you are, I mean, it totally explains, uhhh, I mean I could - -"

"You could what? You could understand why she's like she is? What?" She shrieked. "This is my best friend, and she's hurt and the only thing you can ask is *that*?"

"Just hold on," Kevin demanded, "You're the one she ran off to have coffee with."

"Ran off to --? She may have been *running,* but it sounds more like she was running *from* someone than *to* someone!"

"Are you implying . . . ?"

Someone tapped at the door. They turned their attention to the doctor as he approached Les's bed.

"I think you two should kind of keep it down in here. This can't be good for the patient. She's still out, huh?" He took a small light out of his pocket, lifted her eyelids, and then examined Les's other injuries. "The tests we got back, show Mrs. Jenison is suffering from a pretty severe concussion. We're not sure why she's in and out of consciousness though." The doctor turned to Veronica. "We did call Dr. Whitfield like you suggested."

"Dr. who?" Kevin interrupted.

"Dr. Whitfield," Veronica repeated nervously. "Dr. Whitfield is a psychiatrist. And when I told him Les was here, he wanted to come over and um, see her."

"Why'd you call a psychiatrist?"

"Well, I'm not quite sure." Veronica lied. "It seemed like the thing to do at the time. My God, she hit her head, and she's still unconscious. Doesn't that make you wonder what's wrong? The doctor just said they don't understand why she's in and out of consciousness."

"Yea, I might wonder but I'm not going to run off and call a *psychiatrist!*" Kevin shouted.

"Then who would you call?"

"I don't know. But I think I'd leave it up to the doctor's here to suggest who to call. You pop up out of nowhere, and suddenly you're an expert on the treatment my wife needs."

"I'm not saying I'm an expert."

"Seems to me, you know more about the situation then you care to share, Ms. Moore!"

"At least I care!"

The doctor stepped closer to the door.

"Again, I don't think this is good for the patient. I suggest you two either keep your voices down or step out of the room."

Veronica glared at Kevin.

"I'm not going anywhere." She said, and with as much dignity as she could muster, she placed her crutches under her arms and hobbled to Les's bedside. She clumsily moved the tray out of the way and pulled her chair closer to the bed. The whole ordeal took more time and made more noise than Veronica intended, and she could feel the two men's eyes on her. She plopped down into the chair and would not give them the satisfaction of looking their way.

Kevin walked to the opposite side of the room and sat in a chair facing a window.

Satisfied with the silence, the doctor left the room.

As soon as Les closed her eyes, darkness met her and pulled her deep within it. It was a familiar pulling; one she had experienced many times before, and she prepared herself to fight for control. She listened to the sound of Veronica's voice echoing from the top of the darkness, "Push Les!" Les tried to comply by pushing harder, but she was too weak and needed help. Veronica would help her. "Veronica," she cried out, "Veronica, help me push!" She pleaded. Beads of sweat formed at her brow line and streamed down her face. She became determined "I'm going to win this time. I'm not giving up any more of my life," she demanded, pushing harder. "Ronnie!" she called out, "Please help me. I can't do it by myself. Ronnie!" Veronica appeared in the darkness.

"You have to do it, Les. No one can help you. You have to do it yourself. Remember everything she took from you, Les-- she stole from you. Remember

what you told me? You've always wanted children, and now you have them. She treated them badly, but you can show them what it's like to have a good mom - a mother who loves them. And Kevin, Les. You love him. He deserves to know how you feel. He came back for you. He came back for you. He came back for you." The words echoed in the darkness and got further away as Veronica's image faded.

Les wasn't alone; there was something else there in the darkness with her or someone. She was quiet. The air was stifling. She could barely breathe. All of a sudden, her reflection appeared in front of her. It was her image, but different. The image wore a hairstyle she would never wear, and her lips were covered with bright red lipstick. The image began to mimic Veronica with a sneer, "Push, Les, push," she laughed. "Remember what she stole, Les." She mocked.

The laughing ended abruptly when Les pushed.

Lee was caught off guard and stumbled backward. The push angered her, and she glared at Les, as she steadied herself. "You're not strong enough to win this, Les. Think about it, I've been out for ten years. I'm stronger."

This time, when Les pushed, she focused on the years Lee stripped from her. Steadying herself, she pushed with all her might. Lee was surprised at Les's strength, she staggered and almost fell. The pushing not only shocked Lee, it also frightened her. 'How could Les possess so much strength?'

Les pushed one last time and this time she concentrated on her children; Kelly and Keith. She focused on Kevin, and she concentrated on Veronica. She closed her eyes and pushed with everything she had.

Lee tried to stand against the pushing but was no match for Les. She was too far back into the darkness. There was nothing else to do except concede. She had to admit she underestimated her rival and this time she lost. She tumbled further away until she completely disappeared into the darkness.

Les felt a breeze across her face and knew it meant she had won; she was free.

It was almost an hour since Veronica, and Kevin last spoke. The hospital room they moved Les to was quieter than the emergency room. While Veronica sat at Les's bedside, Kevin found a comfortable chair across the room. He leaned back and propped his feet up on an ottoman. He found and picked up an old newspaper and was leafing through it when Veronica turned to him.

"Would it bother you if I turned on the television?" Veronica asked snippily.

Kevin put the paper down and turned his attention to Veronica, "Not at all."

She picked up the remote and lifted it toward the television. A movement drew her attention to Les's hand. *Did her hand move or --?* It happened again.

"She moved!"

Kevin tossed the newspaper aside and sat forward.

"There she goes again." Veronica pointed to the hand that moved.

Kevin rushed to the other side of Les's bed. "Maybe I should get the doctor."

Les slowly opened her eyes. Veronica waited, not knowing whether to say her name, in case it was Lee and not Les gaining consciousness. Les turned her head and saw her friend looking down at her, "I pushed back, Ronnie," she whispered.

At that moment, Veronica realized she had been holding her breath. The relief was overwhelming as she leaned back on her crutches and gave Les an encouraging thumbs up, "Yes!" she affirmed. "You certainly did, girlfriend."

Les smiled at her friend. The pain in her head was making her sick to her stomach again, but she rushed on, "I could hear you, Ronnie. I could hear you through the darkness."

Veronica cleared her throat and gave an awkward nod toward the other side of the bed. Les slowly turned her head and met Kevin's amber gaze. "Kevin," Les whispered, "I didn't know you were - -" She stopped. "I'm so sorry I missed the appointment. I know it was important to you."

Kevin frowned. He was confused. The thought of his wife being sorry about anything concerning him was absolutely unheard of. How was he supposed to respond to this? He searched for the right words and finally said; "It's okay. Dave - uh rescheduled." He cursed under his breath because he thought his words sounded broken and cold and tried again, "I mean, there may be a cancelation and - - ah, never mind. So, they say, you've got a serious concussion?"

"I do?" Les turned her head slowly, looking from Kevin to Veronica and back to Kevin. "That explains the headache." Les lifted her hand and placed it lightly on her head. " My stomach is kind of queasy too."

"I'll go get the doctor," Kevin said awkwardly and rushed out the door.

Les looked at the door, then shrugged, and turned back to Veronica, "What do you suppose that was about?"

Veronica's eyes were fixed on the door too, and her only response was a slow shrug of her shoulders.

"What's he doing here, Ronnie? Did you call him?" Every word seemed strained and caused more tension, which made the throbbing in her head worse.

"I had to, Les. They were asking questions downstairs I didn't know the answers to, like your telephone number, social security number, address. Questions you couldn't answer either. What was I supposed to do? I had to call him. Don't you remember me saying that?"

"What did you tell him?"

"Nothing, but I don't know how long I can keep this up. He needs to know, but you should be the one to tell him, not me. and, you might as well know; I called Alex Whitfield too."

Les reached up and covered her forehead with both hands, closed her eyes, and moaned against the steady throb.

6

Once out of the room, Kevin tried to compose himself. He leaned against the wall and closed his eyes. Something wasn't right. He glanced up the hall, and then down the other way for the nurses' station, and when he spotted a cluster of nurses standing around, he pulled himself away from the wall and walked toward them. Still, the continual nagging that tugged at the corners of his mind made him aware, something – an important piece of *something* was missing, but what?

The words echoed in his head, *'I'm so sorry I missed the appointment. I know how important it was to you.'* Again her words came. *'I know how important it was to you.'* He couldn't stop thinking about them. There was something not right about how she said it-- not right about the situation altogether. Here she was, regaining consciousness after experiencing a terrifying car accident, and she's sorry she missed an appointment that was important to *him*?

Although Kevin recalled other occasions when he had witnessed his wife's vulnerability, he was certain he had never witnessed her being sorry about how her vulnerability affected him.

His mind was immediately drawn to the day she gave birth to Keith. He thought he caught a glimmer of something--a moment of weakness-- and then it was gone. The way she considered him and reached for the baby was completely out of character. And, in a split second, the glimmer was gone, and she was back to her normal self; cold and manipulative.

But, today was different. This morning at the house and now in the room; he couldn't put his finger on it, but, there was something familiar, yet frightening about the situation, and it nagged him. He closed his eyes for a brief moment and thought about her words again. It wasn't only what she said; it was the way she said it. He continued walking toward the nurses' station almost oblivious to the activity buzzing around him. When he got to the counter, he stopped.

"Can I help you, sir?"

The voice broke his concentration, and it took a second for him to remember why he was there.

"My -uh wife - she's awake. Her head is hurting. She says she needs something for the pain. And I'd like to speak to the doctor in charge, please."

The nurse glanced around the station for the doctor, but he was nowhere in sight.

"Which room is it? I can send him to the room when he gets back," she said.

He leaned forward. "Okay, I'm confused and I don't like to be confused. I'm looking for some simple answers, and I need to talk to the doctor in charge of my wife so I can go home. I'm in room 306. I hope he won't be long." He pivoted and walked toward the room.

"Mr. Jenison?" Kevin turned and stopped as the doctor caught up to him. "I'm Dr. Wilson." The two men shook hands. "You wanted to speak to me?"

Kevin's voice took on a condescending tone, "If you're my wife's doctor, I'd like to speak to you. She's awake, and she's in a lot of pain; her head is hurting, and she's saying she's sick to her stomach. Can she get something for the pain?"

"Of course, I'm on my way to her room now. I'll walk with you."

"I need other information too, Doc. Do you think you can answer a few questions for me?"

Dr. Wilson smiled, "Well, I'm the doctor assigned to your wife until Dr. Whitfield comes in tomorrow. The only thing I can tell you is she's had a serious blow to the head which means she's going to experience a headache for a while, but she'll be fine. Glad to hear she's awake now though?" Kevin nodded, and the two men walked toward Les's room together.

Kevin slowed his pace as they approached the door to the room. "Uh, listen, Doc. I'm not sure how to put this, but there's something you need to be aware of. Something strange is going on with my wife."

"Strange?"

"Yeah, strange, unusual, out of the ordinary. The way she acts, her manner of dress – way off. She's acting really, you know . . ."

The doctor stopped and considered him. "Strange?"

"Yeah."

"Well, let's go in and check her out."

The two men entered Les's hospital room.

"Welcome back, "Dr. Wilson laughed and approached her bed, "I was beginning to think I wasn't going to talk to you again until morning." He thoroughly examined her eyes and listened to her heart. He could tell the slightest movement caused quite a bit of pain. He stood back and thought for a while, then said, "I'm going to suggest you stay here overnight. We mentioned the possibility earlier, but now I'm convinced it's the best thing. I'd like to keep a close eye on you tonight and run more tests in the morning. We're going to try to help you get rid of this headache or, at least, make it tolerable for you to go home. Okay?"

Les didn't want to stay, but she reluctantly nodded her head.

"Okay, I'll stay." She said, raising her hands to her head.

"I'm going to send one of the nurses in to give you something for the pain and make you a little more comfortable. Are you allergic to anything?" He flipped through her chart while he waited for an answer.

Les turned to Kevin and shrugged, "I don't think so."

"No," Kevin finished. "She's not allergic to anything."

"Codeine!" Veronica blurted out. "She's allergic to Codeine."

Both Les and Kevin turned in Veronica's direction. Kevin blurted back, "No, she's not!"

Veronica closed her eyes, nodded her head, "Yes, she is."

Before Kevin had the chance to speak again, Dr. Wilson interjected, "Ah, here it is. You're right. She's allergic to Codeine." Kevin squinted an inquiring eye in Veronica's direction.

The doctor laughed nervously and stepped closer to the door. "I'll send a nurse right in. If everything goes well tomorrow, we'll see about letting you go home, but for right now I think you need more rest. You took a bad bump to the head, and I want to be able to watch you closely for the next 24 hours. On a scale from one to ten; how bad is the pain?"

Les slowly moved her hand to her head and closed her eyes against the throbbing pain. She swallowed back the sickness in her throat and held up both hands for the doctor to see her pain had elevated to a level ten. She whispered, "Please hurry."

"The nurse will be right in, and I suggest," he turned to Kevin and Veronica, "you two need to go get some dinner or something. Let her rest and then come back tomorrow. It's been a trying day for everyone. You need to rest too." He said to Veronica. "Before I leave, are there any more questions for me?" They both shook their heads, and Dr. Wilson left the room.

Veronica turned to Les, "I know where you'll be having dinner tonight," she teased. "I'm going home to get some rest, and I'll be back tomorrow morning; he's right; it has been a tough day, girlfriend, and I'm tired. Not to mention having to deal with these things" She reached for the crutches and placed them under her arms. Les's hands moved to her head again, and she regarded Veronica sympathetically.

"So sorry," Les whispered, holding her head as if holding it somehow controlled the throbbing. "If I hadn't been in such a hurry—"

"Please, girl, don't you even worry about me. You concentrate on getting yourself better. I'm gonna go home, take a pain pill, and get off my feet."

"I'll walk out with you," Kevin said.

Both Kevin and Veronica moved toward the door. Kevin turned one last time to look at Les then he and Veronica walked in awkward silence to the elevator.

Concentrating on developing a rhythm in her movement Veronica stepped, crutch, stepped, crutch, stepped--. Finally, Kevin turned to her, "Do you need me to help you with anything?"

"No, I'm good, thanks."

"So," he began, "how long did you say you and Lee were friends?"

"I didn't."

The elevator doors opened, and they stepped in. The awkward silence engulfed them.

Kevin rushed on.

"I'm asking because, in all the time Lee, and I were married; the only friend she talked about was Brenda Crenshaw. Lee's always been what people call, a loner."

"Lee's friends with Brenda Crenshaw?"

"Yeah, apparently she has two friends, Brenda and now, you. Jealous?"

"Right," was the only answer Veronica gave.

"You're not gonna make this easy for me, are you?"

"Listen, Kevin. You need to talk to Le - - I mean, your wife. She can clear up everything."

"Everything like what?"

"Everything, like *everything.*" The elevator doors opened, and Veronica secured the crutches under her arms and hobbled quickly toward the exit doors. It was when she reached the doors that she realized Kevin had been able to stay at her side with no problem. Knowing all along what Veronica was trying to do, he opened the door wide, and watched as she maneuver the crutches through them, not once letting his smirk fade.

Once outside, Veronica stopped fast and dropped her shoulders, then she let out a loud sigh.

"What's wrong," Kevin asked sarcastically, "forget something?" He smiled, cocking his head.

"It's my car. I don't - I don't have my car. The accident."

"Ohh yeah." Kevin snapped his fingers. "You probably need a ride. Huh?"

Veronica could hear the sarcasm in his voice and fought the urge to tell him to take his ride and shove it. Instead, she surrendered. "You offering?"

He shrugged, "I could save you a lot of inconveniences. And I could also bring you back tomorrow."

Veronica thought of the hours she would spend on a bus as it looped around the valley rather than take a straight, less painful route to Chandler, or a taxi that would overcharge her. All she wanted to do was get off her feet. She brought her crutches together, leaned against them and gave a nod. "I live in Chandler."

"I'll be right back with the car. Would you like to stand here or wait over on the bench?"

"I'll stand here, thanks."

Kevin rushed off through the parking lot to get the car while Veronica waited. She wondered how she could avoid his questions during the ride home.

"Oh boy!" She said, adjusting her weight and pulling the crutches closer, she wished she let Kevin help her to the bench, but it was too late now.

She thought of Les. *What would happen during the night? Would she be strong enough to continue pushing back? Would they walk into the hospital room in the morning and be met by--?* She didn't even want to think about it. She took a deep breath and focused on the black Mercedes pulling close to the curve. When she saw Kevin behind the wheel, she hobbled toward the car. Kevin jumped out and came around to help her.

"I got it." She protested.

He ignored her and opened the door. Veronica moved awkwardly around him to sit down and he took the crutches and placed them on the back seat.

7

As he drove, Kevin stole glimpses of Veronica out of the corner of his eye. Under the circumstances, she was on guard and tense. But he still wondered what a normal conversation would be like with her.

"So how long have you lived in Chandler?" Kevin's attempt to break the ice with small talk was obvious, but Veronica was vague and her answer short.

"A couple of years."

"Were you born in Arizona or did you relocate from somewhere?"

"Why do you ask?" She was grateful for the ride, but not quite ready to be friends with him.

"Listen, Veronica. I'm only trying to understand a few things here, but I'm willing to call a truce for tonight. Despite how you may feel about me; I'm not your enemy. Hell, I don't even know who you are. Tell you what, let's go, sit somewhere, and grab a bite to eat. You've got to be hungry, and once you get home you'll need to get off your feet. You don't have any business hobbling around the kitchen, trying to cook somethin'. Truce?"

Veronica thought for a minute. He was right. She had wondered how she was going to get around at home. She hadn't eaten all day, and she was starving. Dinner sounded good, so she took in a deep breath and conceded.

"Truce." She whispered.

"That's what I'm talkin' about. Now we're making progress." He tapped the steering wheel. "I'm familiar with a couple of restaurants in the area, but I'm partial one."

Kevin drove a few miles and turned into a parking lot that Veronica recognized immediately. He saw Veronica shake her head. "What, you don't like this place?"

"Actually, you've got good taste," Veronica chuckled, "this is one of my favorite spots to eat. Have you eaten here before?"

"Oh yeah, plenty of times." He smiled, "Tom; that's the owner here, he and I are pretty good friends. We've golfed together a couple of times. Well, let me clarify that statement," he laughed. "Tom golfs, I, on the other hand, hit a couple of balls, the grass, and my foot, but I'm determined. I guess that's why he continues to allow me to tag along."

Veronica, didn't want to, but found herself laughing too easily at Kevin's comment.

He pulled into a parking space close to the door and hopped out to help Veronica to the entrance. He waited for her to stand and steady herself and handed her the crutches. She placed a crutch under each arm and hobbled toward the restaurant door. The doors swung open as soon as they reached them, and the hostess was suddenly there with a wide smile.

"Oh, My Goodness. Here, let me help you." She helped Veronica inside and motioned for more help. "Happy to have you dining with us again, Mr. Jenison. We'll get you seated right away."

Kevin nodded. "Thanks, Ashley, is Tom in today?"

"Yes Sir, we'll get you seated, and I'll go tell him you're here. Here comes Christopher now. "Chris, please make sure Mr. Jenison and his friend get seated comfortably?"

"Sure," Christopher said, picking up a few menus and motioning for the couple to follow him. Again, Kevin helped Veronica maneuver until they reached their table.

Seated at a table, Veronica opened and studied the menu. "I think I'm gonna go for the top sirloin today. I'm starved."

"That sounds good to me," Kevin agreed and turned to Christopher. "Make that two top sirloins," he lifted his eyes to Veronica and shrugged. "What do you think - garlic mashed potatoes and mixed veggies for sides?"

"Absolutely," Veronica said. She felt her stomach rumble at the mention of food, and she prayed they'd hurry the preparation of it.

"Can I start you off with something to drink? Do you need a wine list?" Christopher asked.

"Can you bring my wine from the vault? It's under my name, *Jenison.*" Kevin turned to Veronica, "I think you'll enjoy the taste. We can both use a glass or two of wine after our day. Right?"

Veronica chuckled, "Are you kidding? I think, yes."

Kevin handed the menus to Christopher and watched him disappear behind the bar. He turned his attention back to Veronica and studied her for a minute.

Kevin noticed right away that Veronica was an attractive African-American woman. Her eyes were a deep brown that matched her hair. Her body was slender and had no problem filling out the navy blue capris she wore with a white pullover, sleeveless shirt. It was easy to make her laugh, which told Kevin, under normal circumstances, Veronica Moore was probably a fun, vivacious woman.

"So?" Kevin began, "I guess now's the best time to talk about our situation. I have to say, I'm curious. How does one become a best friend to one's wife within a couple of hours? I mean, Lee has never mentioned your name, Ms. Veronica Moore."

"I can tell you this much, Kevin, your wife and I have been friends for a long time. We went to school together. You went to Lexington High, right? We used to go to the football games there when you were playing. You were good. I know this is complicated for you, but I'm sure *Lee* will explain everything to you. It's not my place, Kevin. Even if I wanted to explain it, I wouldn't know where to start."

"Explain what?" Kevin asked leaning forward.

"This whole ordeal--because there is an explanation. Listen, I'm not even going to say I understand what you're thinking or what you're going through. I don't! But I will say this; what you *think* you know, you don't know, Kevin. Please hang in there and everything will be cleared up, but you're gonna have to be patient. It's not my place, and it's too complicated."

Kevin sat back in his chair and studied Veronica. "Ok, Veronica. I'll stop asking questions tonight. I'm kind of liking the ceasefire we've got going on. Let's have a nice dinner, and I'll get you home so you can get some much needed rest."

Christopher appeared with their drinks and Veronica lifted her glass and tipped it toward her nose. She nodded and swirled the wine around in the glass and lifted it to her nose again. "Do I smell violets and blackberries?" She asked.

"Hmm, yes, you're good. You'll love the taste too. A smokey type, earthy flavor. Try it."

Veronica lifted the glass to her mouth and sipped her wine. It was delicious. She closed her eyes and enjoyed the way the flavors blended in her mouth. She allowed the wine to linger a little and rolled it around on her tongue, and swallowed. When she opened her eyes, she saw Kevin watching her, his head cocked to the side, waiting for her response.

"You're absolutely right, Kevin. The wine is extremely good. It'll be excellent with our meal. What is it?"

"Ahhh, you got your secrets. I've got mine. But, I might share it with you one day. I knew you'd like it. I guess I know a little somethin' somethin', huh?" They laughed.

"Kevin, my friend!" the voice came from behind Veronica. Tom Pryor approached the table and over to Kevin, and the two men shook hands. Kevin stood and introduced Tom to Veronica. "It's good to meet you, Ma'am. He glanced at Veronica, and then did a double take. His eyes remained on Veronica as he told Kevin, "I -uh - hope you enjoy your meal." Then to Veronica he said, "Please, *do* enjoy your meal." You're certainly in good company here." He said referring to Kevin, but still having a difficult time tearing his gaze from Veronica.

Tom was a tall man with a pleasant smile, impeccably dressed, and from the appearance of the restaurant and the overflow of patrons, extremely successful.

Veronica smiled and sipped her wine.

"How are you, man? "Tom turned back to Kevin. "Ready to get back on the golf course?" He laughed with a laugh that seemed almost too big for him, and he patted Kevin on the shoulder. To Veronica, he said, "The last time we played golf, I thought Kevin here was gonna dig his way to China."

The two men laughed. "Everything's still on for tomorrow. Right?" Tom asked.

Veronica had been enjoying the banter between the two men, but when Tom asked about tomorrow, she saw Kevin's laugh subside.

"It's kind of too late to change things now," mused Kevin, "so yeah, I suppose everything's still on. Only one minor adjustment and I'm not sure how it's going to work out yet. Lee's been in an accident and the hospital's keeping her overnight for observation. She's got a bad concussion. They say she may be able to come *home* tomorrow, but we'll see."

"Oh, man, sorry to hear that. Uh, you two still, uh?" Tom was searching for the right words.

Kevin interrupted, "Yeah, man – divorce still going through. It's just not working out like I planned." Kevin glanced at Veronica and cleared his throat. He placed his hand nervously on the back of his neck and then looked back at Tom. Tom understood, and so did Veronica.

Tom said, "Yeah, well – that's too bad."

Christopher approached the table with their entrees.

"Here we go. Two orders of our finest top sirloin with a side order of garlic mashed potatoes and mixed veggies. Enjoy, enjoy. Can I get you anything else?"

The aroma of the food was heavenly, and its arrival changed the mood of the conversation as Veronica and Kevin dug in. Veronica took solace knowing it was *Lee,* the two men were referring to, not *Les.*

"We'll talk later, Kevin, Go ahead and enjoy your meal." Tom turned to Veronica. "It was a pleasure meeting you ma'am. I hope to see you again real soon. Kev, I'll see you tomorrow. Keep me posted on things" Tom unhooked his cell phone from the case on his belt then walked off typing what seemed to be an important text. He turned back long enough to say, "By the way, the meal's on me, Kev." Then he disappeared in the back before Kevin could protest.

Christopher stood waiting to see if Veronica or Kevin needed anything else.

"I'm good. How about you, Veronica?"

"I'm good too."

Christopher nodded and left the table.

Kevin's cell phone buzzed. He reached down and pulled it from the belt case to read a new text that completely caught him off guard; he coughed nervously and squinted toward Tom's office, then put the cell away. His lips turned up into a slow smile as he put his napkin in place, picked up his silverware and began to eat.

They ate in silence for a while. It was Veronica who spoke first.

"What are your thoughts about tomorrow?"

"Tomorrow? Oh, you mean for the hospital? I'm not sure. Hopefully, I'll get some of my questions answered so I can move forward. I'm ready to go on with life with my children who deserve to be happy. Please, don't take this the wrong way, I understand she's your friend, but I'm tired of Lee Cramer making a mess of my life. I no longer want to try to make this marriage work. I've tried for eight years. Marriages don't work with only one person trying. It's over. I've had enough of Lee Cramer."

"Don't you mean Lee Jenison?"

"Nope, she made it clear before the wedding, she had no intention of taking my name. At first, I didn't mind, I mean, so what. Right? What's in a name? But after a while, I realized she didn't want my name because she didn't want *me* or anything connected to me. How's that for an eye-opening discovery?"

Veronica laughed, "You mean *experience*? An eye-opening experience?"

"Actually, it's when I '*discovered*' what I was gonna be *experiencing*, that I realized I had a potential disaster on my hands. You have no idea."

They finished their meal with no more talk about Lee Cramer, and Veronica found Kevin to be great company. She understood why Les enjoyed talking to him. He was thoughtful and intelligent. His conversation was light and sometimes funny. She found herself laughing out loud quite often during the meal. It dawned on Veronica that she was having dinner with the man her best friend had fallen in love with many years ago, and now she could appreciate why.

8

Veronica awoke with a horrific shooting pain radiating down her leg. She breathed heavily trying to pull herself out of bed. The doctor said the pain would get worse, but she didn't think he meant excruciatingly. She tried getting out of bed again, but the pain was so fierce that she fell back onto her pillows. An enormous urge to give in to Oprah's famous 'ugly-cry' loomed, but was quickly overpowered by memories of yesterday's events; Les's reappearance, the accident. And then there was Kevin's promise to be there by 8:00 to drive her to the hospital to check, not so much on Les, but whether her friend was still there.

She looked at the clock. Six-thirty, it screamed back at her! She had exactly an hour and a half to get dressed and be ready if she didn't want to strain that rigid air of punctuality she'd sensed in Kevin. Then she thought of Les and the pain she had been in last night. Suddenly, Veronica's aches and pains weren't so bad anymore, and she managed to push herself out of bed.

Pure, painstaking determination had driven her step-by-step process as she prepared for Kevin's arrival. Her face bore a fine sheen of perspiration as she hobbled, fully dressed and groomed, into the kitchen for the coffee; she'd had the foresight to prepare the night before. Much as she tried to ignore it, her pain level had increased, but she bit it back as she poured herself a cup of coffee. She placed a crutch gingerly under one arm, and then the other, after that she picked up her cup and used her hips to maneuver the crutches as she hobbled toward the patio doors. She spied her bottle of pain meds on the counter but forced her eyes straight ahead. She wasn't about to become victim to a pain-med high at a time when clear thinking was so important. But, more shooting pains brought her to an abrupt halt. She held on to the counter until they were tolerable enough for her to catch her breath. She readjusted her crutches, steadied her coffee and opted for the sitting room instead of the patio. This time as she passed the bottle of pills, she palmed them and carried them with her to the nearest chair. She tossed two of them down her throat with her first swig of coffee. Her hand automatically grappled for the remote, and she turned on the TV as she leaned her head back, closed her eyes, and waited for some relief.

She was immersed in the morning news; more fighting in the Middle East, accolades, and criticisms of the President's latest actions, depending upon who was talking. The first part of the weather forecast was beginning when she thought she suffered enough shooting pains to determine her first dose of pain meds didn't work, so she took two more.

By the time the doorbell rang at 8:00 Veronica was feeling no pain. "Come on in, Kev." She sang.

Kevin tried the door. "It's locked."

"Oh! Okay, I'm coming."

Kevin waited and waited. He leaned closer to the door and turned his ear to it. He heard a loud *thud*!

"Veronica?" he called. "Are you ok?

"Uh, Kevin, I have a situation here. If you check under the pot by the door, you'll find an extra key."

Kevin found the key and opened the door to the sight of Veronica trying to get up from the floor. He hurries to help her.

"Are you okay?"

"Oh it hurt like hell this morning, but I took some pain medicine, and I'm *good to go.*" Her last words were exaggerated and loud.

"What pain medicine did you take? Something the doctors gave you?"

"Yep and they work great. I took two this morning before I had my coffee, and then I took another one or two later." She fanned her hand in the air, "I don't remember what time, but I took another one about an hour ago. No pain!"

"What are they? Can I see them?"

Veronica reached into her purse and took the medicine bottle out then handed it to Kevin. Kevin read the label. "Percocet." He looked at Veronica. "How many of these did you take?"

Veronica's brows knitted. "Well, first I took - -"

Kevin watched as she began to count on her fingers and shook his head. "Tell you what. Let me hold on to these, and when we get to the hospital, we'll go talk to the doctor about your pain."

"What? You think I took too many? I'm okay, right?"

Kevin chuckled. "Oh, you're fine." He helped her carefully to the car. Twice her crutches hit him in the face when he tried to retrieve them to put them in the back. Finally, Veronica was secured in a seatbelt with her door firmly closed. Kevin made sure the house was locked and came back and slid behind the wheel. He secured his seatbelt and backed out of the driveway.

"Now, we're ready to go. Right?"

"Right! Thank you, Kev." Still the sing-song tone. "I understand now, why Les loves you so much."

"Who?" Kevin asked.

"Les. You know, Les, your wife?"

He laughed, "You mean Lee. And no, you're wrong. She doesn't love me at all."

"No, I don't mean Lee," Veronica said turning in Kevin's direction, "I don't mean Lee! Lee can't love anyone. She doesn't even love herself."

The smile was gone from Kevin's face. "What are you talking about, Veronica? *Who's Les?*"

"Les is my friend, Kevin. She's my friend."

They rode along in silence while Kevin tried to digest what she was saying. "Okay, so how is she my wife?" He finally asked. "You're saying your friend, Les, is my wife? Girl, you ain't takin' no more of these pills," he laughed, as he drove into the hospital parking lot. He found a parking space and pulled into it.

"You stay right here Veronica. I'm going to get a wheelchair."

Veronica moved to open the door. "No, don't do that. I feel helpless."

"Please, humor me. I want to do this for you. Okay?"

Veronica studied his smile, which was disarming. "Okay, do your thing." She followed him with her eyes as he walked crisply to the entrance. "Hmph, Lee's a fool. I hope Les isn't."

Two interns approached the car with a wheelchair. While one locked the wheels of the chair, the other opened the door. "Ms. Moore, Mr. Jenison said that we needed to come get you."

Veronica scooted to the edge of the seat and allowed the interns to help her to the chair. They wheeled her into emergency, and she caught sight of Kevin at the nurses' window showing them her bottle of pills.

"Her pain has her downing these things like they're candy," He said, "I think she's taken too many and needs to be seen. Can someone just check her out and make sure she's okay, and then bring her to this room number?" He wrote the number on a piece of paper. "I'll leave my cell number as well, in case you need me."

"Sure, Mr. Jenison." The nurse smiled.

Kevin walked to the wheelchair and kneeled down to speak to Veronica.

"Okay Veronica, they're going to take care of you here."

Veronica frowned. "No, I need to go check on my friend and make sure she's still here."

"Honey, I think you took too many of those pills. Let them check you out, okay? Be safe. I'll be back to check on you later unless they finish and bring you to me. If you need me before then, call me on my cell. I left my cell number with the nurses. I'm sure Lee's still here. You don't have to worry about that."

He turned and walked toward the elevators, but glanced back in time to see a nurse wheeling Veronica down the hall to triage. The elevators opened just as he approached them. He wondered if the people exiting the elevator had lives as mixed up and crazy as his. Here he was at the hospital visiting a wife who couldn't stand him. He'd even heard her say, life would be so much better for her if he dropped dead. He shook his head at that memory.

"Who goes through shit like this?" He asked himself. "What the hell am I doing?" He murmured, as he stepped into the elevator and rode it to the third floor.

9

Les was relieved at the sight of the sun's rays finally pressing through the shaded window. She hadn't slept well at all after the probing and prodding of the nurses in their endless parade in and out of her room throughout the night. The blood pressure cuff tightened and hissed its release, and then there had been that incessant beeping sound.

Lord, no wonder the patients were anxious to go home, to get some rest.

Breakfast was served early. She anticipated the taste of a fresh cup of hot coffee, but when it finally arrived, it was lukewarm and weak. Actually, nothing on the tray appeared appetizing.

She glanced up at the clock on the wall. Veronica should be coming any minute. She'd save the food for her. As she pushed the tray away, there came a quick knock at the door. Several people dressed in white coats and one in plain clothes walked in. The one in plain clothes seemed particularly familiar, but she couldn't place why.

Dressed meticulously in a navy blue, double-breasted sports jacket and matching navy slacks. He leaned in with the other doctors trying to view the notes on the chart, then reached over and lifted the chart away from them, and they gathered around him. Les made out words like *concussion*, *head trauma*, and *headache*.

The man who appeared as though he walked off the cover of a GQ magazine finally pulled himself away from the rest and stepped closer to her bed. The masculine scent of his cologne filled the air.

"How are you, Les?" His voice appeared calm, composed, and familiar.

"Dr. Whitfeild?" Confused, she studied him. The Dr. Whitfield she knew was older and no longer among the living according to Veronica.

"*Alex* Whitfield," he smiled. "You knew my dad. Remember me?"

"*Alex.*" She leaned back in pleasant disbelief. "Alex Whitfeild." She laughed, "Oh my God, you're all grown up. The last time I saw you, you were just entering med school. You resemble your dad so much. It's good to see you, Alex. I was so sorry to hear about your loss. I remember how close the two of you were."

Alex nodded and thanked her for her condolences. "He was a good man. I miss him." He admitted. "So, Veronica told you that I took over my father's practice?"

"Yes, she told me and I'm happy for you. You're aware of my case, right?"

"I recall some of it from back then; not much—HIPPA, you know. I got the details from your files after Dad died. I've been waiting, hoping for you to surface, very interesting case. I was blown away by the information. Do you mind?" He motioned the doctor's forward and touched the sides of Les's head. He examined one eye, and then the other, next he held out his hand. One of the doctors gave him a stethoscope, and he listened to her heart. He instructed her to breathe for him, and then motioned for her to lay back down. "Your heart rate is good and so is your blood pressure, a little elevated, probably because of your pain. How's the head feel? You hit it pretty hard."

"Most of my pain is here in this area." Les, held her head as she described the pain she was experiencing. "It's a throbbing pain and the pain makes me sick to my stomach. Is that normal?"

"Well, I got the chance to speak to Dr. Wilson and go over the MRI and CT scan this morning. It didn't indicate any swelling of the brain or bleeding, so we're okay there. Now although these tests come back negative, it doesn't mean there's not an injury, it simply means the damage from the injury isn't severe enough to be visible on the scan. That's why they kept you overnight—for observation, and they want to run a few more test before you go home. Your head is going to hurt, and it'll probably hurt for a couple of days, but they'll make sure you go home with medicine that can help you. Okay?" He gave the chart to one of the doctors, and they thanked him and left the room.

Alex sat on the edge of the bed. "Now let's talk about our other situation. From what I read about your case, we're still unaware of what triggers your transformations. I can tell you this though, we're more knowledgeable about personality disorders today than when my father was alive. However, I don't want you to feel obligated to stay with me. You're free to choose someone else if you like, but I think we'd make a good team."

Les considered him.

He put her at ease. His manner was relaxed and amicable. She could already sense their compatibility and a certain comaraderie – The 'same foe' kind of thing.

"I had confidence in your father, and I trust his judgment explicitly. He left his practice to you, so you're stuck with me."

"Then you're stuck with me too." Alex said with a smile. I'm in with a pretty talented team of psychiatrists and psychotherapists who specialize in Dissociate Identity Disorder. I think we might be able to help you." He reached into his pocket and pulled out a business card. "I wrote my cell number on the back. Let's try to get you to the office as soon as possible. I don't want to wait too long. Also, I wrote a script for a new medication, and I want you to start taking it right away so I'll have them start you on it before you go home." He glanced around the room. "I thought for sure, Veronica would be here by now?"

"She's supposed to be. I don't know where she could be this morning. I even saved her some food." Les nodded toward her breakfast.

Alex chuckled "I thought the two of you were friends. Why you gonna mess up a perfectly good friendship by giving her our hospital food?"

They laughed. It was a welcomed moment for both of them, and Les knew she had found a new psychiatrist and confidant. Les told Alex everything; how she was able to push through yesterday. Her feelings about Lee and discovering she had a husband and children. Finally, she told him about the divorce. By the time she had finished, she had started on her second box of tissues.

***

Kevin slowed his pace the closer he got to Lee's room. He was not in a hurry to begin another awkward visit with her. It certainly would have been easier if Veronica were with him, she seemed to know how to talk to her. He, on the other hand, had a hard time *wanting* to talk to her, let alone finding the words. When he reached Lee's room, he could hear her talking to someone, and he waited outside the door and listened to the conversation.

"So many things are going through my mind right now, Alex. I'm aware of the hard work ahead of me. And I'm so between the familiar old and the unpredictable new. Who I was – who I am now. Him, now you, to which are some heavy shoes for you to fill mind you." She remarked with a tearful smile. "I mean he was the best. But, now I look in your eyes, and I can see your sincerity, and I believe we'll work well; you and me. Still, there's a lot on my plate. Kevin wants me out, and I can't think of anywhere else to go, and now this happens." She broke down, her fingers kneading the wad of tissue. "I want to be done with this, Alex. I want it over and done."

Alex gave Les a comforting hug. "We're going to give it a hell of a ride, dear. Right now, Kevin's not my concern, you are. Of course, he's going to behave this way. He doesn't understand the *situation*, so he's not going to understand *you*. We'll work it out. Don't you worry. So, he's not aware of any of this?"

Kevin's blood was boiling now.

So, this was Lee's mystery man? Kevin thought, wondering what all Lee had told him. It galled him to listen to how *sincere* this guy was – *how good they'll be together!*

Now he understood everything. *How long had this "Alex" been around? No, Alex, I'm now aware of anything.* He thought.

Kevin's large frame appeared in the doorway. Les glanced up and was met with a glare of raw anger. His eyes seemed to burn a hole in hers as he sauntered into the room, his hands stuffed deep into his pockets. His eyes flashed from Alex to Les, and his lips turned up into more of a sneer than a smile.

"Your sincerity is such a relief to her. She's been waiting for you. Frankly, speaking, so have I."

Les's heart sank. She put her hand to her throbbing head and closed her eyes. "Kevin—"

He stepped further into the room still looking from Alex to Lee. "I was wondering when you were going to finally surface," he said to Alex

Alex stood and extended a hand. "I'm sorry. I would have been here sooner, but --"

"You would have been here sooner? Man, I wish you had been here sooner too. You could have saved me a lot of gas and energy. Do us all a favor," Kevin snapped, "and make sure she gets to the attorney's office?"

"Hey," came another voice from the doorway. A hospital aid wheeled Veronica into the room, crutches in hand and her leg elevated. "I had to stop downstairs, thanks to Kevin and talk to—" She was met with the raging fury shown on Kevin's face, and she turned back to Les, and then to Alex.

Veronica's words were careful and unhurried when she said, "Kevin, I see you've met Dr. Whitfield."

Kevin's face went from anger to shock, and then embarrassment. "Dr. Whitfield?" He shook his head slowly and closed his eyes to alleviate the humiliation he felt. "But --"

"Kevin," Les said gesturing toward Alex, "meet my doctor, Dr. Alex Whitfield. His father was my doctor a long time ago. Alex here took over his practice."

Veronica looked from Les to Kevin, and then to Alex. "What'd I miss?"

10

Les sat on the side of the hospital bed. "What could be taking them so long? It's 1:00 in the afternoon. They said I'd be released this morning. Morning has passed."

"Patience is a virtue," Veronica declared under her breath. She was tired of the waiting too, but Les had been complaining enough for both of them. "Kevin went down to the nurses' station. He'll be able to tell us something when he gets back. They might still be observing you. Is your headache better?"

"It's better than it was when they brought me in." She touched the side of her head, "Still hurts though."

"See, that might be what they're waiting for."

"What, Ronnie, for my headache to go away? It's not going to go away." She announced. "They already told me that. They said it might last for at least a couple of days--maybe a week, but I need to get out of here to find out what I'm going to do with my life."

"But what does Alex say?"

"We had a good session. He instructed them to start me on new meds here and suggested that I call to set an appointment with him. In the meantime I need to figure some things out about me."

"Like what?"

"Like where am I going? What am I going to do while I sort through this mess? I don't have any money, a place to live, transportation. There are too many open ends. I need to get out of here, and I'm hoping Kevin lets me go home."

"Home? I thought you could stay with me for a while, Les. Wait until you're feeling better. I've got two extra rooms, pick one. It'll be great to have you. Like old times—roommates."

"You know, I appreciate it, but as crazy as it sounds, I want to go home. I just woke up the other day and found I have two children. I want to get to know them, and I want them to know me. You can understand that. Right? And what about you?" She gestured to Veronica's crutches. "You've got enough to deal with."

"Les, I think you're asking for trouble, and I don't want you to get hurt. Do you realize how dangerous this is? What if Lee makes another unexpected visit? What do we do? You need to be with someone who understands what's going on. Kevin has no idea - -"

Before she could finish her sentence, Kevin walked in. "Kevin has no idea about what?"

The two women exchanged nervous glances, "Uhhh." Veronica stammered, "No idea about - - what it takes to - - -" She rolled her hand over and over to encourage Les to help her out.

Les, caught on and began rolling her hands too. "No idea about what it takes to - - -"

At that moment, the nurse walked in with the release papers for Les to sign. Relieved, Les took the papers and pen and pretended to listen intently to the 'going home' instructions. She signed all the papers and returned them to the nurse.

"Well," the nurse said, "You're released, go home, but take it easy. We don't want to see you back in here. Okay?" The nurse turned to Kevin and smiled. "She needs to relax today, but if her headache gets worse, or she starts vomiting, bring her into emergency."

Kevin walked to the side of the bed where Veronica was. "By home. What exactly do they mean? Is she going home with you?"

"I'm going home," Les stated, "Home, Kevin!"

He took a breath and nodded his head. "That's what I thought you meant, so I guess we have a problem."

"Problem?" Les exclaimed, "What kind of problem, Kevin." She was trying to use a tone that she thought Lee would use.

"You need to understand that I was under the impression you, and I were going to sign divorce papers the other day. We were going our separate ways and to celebrate," Kevin spoke the rest of the sentence under his breath, "I was having a party."

Veronica chuckled nervously, "You mean a 'ding doing. The wicked witch is dead party,' so to speak?"

"Actually, so to speak, yeah," Kevin answered.

"Tonight?!" Les asked.

Kevin nodded, "Yeah. Caterers and everything. It was too late to cancel, so people are at my house right now decorating and cooking for a party."

"Oh well," Les declared loudly, laying the palm of her hand on her head to control the throbbing, "I guess *we're* having a party because I'm going home."

Kevin looked desperate. "Veronica, can't you talk some sense into her? This party is to celebrate freedom from a bad situation." He turned to Les, "*Friends* are coming who are happy for me. Clients wanting to wish me well. You wanted to be gone so bad, Lee, *be gone*! I don't need this today."

"You should have thought about that!" Les shouted. She held her head with both hands.

"Thought about what?" Kevin shouted back. "That you would miss our appointment, get into an accident, and end up here? Oh yeah, lady, that was my well thought out plan. Totally on my agenda! Let me understand -- you're saying I should have thought about the fact that you would want to attend my celebration?"

Les braced her head between her hands. It was pounding. She was sure that at any given moment, her head was going to fall off her shoulders and roll across the floor. "Please," she whispered, "Just take me home." She adjusted her weight to climb off the bed.

Veronica stood and put her crutches under her arms then hobbled clumsily to Les's bedside to help her.

Les gently shooed her away, "Ronnie, move before you hurt yourself."

Veronica stepped aside until Les tried to climb down from the bed again. Veronica rushed to her side and reached up to steady her.

Les gently slapped Veronica's hands away and shooed her aside again, "Ronnie, you're gonna get hurt, move back."

When Veronica was safely out of the way, Les attempted the task once more just to have Veronica awkwardly dart over and take hold of her arm.

"*Ronnie!*" Both Kevin and Les shouted at the same time.

Veronica plopped into a nearby chair. "Fine," she declared, "I was just trying to help."

11

It was quiet during the drive home, and Kevin found himself wishing someone would say something to break the silence. He peered in the rear-view mirror at Veronica, who met his gaze, and shrugged letting him know she had no idea what to say. Les sat in the passenger seat and stared out the window.

"Well, umm," Veronica started. "Is anyone hungry? Cause Kevin took me to an awesome restaurant over on - -"

"I want to go home, Ronnie." Les interrupted. "Anyway, the party's tonight. Remember? There's no time to stop."

"Oh, that's right."

"You're coming to the party, right Ronnie?" Les asked

"Well, I - I, uh, I mean, I'm on crutches. I don't think I'd be much fun at a party, Les."

"Let me rephrase that. Ronnie, you're coming to the party!" Les made sure Veronica understood this time she was making a statement, not asking.

Veronica met Kevin's gaze in the mirror again. He rolled his eyes and nodded his head.

"Kevin, will you be able to pick me up later? I want to get my clothes, and I'll come to your house and get dressed if that's okay with you."

Les didn't give Kevin the chance to answer. "Of course, it's okay with us. What time can you pick her up Kevin?" Les asked.

Defeated, Kevin dropped his shoulders, shrugged, and said, "I'll pick you up around 4:30. I'll let the cleaning people know you're coming, so they can prepare a room for you. That should give you enough time to get there and get dressed. Right?

"Yes, that's plenty of time."

They pulled into Veronica's driveway, and Kevin hopped out at the same time Les opened her car door to help Veronica into the house. "I've got this," Kevin said easing Les's car door closed, encouraging her to stay put.

Les's eyes followed Kevin as he helped Veronica to the door. He waited patiently while she fished in her purse for her keys and unlocked the door. "Thanks, Kevin," she turned back to wave again at Les. "I'll see you at 4:30." She closed the door, and Kevin walked back to the car.

Pulling out of the driveway, Kevin, turned to Les and said, "Amazing friend you've got there."

"I know that." She answered and turned her head to stare out the window.

"Why am I just now meeting her? The only friend you ever allowed me to know was Brenda. I mean—until now."

Les turned to Kevin. "Brenda?"

"Yeah, Brenda. Brenda Crenshaw."

"Hmph, Brenda Crenshaw's no friend of mine."

"Since when?"

"Never was."

"The two of you were inseparable. What happened?"

Les realized he was talking about Lee and didn't answer. She closed her eyes against the throbbing pain in her head. She didn't want to think, but the thoughts came anyway, all jumbled together. No sooner would she dismiss one thought, than another took its place as if an arcade game was going on inside her head. Every thought seemed to lead to one major question, *Why would Brenda and Lee become friends?* The last thing she remembered before going to 'sleep' was having a conversation with Brenda Crenshaw on the telephone. *What was it she said?*

"I think it's only right to tell you, Kevin and I are laying here laughing at you. I can't believe you actually thought he'd be interested in the likes of you? Please! A little orphan girl whose own father tried to get rid of her? Didn't he throw you through a window or something? It's only fair to warn you, dear. Kevin might wander off and play in the dumpster every now and then, but he'll always come back to me."

She remembered Brenda's laugh. The room began to spin, slow at first, but gradually increased until it was spinning out of control at the same time the air in the room was sucked out, and darkness overtook her. She groped for something—anything to hold onto but found nothing. She fell further and further into the darkness. Disappearing within herself—powerless and frightened. When she opened her eyes again, she was married with two children.

She wished she could press a button that would turn her brain off.

Les turned slowly and looked at Kevin. *How did he and Lee get together? What could she have said to make him fall in love with her? Couldn't he tell the difference between them? Why Lee? And where did Brenda Crenshaw fit in all this?*

Kevin sensed her eyes on him and turned to her. "What?" He shrugged.

She turned back and stared out the window. Somehow she needed to find the right words to tell him. He deserved the truth, and she wanted to tell him the truth. But the many gaps in time and uncertainties, made her hesitate. How should she approach him? What would she say—where would she start? Les realized, there were only two things she was certain of, she was *Leslee* Cramer, and she was still in love with Kevin Jenison.

They drove home in awkward silence.

***

Once they got home, Kevin helped Les into the family room.

"Timothy should be here somewhere decorating." He said. "Okay, Listen, Lee, here's how I think this thing should play out tonight."

"No, Kevin, you're not going to tell me how you think *things* are gonna play out. It's a party. I am well aware of how to *behave* at a party."

"That's not what I meant, Lee. Come on, don't make a fool out of yourself. Think about this-- you can stay upstairs. Remember, this is your first day out of the hospital. You're suffering from a serious concussion. You're not going to be able to tolerate the loud music. Why would you want to come down for a party?"

"Make a *fool* of myself?! Don't make a fool of myself? Now, I'm furious, Kevin. Even if I considered not going to the party, I'm certainly going now. I'm going to the party, *and* I'm going to enjoy it. Concussion and all." She put her hand on her head and turned to storm off. She turned in one direction, but because of not being sure, she turned back, pivoted and turned again. Realizing how this must appear to Kevin, she stopped, dropped her shoulders and turned to face him. "Kevin, I don't want to argue with you anymore." Her hand remained on her forehead, and her voice quieted to almost a whisper. "Can we get through one night without an argument? There must be somewhere we can go talk? I really need to talk to you uninterrupted." She closed her eyes against a pain that made her stomach queasy.

Kevin thought it strange but considered Lee's mix-up in direction a consequence from the concussion. "Not right now, Lee. Maybe tomorrow, but right now, there's too much to do!"

Kevin stormed out of the house to his car. He was crunched for time. Only six hours before the party and nothing was completed. He was determined to run his errands and get back in time to get dressed before the guests arrived. Adjusting the rear-view mirror, he put the car in reverse and slowly began backing out. He checked his mirror again then slammed on his breaks. He leaned forward and squinted, hoping he wasn't seeing what he thought he was seeing. He tried fine-tuning his vision without physically turning around.

"*What the hell?*"

He closed his eyes and pinched the bridge of his nose then lifted his eyes to the mirror again. It wasn't bad enough that she missed their appointment and rearranged his plans, now, whatever she needed to talk to him about, of course, took precedence over what *he* needed to do. His anger flared, and the heat from it startled him. He took a deep breath and tried to calm himself, but it didn't work. Kevin unlocked his seat belt, threw the car door open, pulled himself out and stormed to where his wife stood unmoving behind his car.

Les had never seen Kevin so angry, and she stepped back, as he walked toward her. His huge frame overshadowed her petite one, and she stiffened her back to camouflage the fear rising inside her. But, this time he had to hear her out.

The sound of his voice was like uncontrolled thunder, "What the hell are you doing, Lee? I'm sick of these childish games! What are you trying to accomplish here? What?" Kevin used his hands and arms to emphasize what he was saying.

Les stood her ground. "Kevin, all I'm asking is for a few minutes of your time. We need to talk, and I'm not leaving you alone until we do." Her heart was beating so fast and hard, she had to force herself to breathe deeply and speak slowly, "I'm just saying that there are some things you need to know."

Kevin checked his watch. "Guests will be arriving in about six hours. I still have to go get Veronica. I-don't-have-a-few-minutes, Lee, I don't even have a second. This little encounter *here* is taking up more time than I have!"

"Kevin -- I --"

"Don't do this to me, Lee, not now. I'm already fighting the urge to lock you up, so you don't embarrass the hell out of me tonight. Don't push me." He groaned, "You're in my way, kindly move out of my way, so I can back out. I don't understand why you're so bent on ruining my life. Why can't you just go away like you promised."

"Kevin," Les turned and walked toward the house, "I'm staying until you and I talk. The sooner we talk, the sooner you can have me out of your life, since that's what you want so badly. I'll be here when you get back." She walked to the back door.

Kevin chuckled and shook his head, "I have to admit, this is going to be interesting." Les, turned and looked at Kevin. He cocked his head, and his smile turned into a slow smirk. "Yes, this is going to be very interesting indeed. Help yourself to some finger food, Lee. I believe we have some of your favorites. Ask the chef to show you to the— snake meat." When Kevin realized his words didn't make the impact he thought they would, the smirk quickly faded. "Come on, Lee, you don't even like these people."

"I'm stayin' Kevin and I'm going to the party." Les announced as she turned once again and walked through the door.

Kevin yelled behind her, "It's just like you to--"

Les, stepped into the house and cut Kevin's words off by slamming the door. The heat of his words remained with her as she leaned her back against it. She listened to the engine roar, and the car door slam. He backed out of the driveway, and tires screeched loudly as he peeled off down the street.

Her heart raced, and she was irritated from tears threatening to flood over onto her cheeks, she didn't want to cry. *I'm not going to cry!* But the tears came anyway. She closed her eyes and breathed deeply hoping it would somehow help to calm her nerves.

This was going to be a long night, she thought.

Les opened her eyes and was pulling herself away from the door when she was surprised, and a little startled by the two small forms standing in front of her, their wide, curious eyes staring in confusion. She hurried and wiped away her tears, hoping they hadn't seen.

"Hi." She said. The simple word sounded more like a breath than a greeting. Les mustered up a smile.

The children seemed anchored to the floor, and no one moved until Kelly scampered to the most protected place she knew, behind her big brother. She peeked from around his back at the familiar stranger.

"Hi." Keith finally responded. He did a half turn to speak to his sister. "Don't be scared Kelly. It's just Mom." He turned back to Les, "You're not gonna yell at us for being downstairs, are you?"

Les answered softly, "Of course not. Do you usually get yelled at for being downstairs?"

"Not by Dad." He replied.

Les was taken back, "You mean by your—me?" Les asked. "I yell at you for being downstairs? Why?"

"You say we get in the way." Keith responded.

"Underfoot." Came a small voice behind the boy.

"Well, you're definitely not in my way right now." Les moved closer to the children and knelt to their level. She slowly reached for Kelly's hand and pulled her gently from behind Keith's back.

"Don't be frightened" she whispered, "I'm not going to hurt you. I promise."

The little girl, still frightened, allowed Les to gently pull her closer. Kelly peeked through a mass of curly brown hair that had come loose from the French braids cascading down her back. She kept a guarded eye on the woman in front of her. Les slowly reached up and brushed Kelly's long bangs to one side and smiled as the child lifted her gaze, revealing beautiful golden-green eyes. "You have eyes like your father. How old are you?"

As if her arm was made of lead, Kelly slowly held it up and spread out five fingers.

"You're five?"

"No, she's not, she's four." Keith said suddenly. "She tells everybody she's five though, but she's four."

She turned to Keith and still smiling asked, "And how old are you?"

"I'm seven. I'm gonna be eight when I get my next birthday." He adjusted his posture to appear taller, "Dad says I'm gonna be tall like his brother. I'm already up to Dad's waist, and I'll bet, by the summer, I'll be all the way up to his chest."

The sound of Les's laugh caught the children off guard. Kelly darted back behind her brother, and the two stood wide-eyed once again, not because of *the* laugh, but because of *who* laughed.

Keith gulped hard. He lifted his right hand and lightly touched the side of Les's face. Les gently lay her hand on top of his, and slowly guided it around her cheeks, to her eyes, her nose, and then her mouth. Kelly moved closer and laid her hand on the opposite side of her mother's face, and Les did the same for her.

"That's right. It's me," She whispered, nodding to assure them they were safe.

Keith was the first to pull his hand away, and then Kelly.

"What? Ohhhh, don't be frightened."

"You *look* like our mom, but – you don't *act* like her." Keith stammered.

"I know," Les smiled, "I don't have the poofy hair." She teased making an exaggerated up doo motion with her hands. Keith was surprised at his mother's attempt at being funny, and a smile toyed at the corners of his mouth until it had no choice, but to surrender itself to the moment. His smile was big and revealed two empty spaces.

"Woe," Les laughed, "what happened there?" she reached up to take Keith's chin in her hand.

Keith's smile immediately disappeared, he threw his hands over his mouth and stepped away from Les's touch.

"What's wrong? I just wanted to - - ."

In one swift movement, Keith took his sister's hand, and the two darted down the long hallway and around the corner.

"Wait—." Les called to them.

She stood quickly and started after them, but thought better of it and stopped. They were gone anyway-- just that quick, they were gone. A memory tugged and unfolded itself, revealing what she had always thought was a dream. It was a moment -- a brief, wonderful moment in time.

People standing around smiling, but why was there pain . . . so . . . so much pain. She was desperate for someone to make the pain go away. . . No one would listen to her. She pleaded for the nurse . . . "Please!" She cried out. She heard only one word . . . "Push!" If she pushed would it take the pain away? . . . She pushed . . . she pushed harder . . . harder . . . She heard crying . . . a baby . . . crying. The nurse lifted a little infant and laid it on her chest . . . "It's a boy!" she exclaimed. Les's eyes darted from one person to another. "It's mine?" she asked, looking around wildly, "My little boy?" . . . And then it was gone . . . the dream was gone, only to return another day.

This time the nurse lifted the infant, laid it in on her chest, and said, "It's a little girl, Ms. Cramer, you've got yourself a beautiful little girl." Les held on to the baby. "Please, don't take her from me." She pleaded.

"We're not taking her from you, Ms. Cramer, we're going to clean her up, weigh her, take her vitals, and you can have her right back."

Les lifted the infant and cradled her in her arms right beneath her neck. "What a perfect dream," she breathed, "so perfect. She didn't want to let go— didn't want the dream to end, but the nurse was persistent. She took the baby, and Les kept her eyes peeled on the nurse who carried the baby away, following her closely, as she moved to the other side of the room. Finally, Les allowed herself to relax. She rested her head on the pillow behind her.

The presence of someone else in the room was evident. Les turned her head slowly and came face-to-face with the handsome man at her bedside, who seemed totally amazed at what he witnessed. She reached out for him . . . wanted to talk to him . . . ask questions, but the beautiful dream was replaced by darkness, and she was too weak to push it back.

It became clear to Les at that moment, the dream she thought to be so beautiful, was a reality.

She was present when her son, Keith, was born then again, to give birth to Kelly. Lee couldn't do it. She wasn't *strong* enough. Childbirth pain wasn't something she desired to experience, so she withdrew herself, which allowed Les the opportunity to give birth to her own children. She also realized the handsome man who stood at her bedside was Kevin. He remained with her through it all—never left, and she loved him for that. However, the whole ordeal, as beautiful as it was, left Les weak and defenseless, and she surrendered to the darkness.

The awareness and the understanding of that truth was so amazing and unbelievable that Les found herself sobbing uncontrollably. Finally, when no more tears would come, Les wiped her face, and tried to remember other times she thought she was dreaming. Les made a mental note to talk to Alex Whitfield the next time she saw him.

12

Les could hear the clattering of dishes and a sea of voices and turned in the direction to follow it. The sound led her to the kitchen. She stood at the entrance of the doorway as people rushed in and out bowing their heads as they passed her.

"Excuse me, Madam," was all they said. She moved forward and backward, from one side to the other trying to stay out of their way, almost colliding a number of times as the staff hurried around the huge kitchen.

If the Pillsbury dough boy were to take on human form, he would be a replica of the man standing at the stove. His bright white smock barely wrapped around his rotund body and his chef hat slid into his face every time he barked an order at his staff. The table was smothered with plump strawberries, flour, sugar, butter, eggs, and jugs of apple juice.

Chef Orin stopped yelling when he saw her and quickly ended what he was doing and hurried toward her, "Ma'am I'm so sorry. I know I told Mr. Jenison we would be having lemon cake, but I thought the strawberry tarts would top the evening. I hope you don't mind the change. Please, feel free to sample them." Chef Orin picked up a large fork along with one of the tarts, he dipped the fork deep inside the fluffy pastry and pulled out an ample amount. He swirled the forkful of tart around the creamy, homemade whipped crème, then lifted the fork to Les's lips. She couldn't resist it. She opened wide with excited anticipation and Chef Orin gently laid the tart in her mouth.

The pastry was sweet and savory and she closed her eyes to enjoy the flavor. When she opened her eyes she asked, "Do I taste apple?"

Pleased, the chef withdrew a cup of liquid from the counter behind him. He held it out to her, "I added a little apple juice to the glaze to give the tart a more interesting flavor." Everyone in the kitchen came to a complete halt. They expected a scene like the one they witnessed when Chef Orin took it upon himself to change the Madam's menu at an earlier event.

"What do you mean by undermining my authority and going to Mr. Jenison?

When I say I want a certain dish prepared for dinner, I expect you to prepare it with no questions asked. Do you understand me?

The next time this happens, and I hope there won't be a next time, you will have hell to pay, and you can kiss your job here good-bye. I'll make sure you never cook for another of our events or anyone else' if I have anything to do with it!"

"But Mrs. Jenison, ma'am, Mr. Jenison came in this morning and changed the menu himself. I thought surely he had spoken to you about it."

"Listen. I don't care if the Pope comes in and changes my menu. If you don't hear from me personally, the menu is to remain the way I planned it. And don't ever call me Mrs. Jenison. My name is 'Ms.' Cramer," she spat, "Do you understand me?!"

"Yes Ma'am," he said.

But today Mr. Jenison came to the kitchen and gave him free reign over the menu. He said the Mrs. wouldn't be attending the festivities, and he would be allowed to be adventurous and come up with a menu of his own. Kevin only had one request, Chef Orin's lemon cake.

When Ms. Cramer walked in, he expected to be fired on the spot and humiliated in front of the staff. Instead, she smiled up into the man's face and said, "It smells heavenly in here. What are we serving?" His eyes widened in shock and amusement.

The staff relaxed and went back to their work while Chef Orin took Les to each station to sample everything on the menu for the evening. He didn't know what changed her, but whatever it was, he liked it. She listened intently as he described every dish. Educating her on its origin and enlightening her on why he decided to serve it tonight. He even explained how the dish should offer a new and exciting experience to her palate, and with each explanation, he presented a spoonful of another dish. With her eyes closed, she allowed the cuisine to present its fresh flavor as she rolled each bite across her tongue and savored every morsel. She searched around the room for a clock and, when she found it, she realized the time slipped away quicker than she expected. She needed to get somewhere alone and think about the best way to tell Kevin he was wrong about her, and she needed to do it before the party tonight. She said her good-byes and left the kitchen.

Finding her way around the spacious house was a pleasant chore. Each room opened new and exciting hints about the man Kevin came to be. Finally, Les found herself in the living room smiling at each photograph strategically placed on the mantel. She had picked one up to admire it closer, when she heard the sound of a man's voice in the hall. Kevin stopped in the doorway.

"What are you doing in here?" he asked.

"Waiting for you to get back and looking at all the photographs. I love this one," she said quietly. She turned the picture to Kevin. It was the picture of him holding Keith with one protective arm around his waist. His other arm stretched toward Kelly, who held on to his hand, using it as leverage to help her climb onto his lap. "You look so proud here, Kevin."

He tilted his head to the side in disbelief. "Right! Is this one of your jokes? You hate that picture. You say it every time you come in this room. There's a dinner party to get ready for. We can talk later. Please, I'm going to say this again, don't spoil this one, Lee, not tonight. I promise I'll make time to talk tomorrow." He turned to walk out of the room.

"Tomorrow might be too late; we need to talk now, Kevin, there's something you need to know." She turned to place the photograph back on the mantel.

"Okay. Let me help you. You're gonna tell me you haven't been yourself lately, Right?" She tried to ignore his condescending tone.

"You're right. I haven't been myself lately. I'm sure you've noticed some subtle changes, and I know this is going to sound strange to you but -." she moved closer. "Kevin, the truth is, I'm not - --"

"Sir?" Kevin turned to the door. "There's a problem in the kitchen. Apparently, Chef Orin decided *not* to serve lemon cake as you requested. I wanted to make sure you were aware of the change. I checked the written menu Chef Orin submitted. Lemon cake is on the menu, but there's no lemon cake in the kitchen."

It was a simple change, but Timothy Joseph's job as Event Planner was to make sure all changes had the approval of his employer. He certainly didn't expect the outburst that came next.

"What?! Lemon cake is the main desert. What the hell happened to the lemon cake? Chef Orin never ignored one of my requests!" Kevin's voice got louder as he spoke. "Why is it so hard for people to follow simple instructions? For Christ's sake, I asked for lemon cake, and I expect to get lemon cake. First, I have this problem," he gestured carelessly toward Les, "and now - - -." Shaking his head, he gestured toward the Event Planner, then he ran a hurried hand through his hair. "What is this, some kind of conspiracy?"

Timothy Josephs worked for the Jenison's before. It wasn't usually 'Mr.' Jenison who created the problems.

Les stepped forward, "Maybe I can help," She suggested.

Kevin threw his hands up, "No thanks, lady. The last time you were in the kitchen, the whole staff was ready to quit! As it stood, you upset Agnes and Morrine so badly they left here in tears, and it took weeks to convince Orin to come back."

"I was just going to say that I already spent quite a bit of time in the kitchen today with Orin. I believe you'll be pleasantly surprised at his choices for this evening. His substitute for your lemon cake is superb. They're called - - -."

"You're trying to tell me, you were in the kitchen intimidating the help again?" Kevin interrupted.

"No," Les responded taking another step forward. "I'm trying to tell you that I had an amazing *experience* in the kitchen with Orin this afternoon. He's a brilliant Chef and if you'll trust him - - -."

"What the hell do you know about *trust*, lady?" Kevin bellowed.

His fury caused her to take a step back and realizing Kevin had been pushed to his limit, she slowly closed the distance to the couch and sat down.

Josephs stood in the doorway waiting for Mr. Jenison to give him further instructions and was thrilled to witness the heated exchange between the couple. A sly smile curved his lips when he saw Kevin stand up to Lee Cramer and send the ol' bitch running to the nearby sofa. *No better for her.*

Kevin took a deep breath to calm himself before turning back to the doorway. "I'll handle this, Josephs." He said and stormed down the hall toward the kitchen.

Had Kevin stayed in the room any longer he would have been as surprised as Timothy Josephs to see Lee Cramer reach up and brush a single tear from her cheek.

Timothy couldn't believe his eyes.

"Ma'am?" he took a step toward her.

The sound of the man's footsteps caused Les to look up. When she saw the genuine concern in Timothy's eyes, she couldn't contain her tears any longer. She lifted her hands to her face, and Les Cramer began to cry.

Caught up short, Timothy quickly removed a handkerchief from inside his suit jacket pocket.

"Madam?" he soothed, kneeling to console her. "There, there, Madam." He pressed the handkerchief into her palm. He had never seen this side of Lee Cramer.

"He's so angry and I don't know how to get around it. No matter what I say! No matter what I do. I run smack into his anger - - -that - - - that uncontrolled temper of his. I have to find a way to get through to him and make him listen. Is he always like this?" Les lifted the handkerchief to her eyes.

"There, there madam." Timothy soothed again, not knowing what else to say. The Lee Cramer he knew would have spat obscenities in Kevin

Jenison face for daring to speak to her like that in front of the 'help.' Then she would have turned and reprimanded him for interrupting what seemed to be a critical conversation between her and the mister.

He had to admit, though, it was a nice change to see she was capable of experiencing some type of emotion other than rage and animosity.

"Josephs," came a voice from the door. "Please, excuse my *wife* and me. I believe we have some unfinished business to discuss."

Timothy and Les looked up to see Kevin's large form resting against its door frame. Neither knew how long he'd been standing there. The older gentleman stood and moved toward the door.

"I'm sorry, Mr. Jenison, I was just trying to--."

Kevin raised a hand. "It's all right, Josephs. Everything's been taken care of in the kitchen, and I am in agreement with Chef Orin. His choices have superseded my expectations. Instead of the lemon cake, we will have the tarts he prepared. Please, excuse us."

His tone was steady yet firm. Timothy turned, giving Les a quick nod before exiting. Kevin closed the double doors and slowly turned to Lee.

He cleared his throat and walked toward her, "I don't know what you're trying to pull, Lee. I'm usually able to figure out your strategy before you get too far out of hand, but --"

"There's no strategy, Kevin, not on my end anyways." She felt more tears stinging her eyes, but she was determined not to cry anymore, not with Kevin standing there. She needed to pull herself together and face him head-on with news, she knew, wouldn't make sense to him.

"You have fifteen minutes to tell me what you think is so damn important it can't wait, and then I have to go get dressed for tonight." Kevin looked at his watch, and then back to Lee. "Fifteen minutes, Lee."

Les stood slowly. "Kevin, it's going to take longer than fifteen minutes to -"

"----Twelve." Kevin interrupted, looking at his watch again. He cocked his head. "You're wasting my time, Lee. I can't afford to waste this kind of time. What is it?"

"I don't know where to start!"

"Start somewhere damn it!"

"Okay, I'm trying to think." Les paced back and forth with her hands on the side of her head, the throbbing again.

"Lee!"

"Stop shouting at me."

"Well, get to the point!"

"Oh My God, Kevin. You're making it so hard for me to think."

"Well, let's not make *things* too hard for you, Madam. Not after you've made the past eight years of my life so *easy* for me!"

Les, felt her anger rising.

"Oh My God! Why do you hate me so much, Kevin? What the hell did I do to you?"

"What did you do to me?"

Kevin grabbed her and ushered her back into the chair.

"Unlike you," he shouted, "I know what I want to say, *Lee*. I'm sick of your charades, sick of the way you parade around here barking orders at everyone, including me. You think everyone owes you something like the sun rises and sets only for you!

I know things, Lee. I know things you don't think I know. For instance, the little situation you tried to arrange between you and my boss. He told me all about it. That secret's been out for quite some time! My boss has scruples— something you don't know anything about."

Les's, eyes widened, and all she could do was shake her head in disbelief.

"I know all about it, Lee. And -- I even know you told him you were trying to get even with me for doing the same thing to you. That was low! You and I both know that was a lie. I've *never* gone outside this marriage lookin' for anything.' He finally came to my office and gave me the chance to clear that mess up. You had him and the other associates at the firm looking at me like I was some kind of monster.

I'm also aware of the threats you made to the children. No wonder they're so afraid of you. And you told them not to tell me? You're a sick individual! You need help, you know? Thank God they had enough sense to tell me anyway. I didn't want to believe them, I mean, what kind of mother hurts her own children, but then I saw the bruises on Kelly's back and arms."

Les could see the tears of fury threatening to spill over from Kevin's eyes.

Why had Lee hurt him so? And the children --?

94

"But," he continued, "it's when I found the tent in the garage. The one you bought at Hammonds Sporting Goods Store. That's when I started putting things together. The map was rolled up in a box and hidden behind an old tire, along with some rope and duct tape. I saw the map with my own eyes, Lee. You circled the desert. You were taking my children to the desert! And you have the nerve to ask me why I dislike you? -- Don't trust you?

I wonder, could you have really left our children in that tent to die? Are you that evil?

We've talked about all this! You agreed to sign the papers and go, or I was going to call the police and tell them everything. I have all the evidence I need to put you away for a long time. Hell, for what you were planning. I could have you put away for life.

I thought, if you'd go away, it would be so much better than having the children see their mother taken away by police. I gave you the benefit of the doubt, Lee. I did what you asked me to do. I set up the meeting. Dave got the papers ready, and all you had to do was sign them and go away. And what happens? You have a car accident. How convenient! You don't fool me, Lee. I know your tactics, and this is one of them. I'm sick of your games, and I'm sick of you! Your best bet is to stay the hell out of my face tonight. Since you have it made up in your mind to stay for the party. Stay. But you have a choice, either leave on your own tonight, or I'm calling the police first thing in the morning to tell them everything I know. So, if I were you, I'd start packin'." The thunder in his voice seemed to shake the whole house.

Les, couldn't listen to anymore. She bounded from the chair and stormed over to him. Tears of outrage spilling over onto her cheeks again. She was furious! *So, this is the reason Lee decided to disappear?* The rage, confusion, chaos, and the pain in her head all stormed from her voice.

"You look at my face, Kevin Jenison and listen to me very carefully. Lee Cramer is an evil, spiteful, despicable bitch who has devastated my life *and* yours, and now you tell me she hurt my children? I want her gone just as badly as you do. That's what I've been trying to tell you! Ten years ago you asked me not to give up on you. Now, I'm asking for the same courtesy. Can't you see me, Kevin?" She wiped her hand over her face. "Look past this and see me for God sake. I'm not Lee! That's what I've been trying to tell you. I live with a disorder called DID. I'm NOT Lee!" Les shouted at the top of her lungs. She rushed passed him, pulled the doors open and ran as far away from him as she could run.

13

Kevin stood motionless staring at the door. What--? Did Lee say she wasn't herself? No -- he must have heard wrong.

Lee's words kept spinning around in his head, but he didn't have time to think about them or her strange outbursts right now. He looked at his watch, guests will begin arriving in less than three hours. He had time to get dressed and get ready to meet them. He left the room and went looking for Timothy.

Timothy was found making the last adjustments to one of the tables. When he looked up and saw Mr. Jenison approaching, he stopped and moved toward him.

"Mr. Jenison," Timothy fanned his arms around the room. "I hope this is to your liking, Sir."

"It is, Josephs, I stopped in to let you know I'm going upstairs to get dressed. Please, if the guests start arriving before I come down, I'm leaving you in charge.

"Sir?" Timothy asked reluctantly.

"Yes, Timothy."

"How's the Mrs., Sir?"

"She's great, Timothy -- no worries."

Timothy knew not to pursue the matter any further. He nodded toward Kevin and moved on with his work.

Kevin walked up the stairs to get ready for the evening. He could hear the voices of the band members coming in the front door.

Timothy directed them to the area where they could set up their equipment. The area was small but conducive to the needs of the band.

This was not their first time playing for an event given by the Jenison's. On several occasions, others who had attended affairs there, liked what they heard, and hired them for special events of their own. So, the band knew how to set their instruments up for the sound to work best for them. Each member adjusted and tested then readjusted his own instrument. Soon the pleasant sound of all the instruments together harmoniously began to play the tuneful, "Ribbon in the Sky," by Stevie Wonder.

Unable to forget Lee's words, Kevin stood under the shower and allowed the water to cascade down his body.

"I'm NOT Lee, I live with a disorder called DID." he kept hearing over and over again. What did she mean by that? -- *Not Lee --Not Lee -- Not Lee?*

Kevin forced himself to think about the past few days. He considered particular circumstances - *the way she looked at him, as though she was seeing him for the first time. Her transformation at breakfast! During the hospital stay - not knowing her own telephone number or address. Not knowing what day it was -well, everyone forgets a date here and there.* He reasoned as he changed the dial on the shower head and turned to have the pulsating water massage his shoulders and down his back. "This is crazy," he sighed, "it --it can't be --it just doesn't happen." He strained to remember other bizarre occurrences -moments in time when Lee behaved strangely.

Suddenly Kevin's head shot up. *'Ten years ago you asked me not to give up on you. Now, I'm asking for the same courtesy.'* Flashes of memories continued to invade his thoughts. *The day Keith was born -- hell the day Kelly was born! He recalled the way she looked at Kelly after she was born, not knowing he was standing beside her.*

At first, he was confused by her gentleness, her desire to hold on to the baby, as long as she could. When she sensed his presence, she turned to him, and her face changed from affection to pure terror. She reached for him -- but the look was gone as suddenly as it came— and life returned to normal.

He thought about the day they met again. After he returned home after throwing his arm out playing ball in college.

"She didn't even know who I was!" *He whispered.*

Kevin stepped out of the shower and wrapped the towel around his waist. He walked around the room in a daze. Every now and then, he'd remember something else and stop, trying to wrap his brain around the possibility. He turned and picked up his electronic tablet from the dresser, booted up, and entered, 'D-I-D.' Within seconds, a stream of information popped in. The bold words caught his attention, and he read them aloud:

"DID, Dissociative Identity Disorder, also called multiple personality disorder."

"Right, Lee. No way!" He laughed and continued getting dressed.

He chose a double-breasted tuxedo for the evening. Not only did he like the way it fit, but Kevin Jenison was known for his elegance and style, always careful to dress in a way that exuded confidence. But tonight --- standing in front of the mirror— he felt anything, but confident --- getting through the evening was the only thing he could think about right now.

"Where did she run off to anyway?" He wondered. He walked to the window and peered out, squinting against the setting sun trying to see as far away as possible.

"Where could she have gone?"

***

Les, didn't know where she was trying to run. She only knew she had to get away from '*him*'. She didn't want to believe what he was saying and surely didn't want to hear anymore. She needed to get away.

Timothy Josephs put the finishing touches on a centerpiece in the back of the room when Les ran in. He watched as she looked every which way before he asked,

"Are you looking for your friend Madam?"

Les turned to Timothy, "My friend?" she asked.

"Yes Madam, your friend! We put her in the guest room down the hall. Ms. Veronica. We thought it was best because of the crutches. I hope you don't mind. We just thought --"

"Veronica? Veronica's here? Wonderful! Of course. It's perfectly fine," Les rushed to the hall entrance and turned back to Timothy, "Down the hall -- exactly -- where, Timothy?"

Timothy looked up with a puzzled expression on his face, but stopped what he was doing long enough to show Les, which room she could find Veronica. She rapped at the door.

"Ronnie?" She called out. "Ronnie, are you there?"

"Yeah, come on in, Les!"

Les opened the door and walked in. "Veronica, you look beautiful."

"Thank you," she sang, picking up her matching clutch bag. She held the corner of the dresser and exaggerated a pose.

She was dressed in an elegant butterscotch gown with a sweetheart neckline that complimented her long neck. The tight bodice accented her tiny waist while the delicate ruffles layering the bottom of the bodice spread tastefully over the top of its long matching skirt. It wasn't until Veronica hopped over to pick up the crutches that Les was reminded of her friends' temporary disability.

"This is getting real old, girlfriend. I'm so sick of these things, and this cast is as heavy as sin. Everybody else is gonna be having a good time tonight, and there I'll be with these damn crutches under my arms and --." She paused when she realized Les still had on the same clothes as earlier. "Why aren't you dressed, girl? You've only got --. What's going on?"

"I told him, Ronnie."

"You told who?"

"I told *him*! Kevin! I told him about my disorder. Well, actually," Les moved over and sat on the bed, "I told him I live with DID, and I told him I wasn't Lee. That's as much as I could get out. Oh, my God, Ronnie. You should've heard the things he was saying. What he said I did to the children and to him. I could *never* do those things. He's so angry with me -- I mean Lee. He hates her."

Veronica had turned slowly and was now facing her friend --"Did you tell him -- *everything?*"

"He didn't give me a chance to tell him everything! He kept shouting and telling me how evil I was and how he wanted me gone! How I've been an embarrassment to him through the years, and he couldn't wait to be done with me! He said so many awful things!"

"No, Les. He was talking to Lee, not you. You have to talk to him. Wait for him to cool down and try again. Even if he doesn't want anything to do with you, you have the right to be a mother to your children."

"That's the other thing," Les answered, "remember when you said you saw Lee at a sporting goods store?"

"Yeah!?"

"Well, apparently she had plans to -- 'harm' the children." Les couldn't bring herself to say it any other way. "She was going to tie them up, take them to the desert, put them in a tent, and leave them there."

Veronica held up her hands. "Wait a minute . . . what? What are you saying?"

"Veronica, Kevin not only found the tent, he also found a map, duct tape, and the rope. She was planning to take Kelly and Keith, leave them in the desert, and not tell Kevin where they were. When he discovered her plan, he confronted her, and she promised to sign the divorce papers and go away to keep him from calling the police and having her arrested."

"What? - - Wait." Veronica responded quietly. It was all becoming clear to her now. She looked at Les.

"Don't you get it? -- That explains everything! The reason Lee went to sleep so suddenly. She hates you, and it took ten years to get Kevin to hate you too. Now she can go to sleep and have you suffer the consequences of her actions. Everything's coming back on *you*. How would you have known about an agreement between the two of them? This whole thing is playing out exactly as she expected. I mean, think about it, who's gonna believe you have a personality disorder? Kevin's so blinded by his anger and hatred for you that Lee's hoping he has *you* arrested. The evidence he has is what she wanted him to find. If he has you arrested, a trial could --"

Les nodded her head. "I know, Ronnie. And he said he's going to call the police, if I'm still here in the morning. He's going to have me arrested."

"That's exactly what Lee wants. He's playing right into her hands.

"A trial could put me away for life."

"That would kill you, Les."

"Yes, and Lee would win."

Veronica's heart dropped. She put her crutches under her arms and moved to Les's side. "You have to make him listen to you, Les. Go get dressed. You have to talk to him tonight. This can't wait."

"You mean go to his party? Ronnie, I can't do that, especially now."

"Les, you *have* to. You've got to prove you're not Lee! And don't say you don't have anything to wear. I'm sure Lee has some beautiful dresses upstairs."

"I'm not wearing her dresses!" Les shouted.

Veronica thought for a minute and then turned to the closet. "Well, here then," she pulled out a garment bag, unzipped it, and pulled out another beautiful gown, "wear this one. We're about the same size. I brought two dresses with me because I couldn't decide which one I wanted to wear. The color would be beautiful on you."

"I'm really not in the partying mood, Ronnie, but I guess you're right. I don't have a choice." She picked up the gown and looked at Veronica. "Well, here goes nothing."

Les used the shower in the guest bedroom and then opened Veronica's makeup bag. She used the bronzer, blush, and eye shadow. She applied a light coral lipstick and let her hair hang in ringlets down her back. "I need some of your perfume too, Ronnie."

"I think I still have a sample of the new Gucci perfume in my bag. Do you want it?" She reached in her makeup bag and pulled out a small sample bottle of perfume.

Les smelled it.

"I like it." She said as she applied it to her fingertips and dabbed it strategically behind her ears and onto each wrist.

Finally, she picked up the light coral, chiffon gown, unzipped it and stepped into the most beautiful dress she could remember wearing. She pulled the dress up passed her hips and over her breast then stepped closer to Veronica, swept her hair to the side, and Veronica zipped the dress with ease. Les allowed her hands to touch the small rosettes that detailed the bodice of her gown. Each rosette held a tiny crystal that gave the gown a subtle elegance and provided a delicate glow to the tone of her skin.

Veronica could do nothing more than shake her head slowly, "Simply stunning," she said.

Les turned and looked at herself in the mirror. She let go of a long sigh.

"Oh -- my God, it's beautiful. Ronnie, what do you think?"

Veronica said, "You want to know what I *really* think?"

Les, turned and looked at her friend, "Of course I want to know what you really think."

"Well, honestly," she looked down at her dress then back to Les, "I think I chose the wrong dress."

They both laughed.

Timothy was standing outside the door and heard laughter coming from inside the bedroom. It was good to know the lady of the house was in better spirits, and he was surprised when Les opened the door and beckoned him to come in.

"Timothy, is Mr. Jenison downstairs yet?" Les asked.

"Yes Ma'am, he's greeting the guests. Do you want me to get him?"

"No --no" Les stammered, "I don't want you to get him. I need you to do a special favor for me."

"Sure Madam, what do you need me to do?"

"You know where my bedroom is upstairs, right?"

"Yes Ma'am." Timothy gave a quizzical nod.

"Timothy, this is so important. I need you to go upstairs and look in my closet, on the floor, on the right side. You'll find a pair of strappy sandals with rhinestones on them. You won't be able to miss them. They're sitting right there on the floor. Can you do that for me?"

"Of course Madam. I'll be right back."

"Thank you, Timothy. I knew I could depend on you."

While the women waited for Timothy's return, Veronica took some rhinestone hairpins out of her purse, swept Les's loose curls to the top of her head and pinned them. She left only a few ringlets spiraling on the sides and in the back.

Before long, Timothy knocked on the door, and Les opened it. He handed Les the shoes. "Here you are, Madam, and I must say, you look exquisite."

Thank you, Timothy." She smiled and turned from the door. After slipping the shoes on her feet, Les turned to Veronica as if offering a finished product. "Showtime," she whispered.

"Okay, Les," Veronica said, "you have to make an entrance, so I'm going out before you." Veronica reached for her crutches and hopped to the door. She turned and gave Les one last look. "Girlfriend, you've got this. He's not going to be able to resist you. How's your head?"

"Tolerable." She said, crossed her fingers, and then waved Veronica off.

***

Veronica followed the sound of the band playing, George Michael's, "Careless Whisper." She rounded the corner and walked into the room. Immediately heads turned as she made her entrance. Kevin was the first to approach her and tell her how beautiful she looked -- crutches and all. They laughed.

"Thank you, Kevin."

"No, I mean it, you look absolutely stunning. I'm glad you came. You haven't, by chance seen Lee, have you?"

"As a matter of fact, I have. She's in my room getting dressed. She'll be out in a minute, or did you need me to get her?" Veronica pretended to turn awkwardly to go back to her bedroom.

"No-- no," Kevin said, standing in Veronica's way to prevent her from leaving. "I want you to stay here. I'm sure she'll be here soon. Let me help you to a seat." Kevin walked alongside Veronica to settle her at one of the tables.

"Well, I was hoping to see you tonight." Tom Pryor approached them, his eyes sparkling as he took in Veronica's full length. "My God, you look spectacular."

"Thank you, Tom, it's good to see you again." Veronica said as Tom moved to her side.

"Listen, Kevin. Why don't you let me take this beautiful woman off your hands? You have enough to do this evening. Enjoying this lovely lady's company has just become my favorite thing to do."

Kevin turned to Veronica making sure she was alright with those arrangements, but Veronica hadn't taken her eyes off Tom either. So Kevin released Veronica and allowed Tom to step into his place. Tom helped her to a seat then pulled a chair out for himself. They immediately fell into comfortable conversation.

Les sat in the bedroom waiting nervously for the best time to make her entrance. She checked her makeup again and arranged the tresses of her hair, then stood back from the mirror for one last look. "Well, here goes nothing." She whispered again. She crossed the room and laid her hand on the doorknob, "Breathe, Les, breathe," she sighed. Closing her eyes, she inhaled deeply then exhaled, opened the door and left the room.

14

Most of Kevin's guests had attended functions at his home before and knew what to expect. But there were those who were there for the first time and Kevin moved through the crowd greeting them. They were the ones who stopped him and asked about the catering company that provided the delicious hors d'oeuvres for the evening or who was the 'magnificent' band. Everyone else knew Kevin only used one band, one caterer, and one event planner for his events.

He was glad to see couples dancing close. The band was playing, Harold Melvin and The Blue Notes, "If You Don't Know Me by Now." Kevin stood back and watched as more couples gathered on the dance floor.

Tom had stood at his seat and extended his hand to Veronica. She was surprised and declined at first but soon realized his plan was not to take her to the dance floor, but to dance with her right there. She smiled, laid her bag on the table and accepted his invitation. He drew her up to him, put his arms around her waist, and they began to sway back and forth to the music. Veronica was caught up by Tom's gaze and did not notice Kevin watching them.

"Sly dog." Kevin chuckled to himself.

The music was enchanting. The bands' intention was to fill the air with a sense of euphoria and engulf their listeners into a rather long embrace that would linger after the music stopped. So far, they had achieved their purpose. Kevin caught himself a couple of times, singing the words to the songs and tonight, as he watched the band create their magic between Tom and Veronica, he sang quietly,

"If you don't know me by now, you will never, never, never, never, never, never know me.

"Mr. Kevin Jenison!"

Kevin turned slightly toward the feminine voice. He didn't see her come in and was shocked to come face to face with a woman he hadn't spoken to in more than ten years.

"Brenda? Brenda Crenshaw."

Brenda reached up expecting to give Kevin a hug, but stopped as Kevin extended his hand. Hiding her disappointment, Brenda shook his hand then sized Kevin up and down, and nodded. *Yes, he had certainly aged well, and she was very pleased to see it.*

"Yes, Kevin, it's been too long," she uttered. "I hear congratulations are in order?"

Kevin turned his attention back to her. "Congratulations?"

"Yes, rumor has it you're going back on the market as a free man." She smiled.

"Oh that," He chuckled, "Well, I must say there has been some -- uh -- minor changes in that department."

Her smile faded. "Changes?" She asked.

"Yes, Brenda, changes. How'd you get in here? I don't recall sending an invitation your way. Who'd you come with?"

"No one. Lee invited me," she lied.

"Really? Then I'm sure the two of you will have a great time together."

Brenda smiled. By the looks of it, Kevin wasn't even aware that Lee was gone. This was working out better than she'd planned. She stepped closer to him. "There's no reason you and I can't be friends too, Kevin. We were friends once. Remember?"

Kevin's gaze met hers. "That was a long time ago, Brenda. Now, if you'll excuse me."

She caught his arm as he turned to leave. "One dance?"

"Brenda, I--"

Out of the corner of his eye, he saw Veronica and Tom stop dancing and look toward the room's entrance, as did everyone else. His gaze followed theirs and rested upon the angelic figure in the doorway. Although the music never stopped, to Kevin, silence overtook the room providing a chasm for the words, *"I'm not Lee!"* They echoed over and over in his ears. His eyes connected and remained transfixed by hers, pleading with him to see more than her familiar face.

Please, see 'me', Kevin.' Les's thought, *'Please, see ME.*

Forgetting the woman standing beside him, Kevin squinted his eyes and headed slowly to the entrance, toward the familiar guest. The words *'I'M-- NOT— LEE!'* continued to echo.

"Oh, My God," He breathed. He moved closer and thought, *Lee --would never wear a dress like that. But, of course, this wasn't—*

He shook his head and tried to make sense of it all, "It's -- it's Impossible." he said under his breath and squinted again. She was stunning, and he couldn't pull his eyes away from hers. She seemed to plead with him to look beyond the surface and see her.

Suddenly, he heard another voice. Veronica's. He turned and searched the crowd for her. What was it she said? *Now I see why 'Les's loves you so much. No --not Lee! Lee can't love anyone!* He said the words out loud, just as he located Veronica at her table "Lee -- can't love anyone!" He repeated.

Veronica stood with Tom's support, tears in her eyes as she nodded to Kevin. He whirled back around to face Les at the entrance. Now understanding, full well, this was *not* Lee. His eyes soften, and a confused smile played on his lips, as he continued toward her, extending his hand--

Finally, he spoke her name, "Leslee?"

Les nodded and accepted his hand, he led her to the dance floor, put his arms around her waist and swayed with the music, never once taking his eyes away from hers.

At last, breaking the silence between them, Kevin cocked his head to the side, leaned closer to Les's ear, and whispered, "Tell me something?"

Les lifted her eyes to his.

"I don't know what's going on or how this is happening, but what am I going to have to do to keep you from leaving me again?"

Les studied Kevin, "If I knew that -- I promise you -- I would never have left you in the first place."

Kevin pulled Les closer, and they swirled around the dance floor.

Brenda stood mortified in the middle of the floor. She had never been so humiliated in her life. She looked around to see if anyone else noticed Kevin's cold dismissal of her. Ashamed and embarrassed, she walked to her table and sat fuming as Kevin and Les caught the attention of the whole room.

So many thoughts swirled around in Brenda's head, but none of them made any sense. *What just happened? Who did Lee think she was walking in there like that? Looking like that! I was supposed to be the center of attention on Kevin's arm tonight, not Lee. Why was she here? This wasn't the plan.*

Brenda dropped her eyes painfully to her dress, *I -- I chose the perfect dress and did everything I knew to do to make this night perfect— didn't I?* She fought back angry tears. *Yes -- I did! I even bribed the event planner to let me in. Of course, that wasn't too hard to do. At any rate, I'm supposed to be falling into Kevin's arms or-or he in mine. Why is he dancing with— Lee? There's something wrong here! Why was Lee -- here?*

Finally, she gathered her belongings and stormed out of the room. She kept her head down not wanting to make eye contact with anyone; she didn't want to speak to *anyone! This was not the way things were supposed to end up.* She fumed. The last conversation she had with Lee Cramer left her with the impression she was going to disappear. She turned to get one last look at the couple on the dance floor and left.

Pretending to be friends with Lee Cramer was a difficult task what with all her irrational outbursts. Brenda soon found out that Lees' rants could go on for hours as if the woman had forgotten someone else was in the room. She was a peculiar bird, Brenda thought. And she acted as if she had never called her that day many years ago, when she lied about her and Kevin laughing at her, as inflammatory as that should have been. It was as if the incident hadn't occurred. And Brenda was obliged not to bring it up.

Lee was just strange. Brenda walked in during one of Lee's rants. She was so enraged that she was pacing the floor screaming. 'I'm gonna kill that little bitch, I'm gonna kill that little bitch, I --- AM --- gonna --- KILL that little bitch!' When her ranting was over, Brenda remarked. "My, my, what horrible language, who put a spur up your ass?" Brenda laughed nervously. "Obviously, somebody ticked you off royally?"

"It's that little girl!" she seethed.

"What little girl? Your little girl? Are you talking about Kelly?"

"Yes, -- Kelly! I get so angry with her, and she makes me do things. I don't mean to hurt her, but she -- she infuriates me. Why can't she be more like her brother and stay out of my way? I've tried to reason with her and let her know that 'Mommy' needs some 'me' time. I even talked to Kevin about it, but all he says is that she's a child and needs to know she's loved. He says, "Maybe if you try holding her." But she acts like a frighten little rabbit and almost jumps right out of my arms, and then she starts that --- whimpering and when I tell her to SHUT THE HELL UP, she gets louder. It grates on my nerves until I lose it. I -- have to -- hit her. But I apologize afterward and tell her I love her and swear, I'll never do it again, but it happens over and over and over."

"You mean, you -- hurt her? Lee, she's only a little girl. What could a little girl possibly do to make you so angry?" Lee doesn't hear the question. She continues in her rant, oblivious to Brenda's stunned look.

"I say, please, please, please do not tell your father. I mean, I pleaded with that little BITCH; and what does she do? She turns around and tells him anyway. I mean, where's the loyalty? Now Kevin wants me 'out' just because of a few bruises."

"Wants you out?! Are you going?" Brenda asked excitedly.

"Oh -- I have my plans." Lee admitted with a sneer. She fans a dismissing hand. I don't care! They'll all be sorry. Especially Les!"

"Who? Wait a minute! So---- you ARE leaving? But who's Les?" Brenda asked again.

"I have to do something! Kevin said, if I don't quietly disappear, he'll call the police and have me arrested. And prison colors don't look good on me. Les won't mind them though." She sneered

"And who's Les?" Brenda probed.

Lee turned slowly and glared at Brenda, "You didn't, by chance, tell Kevin what I told you about --- you know— the tent?"

"Of course not, Lee!" Brenda pretended to be offended. "Why, would you think that?"

"Because he said he found it in the garage, and I know for a fact it was hidden well. You were the only other person who knew about it." Lee watched Brenda's reaction and knew immediately she was lying.

"Well, I certainly didn't tell him." Brenda lied and went back to her question. "Are you going to leave --- are you getting a divorce--- what?"

"Well, it's been a game of cat and mouse between me and my 'darling' husband. Kevin makes the appointments at the attorney's office to sign divorce papers and I," Lee laughed, "'forget' to show up." She whispered proudly. "However," the smile suddenly left her face, "There's another appointment set, and he's expecting me to be there. I'll be missing that appointment too."

"You know, Brenda," Lee smirked, "when I sign those papers, Kevin's going to be a free man."

Brenda felt a surge of excitement tingle up her spine, and it took everything she had to control the overwhelming desire to smile --- she suppressed it. "Well -- I haven't thought about Kevin Jenison since we were in high school" Brenda lied again.

"Really?" Lee asked, she chuckled and rolled her eyes toward the ceiling.

Brenda's strategy was watertight. All she had to do was find out Lees' little secrets and leave clues for Kevin to find. Once he realized how manipulative and sneaky Lee was, he'd divorce her, and Brenda would be at his side to help him pick up the pieces. The biggest clue was sent through an anonymous email telling Kevin of Lee's plan to take the children on a secret camping trip and disclose the where about of the hidden tent as proof of it all. Brenda expected Kevin to be angry, but she didn't understand why he got *so* angry.

Of course, anyone familiar with Lee Cramer knows; *Lee* and *camping* are two words that would never appear in the same sentence together, when they talk about her. Although Brenda knew Lee was up to something, she didn't know what it was. She was dying to learn what else Kevin found in the garage that warranted the rage that took him over the top, here she was so close to finding out, and *this* happens. Her watertight plan had just been reduced to an annoying drip.

"I can't believe I fell for any of your lies, Lee Cramer. You had no intention of leaving at all."

Everything seemed to backfire right in Brenda's face.

By the time she reached the car, her anger had escalated to sheer rage. She was ready to burst and found it difficult to contain the eruption begging to be set free. She opened the car door, got in, and slammed it so hard, the sound resonated through the air, bounced off the roof, and vibrated through, to the trunk. When the sound finally made its way back around to Brenda's ears, it was presented as a high-pitched ring that was immediately replaced when she braced her back against the seat and screamed at the top of her lungs.

15

When the dance was over, the couple stood still, not wanting the moment to end --- not wanting anything to invade the space where truth had been revealed. Kevin looked deep into Les's eyes again.

"I --I'm sorry. I'm trying to wrap my brain around this whole thing. I don't understand what's happening. I have so many questions but I don't know where to start."

"I know," Les answered, "I'll try to answer them all. I promise."

"D-I-D? What --? How --? Can it be fixed?"

"I hope so Kevin. I can't afford to give up hope."

"My God, I said so many hurtful things to you."

"I had to keep telling myself, you were talking to Lee, not me."

Realizing they were still on the dance floor, Kevin took Les's hand and guided her to a nearby table. He motioned for one of the caterers to bring them a glass of wine.

"You do drink wine, right?"

"Yes," she nodded, "I'd love some but the medicine I'm on for my headache, I think I'd better stay with Ginger Ale if you don't mind."

Kevin couldn't take his eyes off her for fear she'd disappear again.

"Question," Kevin squinted and cocked his head to the side. "I'm curious about something?"

"What's that?" Les asked.

Kevin lowered his eyes then lifted them back to hers, "Lenny's Pizza? It was *you* I talked to for hours?"

Les nodded, "Yes, you were getting ready to go away to college."

The caterer brought a glass of wine and Ginger Ale and sat it in front of the couple, and they thanked him.

"Do you remember anything else?" Kevin asked, tilting his head to wait for her answer.

Les blushed and dropped her eyes, "I remember – everything."

"Everything?"

Les lifted her gaze slowly until she met Kevin's. She nodded again and whispered, "*Everything!*"

Kevin reached out and covered her hand with his and Les leaned forward. Her other hand covered his. Tears brimmed and threatened to spill over.

"We have a lot to talk about," she said.

"Can I ask one more question?" Kevin inquired. "Because it's - it's *really* buggin' me. Please?"

"Of course."

"The day Keith was born. I noticed --"

Before he could finish, Les was nodding her head, "It was m*e!*"

"And Kelly's birth?"

She nodded again, "*Me.*"

"And where exactly," Kevin stammered, trying to find the right words, "where do you --go?"

Les took a while to answer him. Searching for the best way to explain it so he'd understand and then realized there was no other explanation except the truth. Her reply both disturbed and confused him.

"Into the dark. It's as though I can feel myself disappearing, and I can't do anything to stop it."

***

Veronica watched from across the room. She was glad to see the two were actually talking.

"Tom, I'd like to go sit with Les and Kevin. Can you help me?"

When Veronica reached the table with Les and Kevin, she all, but flopped into the seat.

"*Oh my God*," she said loudly, "I'm so tired of these things." She extending the crutches for someone -- *anyone* to take them. Tom obliged her and made sure she was comfortable before sitting beside her.

"So?" was the first word Veronica could think to say to them. "You've been sitting here talking for a while. What do you think?"

"I think we've got to figure out what the hell we have here and what we need to do to fix it," Kevin stated.

Tom had been watching in amazement since Les walked into the room. Still confused he sat forward on his chair and smoothed his hand over his face.

"Okay," he said. "I see you three know something, but can somebody please explain it to me? What's going on?"

Veronica turned to Tom and began explaining the whole situation, and Les would chime in from time to time to fill in the blanks. The women explained their pact about the cell phone. Kevin listened in astonishment. He held up his hands to interject,

"So, when *exactly* did you get back?" Kevin asked and then rushed on answering his own question, "The morning of the accident, Right?"

Veronica and Les nodded together.

Kevin sloped back in his chair. "I knew it. The difference was like night and day. I mean, the ponytail and jeans were a dead give-away. I was just so angry I couldn't see it."

"Okay," Tom said trying to piece all the information together, "You're saying that this," he reached across the table to Les, "is Lee, but ... she's ...not?"

"Uh, right -- I mean --no."

Kevin got ready to explain everything to his friend again, but stopped. "Tell you what, Tom. Let's just say the game board has changed, and we now have a new player." He turned to Tom and then swept his hands slowly to Les, "Tom, meet Les, Leslee Cramer. The woman I *thought* I was marrying eight years ago."

Tom shook his head. "I don't understand."

Veronica turned to Tom, "You will. We've got plenty of time to play catch up, but let's not think about it anymore tonight.

The band was playing, "Endless Love," and Kevin stood and reached his hand toward Les then led her onto the dance floor again. As they swayed to the music, Kevin lifted Les's chin with his hand, so he could look at her. He caressed the side of her face and gently brushed a kiss across her forehead, and then to her cheek. Les moaned with excitement and desire when his lips finally found hers, and they kissed until long after the music was over.

16

Timothy Josephs was extremely proud of the way his team covered a room. Every fifteen minutes two of his servers would make their way around the room with a fresh tray of hors d'oeuvres and another two would pass through with the wine and a variety of cocktails. Tables were strategically placed around the room. White linen table cloths and huge centerpieces created the style and illusion of sophistication and a promise of a luxurious evening. The lighting in the room was dim with an amber glow creating a rather surreal atmosphere. The music set the perfect mood for the evening as if it were familiar with each guest and took the time to create a ripple of emotion that gradually filled the room with elegance and intimacy. Timothy looked around observing the effects of the music and the lighting, he was pleased. He could see the tenderness between the couples as they danced and talked together. Timothy took pride in his ability to design the perfect atmosphere for his client's guests to fall in love with each other all over again. Tonight was definitely one of those nights.

At 8:00 that evening, Timothy showed the guests into the dining room for dinner. A white linen table cloth draped the long dining room table, accented with a lavender runner elegantly placed beneath a huge glass vase that became the center of attention. The vase held freshly cut

Lilacs and white Cali Lilies, but it was the accent of huge purple orchids that the guests raved about when they entered the room. The fragrance of sweet lilacs filled the air, and the guests took their seats. "Sheer elegance!" Timothy heard someone say. He smiled and with a proud bow, he took his leave. The evening's dinner was now in the hands of Chef Orin.

Chef Orin's dinner was a success! Quarter legs of chicken seasoned perfectly and simmered in a crème sauce flavored with a hint of rosemary, lemon, and wine. The chicken was accompanied by roasted green beans and rosemary potatoes, and paired with a crisp young Pinot Grigio.

Kevin lifted his glass in the direction of his friends and made a toast, thanking them all for coming, then turned his glass to Les, who was seated at the far end of the table. Their eyes met, and Les could hardly tear away from his gaze to finish her meal. She wanted to be closer to him, and Kevin felt her desire and nodded then winked, confirming he felt the same way. She had to close her eyes to compose herself, concerned that everyone there would see his effect on her.

Veronica watched the two then turned to see Tom watching her. He held his glass and tipped it toward her. She did the same to him.

"Did I tell you how magnificent you look tonight?" Tom asked.

"Yes," She blushed. "You certainly did, but I'll never get tired of hearing it."

After dinner, Timothy opened the French doors and informed the guests that dessert would be served outside. He stepped aside as the guests filed past him, making their way to the back yard.

Timothy Josephs found it easier to divide a dinner party into three themes. First, there was the 'gathering room' where guests greeted each other and experienced conversation, hors d'oeuvres, and cocktails, while they danced and listened to music. Next, he would lead them into the "dining area" where they were served their entrées for the evening. In the meantime, the band would break from the first setting and reconvene outside for the final theme: Dessert, outside under the stars, the perfect ending to complete the night.

Each setting provided fitting opportunities for his team to remove the dishes and glasses from the previous setting without disturbing his client's guests.

Tables and chairs had been cleverly placed around the lawn, white tablecloths, and centerpieces decorated each one. As the guest spilled over into the yard and found their seats, the band began to play. And while dessert was being served, some of the guests took their dates to the dance floor and swayed with the music of, Howard Hewett's, "How Do I Know I Love You."

Timothy certainly knew how to impress his clients. His designs became known throughout the valley, as 'sheer elegance of love.'

However, on this day he disappointed himself. To think that someone could make him second-guess the integrity of his favorite client, but Brenda Crenshaw did exactly that. She convinced him that sneaking her into the party would be a pleasant surprise for Kevin, seeing that Kevin had been secretly in love with her for years. Timothy obliged her for two reasons, to please Mr. Jenison and to get back at Lee Cramer for the many times she had belittled him in front of his staff. He despised her for trying to make him appear to others as a hired waiter instead of the designer he knew himself to be.

On the other hand, this was not the same Lee Cramer. This was a different person altogether. This person was enchanting and charming, not to mention beautiful beyond words. He was ecstatic when he saw Mr. Jenison leave Brenda Crenshaw in her scheming little tracks and give all his attention to his wife. "How dare Brenda try to pull the wool over my eyes! Kevin Jenison, secretly in love with her? Preposterous! Serves the bitch right," he mumbled under his breath and continued to work.

***

Veronica watched each guest say their good-byes to Les and Kevin and leave with a final wave. It felt good to sit under the stars with the coolness of the breeze blowing across her face. Nights like this didn't often happen in Arizona, but on this March evening, the breeze was light and welcoming. She gave Kevin and Les a hug and told them she would see them the following evening. She secured her crutches under each arm and hopped to a nearby bench that sat in the front of the house to wait for Tom, who gathered their things. She felt something tug at her heart as she watched Les standing beside Kevin in the doorway. The beauty of the night mixed with the excitement of having truth revealed was more a relief than Veronica could imagine.

Throughout the years, Veronica had to admit she felt as far in the dark as Les. They became the best of friends when they were children, inseparable. Because of the talk around town, Veronica's mother wouldn't allow Veronica to spend the night at Les's house. The 'little girl,' as her mom called her, could come spend the night with them. It was during those nights, Les and 'Ronnie' would sit up most the night giggling, sharing stories, and sharing secrets. At some stage around that time, Les told Veronica about Lee. She told her how Lee would push her back into the dark and when she finally found her way back, hours would have passed and sometimes days. Lee usually would have done something ridiculous and leave Les to clean up her mess.

Les was also realizing, if she'd concentrate hard enough she could push back and make Lee go away. That's what happened the day they were in school, and Veronica was sitting in the nurses' office, crying. She waited for Les to wake up and when she finally did, the first thing she whispered to Veronica was: "I'm okay, Ronnie -- I pushed back." At first, Veronica didn't understand what Les meant, but after Nurse Flemings shooed her out of the office, she remembered and smiled.

Veronica promised Les she would always be there for her, and she kept her promise. They continued into high school and then to college together. If Lee surfaced, Veronica kept her distance and waited it out until Les was strong enough to push back. And that's when Veronica would fill her in on all the mess Lee left behind so Les could either fix it without looking too crazy or try to explain it away.

One of those instances occurred when she and Les were eating lunch with the girls from the swim team. One of them leaned over and whispered into Les's ear, and immediately Les's face changed -- a change Veronica had become too familiar with. Veronica bolted from the table and ran to Les's side, "What did she say to you, Les?" Veronica asked. "What did she say?!" Her eyes flared at the girl, "What did you say to her?"

Before the girl could answer, Les's eyes went blank, and she pleaded with anyone who would listen, "I need Aunt Marie, can someone please call my Aunt Marie?"

Veronica didn't care who was watching or what they thought, she kept repeating, "Push back, Les! Please, look at me. Look at me and — push back!" However, after a while, she could see, Les was gone. Veronica moved away from Lee and allowed the space between them to become cold and unfamiliar until her friend returned.

Fortunately for them, Lee was interested in education. However, she wasn't as good a student as Les academically. Lee got by with a 'C' average, when Les was an 'A' student without even trying. Lee was an excellent artist and designed masterpieces that amazed her art teachers, but Les couldn't draw a straight line without a ruler. People would talk about how quickly Les could change —she could be fun and caring one minute, and cold and calculating the next. Isolated and callous about her school work and then a couple of days later studious and catching up on assignments that fell below her usual outstanding grades.

Like Les, Veronica was always on edge, trying to find a way to help her, a new remedy or a new book. She started working after school as a receptionist for Dr. Paul Whitfield, a well-known psychiatrist and thought she might be able to find help in one of the many books from his personal library. She got caught 'stealing' and to keep her job, she told Dr. Whitfield everything. It took some coercing, but Les finally agreed to meet with him and he became her doctor. He encountered Lee a few times during their sessions and considered her case 'fascinating'. So much so, he remained available if Veronica needed to call him at any time for help.

'On edge' was an understatement when Veronica thought about how she felt most of the time, not knowing when Lee was going to make an appearance.

Even now, she wondered how much time she had with her friend. She wasn't sure if she was going to wake up in the morning and have Kevin tell her Les was gone. Although no one understood what triggered Lee's unexpected surfacing, the most important question was whether Les was strong enough to continue to 'push back'. If she was, there was a chance she could keep Lee suppressed and dormant. Veronica couldn't help, but wonder what it was that made Les so weak Lee was able to surface for ten years?

"A penny for your thoughts," Tom said as he came around the bench and sat beside her. "I put your things in the car, and I'm ready when you are. He took in a breath and looked around, "It's a beautiful night, isn't it? Did you have a good time?"

"I had a great time tonight thanks to you. You were the perfect gentleman. I don't know what I would have done without you, Mr. Pryor. Who else would have carried my purse, adjusted my crutches, and walked beside me to make sure I kept my balance? You even took the time to dance with me."

"It was my pleasure, Veronica. I had been looking forward to spending time with you since Kevin brought you into my restaurant. I could barely keep my eyes off you, didn't you see that? I called Kevin about ten times that night to get more information about you. I felt like a teenage school kid. Asking dumb questions, 'Do you think she thinks I'm good lookin'? Do you think I have a chance?'"

Veronica looked shocked. *"No you didn't,"* She laughed.

"Oh yes, I did! Kevin threatened to block my number." Tom laughed. "And then when you came through those doors in that dress tonight, I about had a heart attack." He put his hand over his heart and fell back on the bench. "Girl, you have no idea what you did to me."

"So, wait a minute?" Veronica studied him. "Is that why Kevin turned me over to you so quickly tonight?"

"That's right. After all those texts and telephone calls, he was very happy to do it. He called me earlier to let me know you'd be here tonight. I was watching for you."

"I see. So, this was all a plan?"

Tom searched Veronica's face, "Are you upset?"

"No!"

"Then yes, it was a plan, and it worked."

They laughed again.

"In that case, I'm glad you agreed to take me home tonight."

"No problem." Tom smiled.

"Kevin was going to do it, but I think they've got a lot to talk about tonight, and I didn't want to be a hindrance."

"Say no more. It's my pleasure to take you home, Veronica."

"I've got a confession to make, Tom," Veronica whispered.

"What's that, pretty lady?" Tom asked, brushing a stray hair away from her eye.

"The day at your restaurant, that wasn't the first time I've been there."

Tom leaned down, never once taking his eyes from hers. "I know," he whispered and kissed her lips softly.

Veronica was breathless by the time the kiss was over. She wanted more, and she could tell Tom did too. Finally able to speak, Veronica said, "Take me home."

Tom winked at her, helped her secure her crutches, and then assisted her to his car.

17

Kevin and Les stood at the door saying goodnight to the last of their guests. They were exhausted, but they had to admit the evening had been lovely and full of surprises. The last to leave was Judge Matthews. He wasn't a real a judge. He earned the title by remaining a successful divorce attorney for over 30 years. He was the 'Matthews' in the law firm, 'Hinkle, Matthews, and Irons,' where Dave practiced.

Judge Matthews patted Kevin hard on the shoulder and shook his hand at the same time. He leaned back on his heels and let out a hearty laugh that seemed to affect his whole body. "Son, this was the best 'divorce' party I've ever been to," he joked. "Better yet, this is the *only* divorce party I've ever been to." He laughed again. "The two people getting the divorce reconcile right in front of about 50 folks, now that's one for the books. That's what I'm talkin' about, son. Fight for her! Men always let the good ones walk away! I see that almost every day. People walk in and out of my office all day long, DIVORCE, DIVORCE, DIVORCE! Just given up on their marriages. 'Bout time I see somethin' different, and it looks good on you, son." He smacked Kevin on the shoulder again, "Looks damn good. I sure wish Dave could've been here to see it."

Kevin pulled Les closer to him and gave her a playful hug. "Oh, I'm fightin' all right, Judge. You have no idea how hard I'm fightin'."

The judge threw his head back and laughed again. He looked at Les and nodded his head. "You look beautiful tonight, Ms. Lee. Can't say that I've ever seen you look more elegant. Good to see you two working things out." With that, Judge Matthews was out the door.

Kevin and Les closed the door and walked into the sitting room. They could hear the sounds of Timothy's team packing the last of the serving trays, and talking quietly among themselves.

Les looked up at Kevin, "Whew, this night was amazing, Kevin. I never danced so much in my life" She exclaimed as she sat on a chair to remove her shoes. Kevin watched her struggling to unbuckle the strap and bent down and playfully brushed her hands away so he could unbuckle it for her.

"I had a blast too, How's your headache? I didn't hear you complain about it all night."

"Well," she smiled as she watched him remove one shoe and bring her other foot up to unbuckle the other. "My head is pounding but it wasn't going to stop me from enjoying myself or enjoying you."

"You made everything so perfect."

"Yeah?" she asked playfully.

"Yeah!" He looked at her and nodded. "So tell me somethin', where did you get that dress? I know it couldn't have been anything Lee owned. It doesn't look like something she'd wear."

"That's because it was something 'I' would wear, and I'm not Lee. Actually, it was Veronica's dress. She brought two with her because she couldn't make up her mind which one she wanted to wear. She chose the one she had on, and I got this one."

"And you wear it well," Kevin said moving closer to her. "But I don't think it would have mattered what you had on, you still would've melted my heart when you came through those doors."

He caressed her cheek. "It's been a long time, lady, and we've got some catching up to do."

"Yes, you're right. But let's get some sleep tonight and start fresh tomorrow. Tomorrow the real work begins." Les stated.

"Real work?"

"Yes, the real work! I want my own life, Kevin. I want to enjoy my children and you if you let me." Les leaned in and allowed Kevin to kiss her softly, she reached up and touched his face.

"Oh My God," Kevin moaned. "I remember that touch, the way your hands feel on my face."

She opened her mouth slightly, inviting him. He accepted the invitation and kissed her deeper.

Les slightly pulled back and looked at Kevin. His eyes were heavy with desire. He wanted her so bad and searched for signs that told him she wanted him too. She caught his face between her palms.

"I've always loved you, Kevin Jenison, you know that, don't you? You asked me not to give up on you. Remember?"

"Of course, I do," Kevin nodded. "You were the reason I came back." Kevin stood slowly and held out his hand. "Come on, let's go upstairs."

Les stood facing Kevin. "Do you think it's wise that we --"

"Woman," Kevin assured her, "I wouldn't have it any other way."

18

When Les reached the bedroom door and turned the knob, she felt a tingle run up her spine.

Why am I so nervous? She asked herself. *It's not like I've never slept with Kevin Jenison. I've just never 'slept' with Kevin Jenison as his wife. But, I'm NOT his wife, Lee is. What the hell am I thinking?*

She felt Kevin come up behind her, and his hands caressed the full length of her arms before he drew her into him. She could feel him and knew he wanted her. Kevin reached up and carefully removed the rhinestone pins from her hair and laid them on the dresser. Her hair fell in ringlets around her shoulders and down her back, and he swept them to one side to place a long, tender kiss on her neck.

"You smell so good." He whispered.

Les closed her eyes and moved back, molding her body to his. She wanted him too, and she needed him to know it. She reached up, found his hands, and slowly guided them around to her breast. She heard Kevin moan.

"Baby," He whispered again, "you – are – driving – me - crazy."

His raspy voice made Les quake. Kevin's hands trembled as he reached up and fumbled with the zipper on her dress. She smiled, he was as nervous as she. Knowing this somehow made him sexier. He unzipped her dress, and she let it fall to the floor. She stepped out of it and turned to face him. His face was flushed, and she wondered what he was thinking. When he looked into her face, did he see Lee? She didn't want him to see Lee -- not tonight.

Les searched Kevin's eyes while she unbutton his shirt. He pulled the shirt off and threw it across the room. "Who do you see, Kevin?" She rose onto her toes and kissed him softly. She opened her mouth slightly and brushed his bottom lip with her tongue. "Who do you see?" Kevin trembled and tore at his belt. He fumbled with his pants until they lay in a heap on the floor; he kicked them away. He removed his shorts and helped her out of her slip. They stripped away every piece of clothing in their way until they both stood naked facing each other. "Please Kevin, tell me who you see?" She pleaded as a tear streamed slowly down her cheek.

Kevin framed her face with his hands and looked deep into her eyes, then he nodded. "I see you, Baby." He said as he walked with her backward to the bed. "I see the woman I fell in love with years ago." He laid her down gently and kissed her, "I see the mother of my children." He kissed her again and finally he said the words Les was waiting to hear, "I see you, Leslee. I see you."

She pulled him down to her, and they made love slow, and he repeated her name deliberately so she could hear it roll off his lips and know that he knew she was Les.

***

When Les opened her eyes, Kevin was sitting up on his elbow, watching her.

"You snore, ya know?" He said playfully.

"I do not!" She laughed.

"'Fraid so."

"What are you doing? What time is it?" She looked around at the clock.

"2:30."

"In the morning? Kevin, why are you awake?"

He cocked his head to the side and a warm smile touched his lips, "I'm busy."

She laughed again, "Busy doing what?"

"Looking at you and willing you to wake up." He bent down and kissed her.

"Okay, so I'm awake. Now what?" She snuggled closer to him.

Kevin caressed the side of her face then tilted her chin up. "Now I--" He wrapped his arms around her and pulled her gently into a warm embrace. He kissed her again, "I can't get enough of you, Leslee," He whispered against her hair.

"That's good to hear," she chuckled. Les laid her hand on his chest and slowly moved it up around his shoulder then down his arm. She kissed his chest and moved her hand down to his hips. His eyes were closed, and hot desire shone on his face as he waited for her to touch him. But she waited. "You're driving me crazy, woman," he whispered. She kissed his chest again. Her lips were hot and wet. Finally, she gently touched him. His body shuddered and he moaned from deep within.

He rolled her on top of him, and he watched her take control while his desire built. Her breathing deepened as she bent down to kiss him, exploring his mouth with her tongue; driving him wild! He lifted her from him and turned with her in his arms. He laid her down, and the heat from their lovemaking became intoxicating. Their bodies swayed together -- melted together like liquid fire. When she whispered his name, he opened his eyes and immediately understood, she wanted him to see her -- watch her. It drove him to the apex of his desire and at that moment, Kevin lost control. He moaned as he released all of his love for her over and over and over before he collapsed then rolled onto his side.

"Woman, woman, woman," he whispered. When he finally opened his eyes, she was watching him. "You are somethin' else," he said.

A lazy smile tugged at her lips. "I was worried at first that you wouldn't be satisfied with me."

"What? Are you kidding me? Les, what would give you that idea? Don't you remember how good we were together?"

"I remember how good it was for me. However, *you*, I believe, had other plans because you waited until you thought I was asleep and made a phone call to Brenda Crenshaw. Remember that?"

"Oh, brother, here we go again." He laughed.

"Don't give me that, Kevin Jenison. You know I'm talking the truth."
They both laughed. It felt good to be able to talk about old times.

"You know," Kevin laid back onto the bed with his arms behind his head, "I should have known something was off. The fact that Lee couldn't recall, certain significant facts, like when we first met, my football career, or my injury should have been a clue for me. I thought you were messin' with me. Lee would turn to me with that sneer of hers and asked, "Oh, so you played ball? She didn't know anything about me. Now I understand, there's no way she could've known. Oh and speaking of Brenda, did you know she was at the party tonight?"

"She was here?" Les let out a long yawn and snuggled deeper under the covers.

"Yeah, she said, Lee invited her, and she wanted to congratulate me on my divorce. I didn't see her anymore. Once you came through that door, baby, you had my full attention" He bent down and kissed her neck.

"I wonder how she knew about the divorce." Les yawned again. She pulled Kevin's arm around her and scooted backward into him.

"I wonder how Lee knew about the party." Kevin answered.

"Maybe Brenda was trying to get her old position back."

Kevin chuckled and tightened his arm around her, "That spots taken."
Les smiled and fell asleep.

19

Kevin awoke with someone tapping at the door.

"Daddy--Daddy?" He knew by the shyness in the voice and the way the words seemed to curl at the end; it was Kelly. She was usually the first one awake in the morning. She wanted breakfast and wanted to fix it herself, but knew she would need his help.

Kevin slid out of bed trying not to disturb Les. He quickly slipped on a pair of pajama bottoms and his bathrobe and went to the door. As he opened the door, he held a finger to his lips to let Kelly know to keep quiet.

"Shhhh, sweetie, Mommy's still asleep and we don't want to wake her. She's very tired."

"Mommy, which Mommy?" She shrugged.

Kevin was taken aback by Kelly's question. "What do you mean *which* Mommy?"

"I have two Mommies' now. I hope it's the nice one."

"Kelly, when did you see the nice Mommy?" Kevin asked bending down to pick her up.

"Yesterday before the babysitter came. Me and Keith were downstairs, and she came in the back door. I think she was crying." Kelly answered.

"Really?" Kevin recalled the incident that had taken place outside the day before and felt his heart drop. He had been angry at Lee and was desperately trying to say anything to hurt her. And now, it tore at his heart to know it was Les at the end of his wrath and not Lee. His angry outbursts had done exactly what he intended it to do, but it was Les, who was affected by it. Having Kelly reveal that he'd hurt Les so badly that it made her cry, brought an agonizing sadness.

"And then," Kelly rushed on, "She *talked* to us and asked how old we were. I told her I was five, but Keith wouldn't let me be it, so he told her I was four." She held up four fingers, "I'm this many, huh Daddy?"

"You sure are." Kevin agreed.

The bedroom door opened, and Les walked out with Lee's bathrobe on. "*Hey*," she whispered loudly, "What's going on out here? Well, good morning, Kelly. Where's your brother?"

"He's downstairs, I told him that I was coming to wake Daddy up, but he's playing a game and didn't want to come."

"It's okay, he doesn't have to come up," Les said.

"Since everyone seems to be awake, how about we go find him?" She reached out to take Kelly out of Kevin's arms. Kelly quickly leaned away and put her arms tighter around her daddy's neck, with a guarded, "Daaaddy?"

Les stepped back understanding Kelly's fear and accepted it. "It's okay, Kelly. I say we go downstairs and make breakfast. Who wants pancakes?"

Kevin looked at Les and shrugged his apology.

Kelly squealed, "Me! I want pancakes! Keith does too. He loves pancakes" Kelly did everything to wiggle out of her daddy's arms. Kevin put her down, and she ran down the hall and the stairs.

"Keith!" she yelled, "We're gonna have pancakes today, and Mommy's coming down to help."

Kevin and Les stood in their bathrobes and watched the excited little girl hurry away. Then they turned to each other and laughed.

"I think she's excited," Les laughed.

"So am I," Kevin said pulling her into his arms. He cocked his head to the side, "Good morning." He kissed her.

The kiss sent a surge of excitement through Les's body. "Good morning."

"Should we put on some clothes or are you okay like this?" He asked.

Les looked down at the bathrobe, "What's wrong with my bathrobe? Come on, let's go." She said walking toward the stairs.

Kevin watched with mild amazement. This was going to take some getting used to. Lee would never think about walking around the house in her bathrobe. But, of course, this wasn't Lee. Thank God.

***

The day was full of excitement. Keith and Kelly had never seen Mommy and Daddy holding hands before, but today, not only did they hold hands, they actually kissed right on the mouth. Kelly looked stunned and turned to Keith, who stood with his mouth open until Kelly nudged him.

Allowing the children to choose an outing for the day landed them at the Phoenix Zoo where they ran from one animal cage to the other.

Kelly called to Les, "Mommy, look at the lion."

Les walked to the sign near the lion's cage and began reading it aloud. The massive creature strolled back and forth, laying claim to his title, King of the Jungle. But, when the ferocious beast let go a thunderous roar, Les ran to Kelly and ushered her away from the cage. They walked around the entire zoo and were standing at the monkey's cages when Les felt a little hand place itself warmly into hers. Her gaze dipped to Kelly and the tentative hope in the child's face as she searched Les's. Les said nothing, just smiled, squeezed the child's hand gently and walked to the next cage. She was on cloud nine, and Kevin smiled.

By the end of the day, Kevin could see that Les was a gigantic hit with the children. Like him, they couldn't get enough of her. It was Mommy this and Mommy that. Mommy, Mommy, Mommy and Les loved it!

20

Les stood at the sink, drying dishes after dinner. Kevin came up behind her and caressed her shoulders. His hand slid down her arms as usual before encasing her in his arms and pulling her into him. Les closed her eyes trying to control the desire rising inside her. He kissed her hair and the side of her face. She tilted her head to the side so he could kiss her neck. "What are we going to do about this, Kevin Jenison?" She put the towel down and turned to him.

"I know what I'd like to do," he breathed.

Les pulled his face down, and they kissed. Kevin groaned and drew her in closer.

"Baby, you have no idea what you do to me." He said.

"I can say the same thing about you, Mr. Jenison," Les whispered teasingly "but we have company coming today, and the children are in the other room."

"Company?"

"Yes, Ronnie's coming. Your friend, Tom, is bringing her over. It was nice of Tom to offer to drive her home after the party. If you ask me, I think he rather likes her."

"Likes her?" Kevin chuckled. That's an understatement."

"What do you mean?"

"When you were in the hospital, I took Veronica home since her car was totaled in the accident, we'd been at the hospital all day and hadn't eaten. Tom owns a restaurant in Chandler, so we stopped there to have a bite to eat. He would not leave me alone about her. Immediately obsessed I tell you!" Kevin laughed.

"How long have you and Tom known each other?"

"Ohh," Kevin thought, "Fifteen maybe sixteen years. I'm not sure. I helped him open his restaurant and in return, he lets me win a couple games of golf."

"You golf?"

Kevin rubbed the back of his neck, "Uhh, yeah. I guess I do."

Les laughed, "That means no."

"It means I'm hopeful." Kevin countered. "What time are they coming?"

Les glanced at the clock, "They should be here by now."

"Well, before they get here," he kissed her softly, "let me tell you how awesome it is to have you around and I'm sure the children feel the same way. You're a natural. They have a good time with you. I wasn't sure how they were going to accept you at first, but since the zoo, you've got them eating out the palm of your hand. The same way you have me." His kiss was warm and inviting.

"I love them, Kevin. I just want them to trust me."

"But, how do you tell children, the mother they couldn't trust before is now someone they can trust? I believe they'll come around, but it's going to take time for them to trust you. I watched Keith at breakfast this morning, when you poured the syrup on his pancakes, every time you moved, he'd move. They're not liberal in the trust department yet."

"And you?"

Kevin's eyes softened. "Me?"

"I feel you watching me, Kevin. You're not sure about me either. Are you?"

He stepped back and rubbed his neck. "I'm going to be honest with you, Leslee. When you ran out of the living room after our discussion, I was stunned. But, I started putting things together – thinking about inconsistencies of the past. I mean, multiple personality disorder isn't something you run into every day. What was it you called it; D-I-D? Either you're telling the truth about it, which is why I'm standing here talking to Leslee and not Lee, or you're deceiving the hell out of me right now. I catch myself thinking about it all the time."

"I understand. Believe me, I'm not trying to deceive you, Kevin."

"Then I need you to do something for me."

"Anything."

"I need you to call Dr. Whitfield and make an appointment to see him as soon as possible. I don't want to take any chances. I can't lose you again."

"I will. I'll call him."

"No, Sweetheart, I don't want you to wait on this. I need you to call him now."

"Now?"

Kevin nodded.

Les walked to the cabinets and drew out Alex Whitfield's card. She picked up the phone. "I don't know why I'm so nervous."

Kevin came up behind her and raised a comforting hand to her shoulder. "I'm nervous too, babe, but you've got to see him. You said you wanted to live your own life. This is your chance. Let's see what he can do to help you? I'll go with you if you want me to."

"You promise?" She asked.

"Of course, I promise. I'll be there."

Les dialed the number. Dr. Whitfield's receptionist answered the phone. She had a friendly southern accent.

"Good afternoon, Dr. Whitfield's office. This is Heather, how may I direct your call?"

"Yes, Hello Heather, my name is Les Cramer. I would like to make an appointment to see Dr. Whitfield."

"Okay, sure. Have we seen you here before, Ms. Cramer? She asked.

"I use to be a patient of Dr. Paul Whitfield before he passed away. Dr. Alex Whitfield came to visit me at the hospital and asked me to make an appointment. But, no, I've never been to his office."

"Can you please hold?"

"Sure," She lifted her eyes to Kevin's and shrugged. "She put me on hold."

The receptionist came back, "Ms. Cramer?"

"Yes?"

"I'm going to transfer the call. Dr. Whitfield has been waiting to hear from you. Please, hold."

"What?" Kevin asked.

"She's transferring my call. He's been waiting to hear from me."

"I like this guy already."

"Les?" Came Alex Whitfield's voice.

"Yes, Alex. It's me. I was calling to set up an appointment with you. I'd like to see you as soon as possible. Do you have time available?"

"Of course, I can see you. How's Tuesday sound? Can you get here by 4:00?"

Les turned a quizzical face to Kevin and covered the phone, "Tuesday at 4:00?"

Kevin nodded.

"Tuesday at 4:00 would be fine," she confirmed. "I'll see you then. Is there anything you need me to bring with me?"

"No, Les. I have everything right here. I'll have Heather make a note of the appointment, and I'll see you on Tuesday. Have a good evening."

"You too and thank you. Bye."

She hung up the phone and turned to Kevin.

"This is good, Sweetheart."

"Yes, I know," She put her arms around Kevin and held him close, thinking about the 'what if's'. *What if Alex Whitfield can't find the answers to her problems?* And then, the other question came just as quickly, *What if he does?*

21

That evening, Kevin and Les sat in the living room with Veronica and Tom. Kevin watched the two women laugh as they told stories about their childhood. Some of the stories had them both wiping away tears from laughing so hard. Kevin found himself studying Les, inspecting the way she walked, paying attention to the tone of her voice, and dissecting each story, looking for inconsistencies and contradictions that never came. Eight years of marriage and he knew nothing about her childhood. He closed his eyes against the thoughts that seemed all over the place and realized, the eight years didn't matter at this point because it was Leslee, not Lee, who was present at this moment.

Kevin watched her and smiled. Veronica would joke about one incident or another, and Les would fall back in her chair and laugh. Kevin shook his head in amazement. *How could he have missed this side of her,* he wondered. He remembered her laugh being genuine and contagious, and her light-heartedness was just one of the qualities that made her wonderful to be around when they first met. These same qualities had him thinking about her constantly while he was away at college and, as he continued to watch her tonight, he realized these same qualities is what made him come back for her too.

He was reminded of the telephone call to the doctor and wondered what was going to happen on Tuesday? He succumbed to the fact that, whatever happened, they would get through it together.

Kevin walked across the room, positioned himself behind Les and gently laid his hand on her shoulder. Les automatically reached up and caressed it. Her touch caused a stir in him, a warm tug at his heart. He bent down and whispered in Les's ear, "I love you."

A smile spread across her face. She closed her eyes, then turned her head toward the hand on her shoulder and planted a warm kiss on it. She had been longing to hear those words, but she knew Lee had hurt him so badly it would take time for him to trust her. She'd been willing to wait.

Veronica watched the couple. "I'm likin' this chemistry between you two," she said.

Kevin smiled, "It's hard to believe that I've been married to this wonderful woman for over eight years."

Les smile slowly left her face, *"You haven't!"*

Kevin frowned, "What do you mean? We've been married for eight years, Babe!"

"No, Kevin, you've been married to *Lee* Cramer for eight years," Les stated.

"Well," Kevin stated, "Let me take care of that right here and now." He turned Les around to face him and said. "Les Cramer, I fell in love with you the day we sat at Lenny's Pizza and talked for hours. I don't want to live another day without you as my wife." He dropped to one knee and took Les's hand. "I promise, Sweetheart, that I will protect you, care for you, and love you for the rest of your life or the remainder of mine. Will you do me the honor of becoming my wife?"

Veronica stood slowly to her feet when she realized what Kevin was doing. She balanced herself with her crutches in one hand and the other covered her mouth. "Oh, my."

Les couldn't believe what was happening either. Tears pooled her eyes.

Veronica broke the stunned silence. "Well, say something, girlfriend, what's wrong with you? He's waiting for an answer."

Les nodded her head wildly before shouting, "Yes! Yes, I'll marry you Kevin Jenison."

Kevin rose from the floor, pulled Les into an embrace, and kissed her.

"Woo Hoo!" Veronica yelled repeatedly.

The excitement brought Riley in from the other room, and he began to bark until Les bent down, picked up the white bundle of fur, and held him close.

Tom closed the distance between him and Kevin. He smiled at his friend then congratulated him with a handshake. "Kevin?" he spoke softly so the others couldn't hear, "Are you sure about this?"

Kevin understood Tom's concern but still he nodded his head and said, "I'm surer about this than anything in my life."

Veronica adjusted her crutches and moved closer to Tom. He took a step back from Kevin and forced a smile, but concern creased his brow."

"What is it, Tom?" Veronica asked quietly.

"Come on, Ronnie," he said. "You and I both know we're taking a gamble here. You can't tell me that the chance of Lee resurfacing hasn't crossed your mind."

"It's on my mind all the time, Tom, but at this moment, *Les* and Kevin are happy. Let's just be happy for them."

He nodded slowly and surrendered to the excitement in the room. "We need to pull out the champagne, if there's going to be a wedding." He walked toward the bar in the corner and removed champagne glasses from the cabinet.

Kevin joined him, poured the champagne and they all toasted to the occasion.

Keith and Kelly were frightened at first and approached the door of the room cautiously, but soon realized the outbursts were from excitement and not anger. They began to jump and skip around in circles, singing, "Mommy and Daddy are getting married again! Mommy and Daddy are getting married again!" Riley jumped out of Les's arms and started barking, running around Keith and then Kelly.

Keith and Kelly jumped on their dad, "Yay. Yay. Yay, Mommy and Daddy are getting married."

Kelly looked at Les, "Can I hug you?" she asked timidly.

"Of course, you can. I was hoping I could get the biggest and longest hug you can give me." Les put her arms out so Kelly could climb into her lap. She gave her a gentle hug. Kelly's little arms circled Les's neck, and she hugged her Mom with all her might.

Curiously, Kelly asked, "What about the *other* Mommy?"

"The other Mommy has to stay away. She's not allowed to come back, honey. She won't ever be able to hurt you again. And you want to know something else?"

Kelly was very excited, "What?"

"You and I are gonna go shopping, and we're going to buy you a beautiful dress so you can be my flower girl. That's a very important job. Can you do that for me?"

"Yeah!" Kelly shouted, "Keith, Keith, I get to have a important job! I'm gonna be a flower girl and wear a beautiful dress." She reached up and hugged Les again.

"What about me, Dad, I want to do something?" Keith inquired.

"Well son, I don't know if you'll be able to handle the job I need you to do for me." Kevin teased.

"Yes, I can, Dad! Really, I can." Keith exclaimed.

Kevin knelt down and put his hand on Keith's shoulder, "Son, I'm gonna be buying your Mom a very special ring." He whispered, "Do you think you can go with me and help to pick it out?"

"Yeah, Dad!" Keith whispered back and nodded his head excitedly.

"Now this is what we're gonna do --" Kevin led Keith to the opposite side of the room where Tom was, and they began speaking quietly. When they were finished, Kevin said, "Now this is only between us guys. Okay?"

Tom chuckled and nodded. Keith took an imaginary key and locked his mouth then pretended to throw the key away. He turned to Kelly and Les and made a 'my-lips-are-glued-shut' face that made them laugh.

"Well, what am I gonna do?" Veronica pouted.

Les went to her friend, "You are and always will be my very best friend, and I wouldn't have anyone, but you at my side as my Maid of Honor."

"I accept, girlfriend." The two women laughed and embraced.

Keith ran to the middle of the room to play with Riley, which gave Tom the chance to speak confidentially to Kevin.

"Listen Kev, I'm not going to even pretend like I understand everything that's going on here, but with all the excitement, are you sure Les is gonna be able to handle it? I mean, what if Lee --"

"I've thought about that too, man, and honestly, I don't know. I know we're here now, and I'm willing to take it a day at a time, but most importantly I'm willing to fight for her and give us a chance. I promised I was going to be there for her, and I'm gonna keep my word. Let's pray for best."

"Okay, man, right. I just want you to know that *I'll* be here for *you*."

"Right. Thanks, Tom. While we're talkin', I've got two questions for you."

"Okay?"

"Number one, will you consider being my best man? And number two, what's going on with you and Veronica?"

Tom laughed. "The answer to your first question is, hell yeah, I'll be your best man. And as far as the second question is concerned, all I can say is, I really like her. We have a great time together. What can I say? When it's right, it's right."

Kevin laughed and patted Tom on the shoulder. "She's good people, man, and so are you. You can't get any better than that."

Les glanced at Kevin and Tom, then to Veronica. "What do you suppose they're talking about?"

Veronica glanced over at the two men and laughed, *"Us!"*

Les gave Veronica a long look.

"What?" Veronica asked.

"What's going on with you and Tom? First the party, he takes you home, and now -- here? What's going on Ronnie?"

"You really want to know? Veronica laughed.

"Yes, I do," Les whispered loudly. She helped Veronica to the sofa and sat down.

Veronica's gaze lifted and fell on Tom, "Well, I believe, I mean--I think--he's great. He's attentive, affectionate, and he's so smart, Les. I like him."

"I can tell," Les smiled. "So what does he say about my situation?"

"Well, he doesn't quite understand it but, he's gonna be there for Kevin. He's concerned about Lee finding her way back."

"Hell, I'm concerned about Lee finding her way back too!" Les said.

"But he thinks Kevin is setting himself up to get hurt again. It would devastate him if Lee came back, and there wouldn't be anything he could do about it. Tom's worried about his friend."

"How's all this affecting you, Ronnie?" Les asked.

"Well, I can't say that I haven't been thinking the same thing. Les, you and I will always be friends, but it tears me up when Lee shows up because I miss you and this last time you were gone entirely too long. Look at Kevin, he's so happy. Lees' coming back would devastate him. I know that because it has already devastated me. Look around the room, Les. If Lee comes back, everyone in this room will be affected."

Les looked at Kevin and Tom, who were deep in conversation. Then she turned to Keith and Kelly playing carelessly on the floor with Riley. And next she turned her attention to Ronnie, who seemed to have had a weight lifted from her shoulders, and she knew she was right. They were all making plans and enjoying life like everything was normal, but there was nothing normal about it. There was a huge elephant in the room, and somebody had to remove it. She was going to have to talk to Kevin, and they needed to talk tonight.

"You're right, Ronnie, but I want you to know that I'm concerned too. I don't know if I'm gonna wake up tomorrow with another ten years gone, or wake up in another city, or in someone else's bed. You have no idea the thoughts that go through my mind. Hell with what Lee was planning, what if she comes back and follows through on it. I could wake up in jail. I'm scared too, Ronnie."

Veronica's eyes glistened. The more reason to push back and push hard. Lee needs to stay gone."

"I called Alex Whitfield today."

"Great, what did he say?"

"I have an appointment with him on Tuesday at 4:00. I'll let you know what happens. Kevin's going with me, but, I'm *so frightened*, Ronnie."

"Of what?"

"We still don't know the triggers. What if Alex can't help me? What if I have to continue to live like this? I don't want to, and I can't ask Kevin to live like this either".

"You gotta get tough and stay that way. Look, Lee's the imposter, you rightfully deserve to exist, not her."

***

The evening with Tom and Veronica ended at 9:00. In time for Les to join Kevin in saying goodnight to the children. They were excited to have Mommy there too. When Les bent down to kiss Keith on the forehead, he reached up and laid his hand on her cheek,

"Mommy?"

"Uh-huh."

"Will you be here tomorrow?"

Les turned and looked at Kevin not knowing exactly how to answer him. But when Kevin took a step toward her, she put her hand up to stop him. She had to do this herself.

She covered his hand with hers, and tears stung her eyes.

"Sweetheart, I plan to stay with you for the rest of my life."

Keith smiled, exposing the two empty spaces in his mouth.

Les used the opportunity to lighten the mood, "I think I see something happening here, Daddy. Come look."

Kevin walked to Les's side and peered down into Keith's mouth.

"Woe," Kevin said, "I see some teeth coming in, son."

"Really?" The boy jumped out of the bed and ran to the dresser mirror. He opened his mouth wide and saw two small teeth peeking through the gums. "They're coming back!" he shouted, "They're really coming back!"

"No, son, these are brand new."

Happy with his exciting discovery, Keith hugged both his parents and jumped back into bed. They were still laughing when they tucked him in again and left the room.

When they closed Keith's bedroom door, Kevin pulled Les into an embrace and kissed her softly on the lips.

"I've been wanting to do that all night." He whispered.

"Me too."

"You were awfully quiet after Tom and Veronica left." Kevin put his arm around Les's shoulders, and they walked to their bedroom together. "Something's bothering you. What is it?"

"I have so much on my mind, Kevin."

Kevin closed their bedroom door and turned to Les. He tilted his head to the side.

"Then let's talk. Tell me what's going on."

Les took a deep breath, "Kevin. I'm frightened. I don't want us to be making all these plans, and then something happens. You know what I mean? What if I'm not strong enough to continue to push Lee back? What if you wake up tomorrow morning, and I'm gone or you sit down to dinner and --."

"You don't think I've thought about that? I think about it all the time."

"What are you gonna do if it happens, Kevin? The thought that you might have to face that woman frightens me and makes me wonder if we should be making definite plans right now."

He raised his hand, "Wait -- What? What are you talking about?"

"I'm talking about what's best for everyone."

"What are you saying?"

"I'm saying I love you, but I can't ask you to take a chance on me right now. I have to get fixed first. I can't do this to you or Kelly and Keith."

"You're not asking me! I'm *telling* you, I'm in this with you, Sweetheart." Kevin walked to Les and hugged her tight. "I'm not letting you go through this alone. We're both taking a chance here, but it's worth the chance we're taking." He held her back. "It's worth it!"

Les pulled away from him. She thought for a minute, and then she shook her head.

"I'm sorry, Kevin, I can't --"

"It's not your choice!" He yelled.

The sudden outburst startled Les. Kevin quickly closed the distance between them. He pulled Les close and kissed her hair.

"Don't you understand, baby? It's not your choice to make! I don't profess to understand everything that's happening, but I know this– I've made a decision to fight, and you can't take that away from me. Do you understand? It's my decision, not yours."

Les's tears were flowing freely, and Kevin tilted her face up and wiped them away.

"You just have to understand you can't run me away." He shook his head. "You can't do it. I won't let you."

She nodded. Her head snapped up, and she gave him a long look. "Then you have to promise me something."

"I'm --"

"No! Now, Kevin, I can accept your decision if you make this promise to me."

Kevin took a deep breath and a step back. He crossed his arms and nodded.

"Promise me that, if Alex can't help me, or you wake up and find Lee here. You gather our children and get the *hell* out. Keep them away from her. Get them as far away as possible. Take them to Ronnie or out of town or something, but don't let her near my babies."

Kevin nodded wildly, "I promise. I promise," he agreed and that night, he made love to Les and repeated how much he loved her over and over again.

22

Dr. Whitfield's office was different than Les remembered. The pictures on the walls were abstract and included neutral colors of brown and beige that were also present in the chairs and the carpeting in the room. It was accented with a few splashes of orange and gold, which made the room brighter and more welcoming than before. Although she found it difficult to relax, she was able to muster up a nervous smile at the pleasant change. She walked to the receptionist's window and signed her name on the list. When she looked through the glass, a short plump lady, her glasses perched awkwardly on the tip of her nose, smiled up at her. Les anxiously smiled back and followed Kevin to the side of the room where there were two chairs together. Les continued to look around nervously.

"Calm down," Kevin said softly.

"I'm trying to. I've never been here to see *this* Dr. Whitfield. My sessions were with his father. What if we're not compatible? I mean, he was so young when I was coming here before. Kevin, what if I'm opening up a whole new can of worms? What if he and I don't --?"

"You guys hit it off pretty good back at the hospital."

"Yeah, but that was then. What if it was a false start? What if --?"

Kevin put his arm around her, "You're workin' yourself up into a frenzy, Baby. Take a couple of deep breaths and relax. We'll go in and feel him out, and if you don't like him, I promise, you won't have to come back. We'll find another doctor. Okay?" He squeezed her against him then turned her chin until she looked at him. "Okay?"

"Okay." She smiled.

The door opened and the little plump lady from behind the glass, walked out. "Les Cramer?" Les knew by the southern accent that she was Heather.

Les and Kevin got up and walked toward the door to follow her. Les took Kevin's hand.

Heather guided them to an office where they waited for Dr. Whitfield.

Dr. Alex Whitfield's office was larger than Kevin expected. On one side of the room, a bookshelf encompassed the entire wall. Rows of books were stacked neatly on some of the shelves and statues of lions and eagles were displayed on the others with a hint of lighting in the background to give the statues more depth. As Kevin looked around the room, it became apparent that the lion/eagle theme was the main décor for the office. Two of the walls exhibited huge paintings, one of a lion and the other an eagle with painting lights perched above them both. The furniture was a deep mahogany and made the room feel comfortable and warm. But it was the display on the wall behind Alex's desk that seized Kevin's attention.

Dr. Alexander Whitfield's, degrees earned, certificates and awards presented, and recognized accomplishments. Kevin walked to the wall and read each one, and as he moved from one frame to another, he whistled quietly and said, "I'm impressed."

"What?"

"He's accomplished so much for someone his age. He can't be much older than you and Ronnie."

"Actually, he's a little younger than us. He finished high school at an early age, and before we knew it, he was entering med school."

Alex entered the office and smiled. He was again impeccably dressed. Today he wore a black suit with a light grey shirt, a black-and-white striped tie, and matching pocket square. Les was impressed remembering the loose dress of his college days. Now he looked like he belonged in a magazine.

Kevin moved toward Alex, and the two shook hands. "I believe we've met." Alex chuckled, then turned and gave Les a light hug before moving behind his desk to sit down.

"Listen Doc, about that scene at the hospital --." Kevin began apologetically as he walked to the seat beside Les.

Dr. Whitfield held up his hands, "No need, Kevin. I'd be surprised if you acted any other way." He chuckled. "This whole thing must have you in a state of shock, but I'm going to do what I can to help you understand what's going on. Let me say, first of all, I'm glad to see you here. I've been looking over my files and reading my father's notes about you since I took over his practice, and I was hoping to get a chance to talk to you. As you can see," He held up the thick folder, "My father took lots of notes." He laughed. "Five years' worth and there's more in the cabinet" He pointed at a file cabinet across the room. "Looks like you and my dad worked together for a long time before you -- went to-- uh --'sleep.'"

"Yes," Les nodded, "I remember. He had me try every possible remedy he could find, but nothing worked. This last time is the longest I've ever been gone, but it doesn't seem long until I look in the mirror. How was that possible?"

"Oh, it's possible, Les. It doesn't happen often though. I've researched some pretty extreme cases of Dissociative Identity Disorder. For instance, there's a case study where the host personality, which would be you, Les, woke up in an entirely different state. She was wearing clothes she would never have worn, and people were calling her by a name that she didn't recognize. It was a reoccurring problem for her. All this had happened before she was diagnosed with MPD, Multiple Personality Disorder, today we call it DID, Dissociative Identity Disorder. She actually thought she was going crazy and tried to kill herself, and that's when we were called in. Like I was telling you at the hospital, I have a team of doctors who work with me on many of these cases, and we've been pretty successful helping individuals who want to be helped. Today we have a better understanding of DID, and I believe we might be able to help you.

Let me explain some of what happens to a person with DID. Kevin, what is your profession?"

"I'm an attorney."

"Okay, let's look at that. You, being an attorney is the professional side of your personality, and you have a certain way you behave during that time. You, as Les's spouse, is another side of your personality, and you take on that role and behave as her husband. The way you are with your friends is yet another side. Now, imagine not being able to intersect the three personalities, and each one becomes individually magnified at any given moment. That's what Les is going through. And not knowing what triggers the switch can be very frightening. What has to happen is the host personality has to come to terms with the fact that each alter is actually a crucial side of them. They have to do the work to bring all the personalities together as a whole.

The brain is miraculous, and it can process trauma, but it's not always good at processing *severe* trauma. A small child who is traumatized by severe abuse, might not be able to deal with the staggering effects of it, so he or she creates a personality who *can* deal with it. That personality becomes real and surfaces every time the child encounters a smell, a thought, or anything that reminds them of the trauma. They create the personality to deal with it for them. Are you following me?"

Kevin and Les nodded that they understood.

The woman I spoke of earlier, the one who woke up in different states with her name changed, is living a normal life now." He chuckled. "If you consider a husband and *six* children normal."

Both Les and Kevin sat up in their chairs, "You were able to help her?" Les whispered.

Alex Whitfield nodded.

"But your father said that there's no--"

"I know what my father said, but he didn't have the knowledge we have today about this disorder. I am confident, in *your* case, we can treat it and help you to live a normal life too. Look, Les, I've been studying your case for a very long time, and I think you'll be amazed at what we can do. But, you're going to have to give me your word that you'll participate and trust me. Do I have your word?"

"Yes, of course." Les blurted.

Alex excused himself, picked up the phone and asked Heather to hold all his calls. He hung up and turned back to Les.

"Okay good! I'd like to get some information from you, Les. Can you tell me a little about your childhood? Did you have a good childhood?"

"Well, yes, my - my - childhood was very normal. I went to school. I came home, did my homework -- yeah, very normal." She shrugged.

"Do you remember anything out of the ordinary about your childhood?"

"No, not really. It was a normal childhood. I suppose. Except for the time gaps but your father knew about those. They should be there in his notes."

"Can you be a little more specific about the time gaps?"

"Sure. I'd be at school on Tuesday and then, all of a sudden, it's Friday. I don't know what happened to the other days. It's like I time traveled to the future or something."

"Would you be wearing the same clothes?"

"No."

"Okay," Alex Whitfield picked up his pen and began to write. He looked up from his writing, "Would you consider time travel or time gaps normal?"

"No."

"I'm asking because you just said that your childhood was normal."

"I meant, normal to me."

"Did anyone say anything to you about acting different during that time?"

"You mean, the other kids?"

"Yes, or the teachers --- anyone?"

"The kids teased me about my red lipstick. I was in elementary school. I didn't wear lipstick. To this day, I can't wear red lipstick but Lee does. That's how I'd know Lee had surfaced, I'd find tubes of lipstick in my pockets or my backpack. The teachers never said anything or acted differently that I can remember. Ronnie was the one I depended on to tell me what happened."

"Where was your mother during this time? Tell me about her?"

"I don't know anything about my mother. She died in a car accident when I was a baby. My father never talked much about her."

"Then it was your father who raised you, right?"

Les nodded.

"How did you feel about him?"

"What do you mean?"

"Was he a good father? Bad father? I mean, what did you feel about him?"

"He was a very loving man," Les said calmly. "He worked hard and taught me the value of a dollar. He was - a - good man. I was told that he died of cancer about six years ago."

"Oh, I'm sorry to hear that."

"Thank you." Les nodded.

"Interesting," Dr. Whitfield addressed Kevin, "When a person suffers from a DID, it's because of some type of severe trauma as a child. Some abuse. Like I said earlier, it always alludes to something happening that was so terrible the child disassociates and develops a personality who can handle the abuse."

"But I was never abused!" Les insisted.

"Hmmm, that's why I find this so interesting. According to my father's records, he spoke to your alter personality -- *Lee*." His voice was steady and soothing.

Les nodded her head slowly, "Yes, I'm familiar with her. I remember he had sessions with us both. I know that she's my other personality, and I know what she told your father. She's lying! And I don't understand why she's here. I mean, if the *only* reason a person develops another personality is because of abuse - I - don't understand."

Alex held up his hands, "Les, I know you've heard this before, but do you mind if I share it with you again? What Lee told my father?"

"Sure." She shrugged.

"You okay with your husband being here?"

She grabbed Kevin's arm. "Yes, I need him here."

"Okay. Kevin, how are you holding up?"

"I'm good, Doc."

Alex opened the folder and drew out a few pages of notes. "This is what Lee told my father."

"My father asked her, "Who is Les Cramer?"

Lee answered, 'Someone who doesn't deserve to live.'

"He asked her, why do you think Les deserves to die?"

Lee answered, 'Because *everything* is her fault.'

"When he asked her, "What specifically is her fault?""

"She said, 'Daddy loved me, and she didn't let him get to me. I could have helped him! Instead, all because of her, he had to go away. All she had to do was stop pushing and everything would have been okay. She thinks she's stronger than me, but I have ways of getting out. I'll show her. I have my ways.'

Alex Whitfield looked over the top of his notes to see Les's reaction. She was looking intently out into thin air. He went to the next page of notes.

"Here again, Lee was asked, 'Your father raised you, right?'

Lee says, 'Right, for a while.'

Then she was asked, "What kind of relationship did you have with your father?

And Lee answers, 'Very sexual.'

My father asked, "Sexual?" and Lee said, 'Yes, very!'"

Les was remembering the day Dr. Paul Whitfield shared these very same notes with her. She didn't believe it then, and she wouldn't believe it now. "She's lying! My father was the kindest, most gentle - kind - loving man I know." She turned to Kevin, "He was!"

Kevin was puzzled. He was trying to put the mixed-up pieces together. He listened as Dr. Whitfield read the notes and he also listened to Les's response as she denied, denied, denied. *Had her father done something so heinous that --?* Kevin didn't want to think about it. He sat plastered in his chair with his arm around Les and waited for Alex to finish then asked, "Okay, Doc, what do we do? Where do we go from here?"

Les turned to face Kevin in disbelief. "Kevin, you don't believe this, do you?"

"Les, baby, listen to me" we know *something* had to have happened to cause a -- a personality disorder. I don't care what it was!" Kevin held her face between his hands. He shook his head. "I don't care what happened." He could feel tears stinging his eyes. "I don't want you to think that I'm going to love you any less, Sweetheart. Think, Babe, how would he have these answers from Lee if he didn't *speak* to her? Let's just get to the bottom of it and get you the help you need. It sounds like Alex here knows something about your problem. Let's work with him. I promise you, Baby,

I promise you. I'm gonna be right here -- I'm not going anywhere. We'll do this together."

Les turned back to Alex, "My father was a good man. He raised me the best he knew how. I don't know why *she* would say something like that about him."

"Les, your father didn't raise you. Do you remember who actually raised you?" Alex asked.

"Sure I do," Les answered, "My Aunt Marie. She came when my father had to go away - he was - *called* away, but he checked on me to make sure I was alright all the time!"

"Where is your Aunt Marie now?" Kevin asked.

"I don't know. She left before I went to college."

Kevin shrugged to Alex, "I've never heard of an *Aunt Marie.*"

Alex held up his hands to let Kevin know to hold on.

"Les, my father's notes show that he used hypnosis on you to speak to Lee. He was confident enough about his diagnosis that he felt you were ready to move toward a fusion of the personalities when something happened to cause you to go 'to sleep.' Lee took over and was in control for ten years. She came in for treatment for a while and then, one day she stopped. The last entry here is dated Thursday, April 13, 2006."

Kevin sat back and wiped his hands across his face. "Lee and I were married on April 15, 2006. Her last day of treatment was right before we got married."

Alex nodded "Ohh that explains it." He went back to his notes.

"Now, here's where things get confusing. Les, you say your father was 'called' away? So he wasn't in your home while Aunt Marie was there. He didn't come back for your high-school graduation or any of your birthdays -- Christmas? He just went away?"

Les was quiet and nodded slowly, "Yes," she whispered. My father was— *called* away."

"And your Aunt Marie, she moved away when you started college? You haven't heard from her since. She hasn't dropped in to see how you were doing, never called, sent a card or --anything?

"I'm not sure," Les stated. "I believe it was when I went to college."

"So," Alex asked, "you woke up one day, and she was gone? No explanations - no good-byes— anything— just - gone?"

"Yes, she was -- just gone."

"Interesting." He nodded and wrote on his notepad.

When you were a child, Les, do you remember having any nightmares, dreams, or imaginary friends?"

"Imaginary friends -- nightmares? . . ." She shook her head, "N-N-N-No. "Wait, yes, I remember a dream about a little girl who used to come to play with me. She would tell me that she wasn't supposed to be out. I didn't know what she meant. She said it was supposed to be our secret, and then her face would become distorted and ugly, and she'd go away or I'd wake up."

"Uh-huh, I see. Was it -- Lee by any chance?"

Les thought for a while, "I'm not sure. I think she did say her name was Lee."

Alex could see that the question was making Les uncomfortable.

"It's okay, don't worry about it. We're just gathering information here." He said and smiled soothingly.

Suddenly Les's head shot up, "Wait! I remember another dream. I dreamed that I suddenly woke up with someone towering over me. I was frightened, and the person put his hand over my mouth and tried to touch me. I started fighting and screaming. I fought with all my might, but I was no match for him; he was huge. He bent down and picked me up and . . . I don't know what happened after that, but I remember being so frightened at bedtime. I was afraid of going to sleep and having the dream again."

"And did you?"

"Almost every night. I hated bedtime."

Alex Whitfield nodded and jotted more notes.

"Les, Do you remember being in the hospital when you were a little girl?"

"Yes, I remember. The nurses were very nice." Les replied.

"Why were you in the hospital, Les?" Alex asked.

Kevin sat quietly - listening.

Les didn't answer. She was trying to remember.

"I've never heard of you being in the hospital as a child." Kevin whispered.

"I think I fell." She answered. "I only remember waking up in the hospital and the nurses bringing me ice-cream. They were nice, very, very nice." She looked at Alex as confusion coursed her features.

Alex sat forward, "Les, I need you to think about something. Don't you think it's strange that your father was called away the same time you fell so hard that you required hospitalization? And suddenly your Aunt Marie came to take care of you?"

Kevin tensed and sat straight up in his chair.

"Like I said earlier," Alex continued, "I believe my father was right on the verge of a breakthrough when you went to 'sleep'. I'm almost positive I know what the trigger is."

Kevin and Les exchanged hopeful glances.

"Although my dad continued talking to Lee, she stopped coming to see him despite my father's urges. Then he got sick and lost touch altogether. One of his greatest regrets was that he didn't get a chance to finish his work with you. However, he made me promise to continue his work, and that's what I'm prepared to do."

"What do you need from us, Doc?" Kevin asked.

"Well, I'd like to try hypnosis." Alex announced.

"Hypnosis?" Les repeated, "You want to hypnotize me? You said the last time I was hypnotized, Lee surfaced for *ten years*!"

"Yes, but the difference is, I know what the problem is. Actually, my father uncovered it without realizing what he'd done. He was looking in the wrong place. Listen, Les, you have an advantage that many in your condition don't have. You're, at least, familiar with your other personality. Usually, the host personality has no idea about alters but alters know about each other. You know her name, and you know some things she's done. All we're going to do is help you to understand why she was developed so you can come together. You'll learn the truth about your childhood and come to terms with it and be able to live a normal life. There's more but, first I need to speak with my team and run it by them before I make any decisions."

"*You know my trigger?* Les asked.

"You've split into more than one personality so you can attribute some traumatic childhood events to someone else. You even gave the other personality a name. The personality has become real and takes over whenever there's a risk of you having to acknowledge these events. What I need to do is talk to Lee and find out if I'm on the right track. She can give me the answers I need."

"But --" She looked frantically from Kevin to Alex. "Isn't that risk here? And you want to bring her out? On purpose? Are you kidding me? Kevin, we need to go." Les stood and turned toward the door.

Kevin came to his feet, grabbed her arms, and held her fast. "No, let's listen to him, please." He tilted her face to look at him. "He said he knows your trigger. Isn't that what you wanted to find out? Let's hear him out." He pleaded.

"Do you want her to come back, Kevin? Is that what you want?" Les shouted, "What if I'm not strong enough? What if she takes over for another ten years? I don't want to go to sleep and wake up with *another* ten years behind me?" Les began crying and couldn't stop.

"Les, that's not going to happen," Alex interjected, "You have to trust me. As long as you're here in my office, you're safe, I promise! You were right on the edge ten years ago, and something happened to trigger a memory and your personality, *Lee*, surfaced. Something made you feel unsafe. Every time your personality came out, you were feeling threatened. I think I know what it is, but it's Lee who can give me the answers I need to help you. You have to let me do this. I know I can help you. Trust me."

Les considered him, her brow furled, and she allowed Kevin to guide her back to her chair. "It's not you who I don't trust. It's Lee. She can't take over again. I can't let her do that."

"She won't! The session is safe." Alex assured her. "But we have to work expeditiously. We can't afford to let her surface on her own. If that happens, I can't guarantee anything."

"Can Kevin be here with me?" she asked.

Alex looked at Kevin. You'll have to be totally out of the way and quiet."

Kevin nodded. "When do you want to start these sessions?"

"As soon as possible. I'll consult my team tonight and see if they agree with my assessment and treatment recommendations, I know they will. We can meet back here as early as tomorrow if everything goes according to plan. There's a special room here where I conduct those type of sessions. Hypnosis is a safe way for me to get the information I need to help you deal with Lee. We need to exert caution by moving forward with this as soon as we can. If Lee resurfaces on her own, I don't think I'd be able to convince her to come in and see me, and we'll be right back where we started. You know what I mean? We don't want to get stuck again. Right?"

Les considered him. "Right. Do you think Lee, can resurface?"

Alex gave her a thoughtful look, then said, "Yes, but you're not going to let her." Alex's confidence encouraged her a little more.

Kevin went back around to his chair and sat down. "Listen Doc," He took Les's hand. "Les and I are getting married at the end of the month. Do you think it's wise? I mean with her going through this and the stress of getting ready for a wedding. In your opinion, is it going to be too much?"

Alex frowned, "I thought you were already married."

"Well, it's kind of complicated. I was married to Lee, but only because I fell in love with Les, and I thought Lee was her so --"

Alex held up his hands and nodded, "I understand. The wedding is to bring the two of *you* together, you with Les and not Lee." He chuckled.

"Exactly."

He looked at Les, "Look, as long as you're not stressed, then it's not too stressful."

"You taking the new meds?"

Les nodded.

"Then I think we'll be okay. Tomorrow, after we see how the session goes, I may want to attempt a fusion.

"This fusion?" Kevin asked, "What exactly does it entail?"

"That's when we integrate the personalities into one entity. That's what my father was moving toward when Les went to sleep. It takes at least five years of consulting before a doctor is at the point that he or she believes the patient is ready for the fusion. In this case, my father did most of the work. I believe I have -- hold on --" Alex opened the folder again, skimmed down the side tabs, and stopped, "Ahh, here it is." He said removing a few more papers from the stack. "The last couple of sessions you had with my dad, he wrote that you had become strong enough to push Lee back. Which tells me something else must've happened that made you so weak, Lee was able to overpower you and stay out for ten years. Something happened to dreg up the truth about your life, and you weren't ready to know the truth. So, you have to make it up in your mind that you're not going to allow *anything* to stand in the way of the truth. That's another reason I want to start these sessions as soon as possible. I don't want to take the chance of you being that vulnerable again."

"Can you give me an approximate time as to when we'll be finished, two weeks, a month, a year?" Les asked.

"I'll probably be able to tell you better after I speak to Lee. It could be finished as early as tomorrow, or it could be a year from now." Alex replied.

Les looked at Kevin, "What do you think?"

"You already know what I think. I think you should do it. And the sooner, the better."

Les looked at Alex, "What time tomorrow?" She asked.

"First thing, 9:00." Alex looked from Kevin to Les.

"I can have her here by 9:00." Kevin assured him. And the two stood to leave.

"There is one other subject I need to talk to you about, Les." Alex said. Les turned to him. "Among the papers in the file, I found something else that was very interesting. I guess my father was holding on to it, hoping to give it to you when you surfaced, but he passed away before you came back." Alex removed a long envelope from the folder. "I have a letter here with your name on it. It's from your father. He asked my father to make sure you got it. It's yours if you want it."

Les felt as though the whole earth had stopped and started again in slow motion. "A letter from my father?" she repeated in a whisper. She walked to Alex and slowly took the letter from his hand. She studied the writing on the envelope, and then used her finger to trace the words: *To Leslee Cramer.* She closed her eyes and held the letter to her heart. *From my father*, she thought. Les took a few steps trying to get back to Kevin. She couldn't breathe -- the room was spinning. She reached for him. "Kev --" Kevin ran to her side, and she collapsed in his arms.

Alex rushed around the desk, opened a bottle and positioned it under Les's nose. She gasped for air, and her eyes fluttered. Kevin and Alex were above her.

"Sweetheart?" Kevin called to her, "That's right, Baby. Open your eyes." Her eyes fluttered again and this time they opened.

"Les, are you alright?" Alex asked.

"What-- what --?" she asked. Her hand went to her head.

"You fainted, Les." Alex answered.

Les sat up quickly and looked around the room. "Where's Dr. Whitfield?" She asked in a childlike voice.

"I'm here, Les." Alex assured her. He reached out to help her to her feet.

"Ouch!" She jerked away from his touch. "You're not Dr. Whitfield!" She scrambled to a corner of the room and began to cry. "Don't touch me! You're not *allowed* to touch me."

"Okay, we won't touch you." Alex assured her.

Les whispered, "Shhh, you have to be quiet. She can't know I'm here. Where's Ronnie? Can somebody find Ronnie? She can help me. She always helps me. Tell her we need to call Aunt Marie." She closed her eyes and slumped to the ground.

Kevin and Alex moved in and caught her before her head could hit the floor.

Kevin looked at Alex. "What the hell?"

Les opened her eyes and took a deep breath. "What happened?"

"You fainted. I handed you a letter from your father, and you fainted."

Kevin stood speechless. He helped Les stand and stable herself.

Les looked around frantically for her letter.

"I have it, baby." Kevin said patting the breast pocket of his jacket. He turned slightly with a quizzical look at Alex.

Alex met Kevin's gaze and nodded, confirming Kevin's unasked question. They had just witnessed the surfacing of yet another alter personality.

23

During the ride home, the two barely spoke. Kevin knew he had to be careful not to elude to what he had witnessed in Alex's office. He thought, if Alex hadn't addressed it, he must've had a good reason so he'd leave it alone too. However, there were other concerns he had, and he was trying to decide on the best way to address them.

Les, used the time to mull over the statements from Dr. Whitfield's notes. *Lee said her relationship with Daddy was very sexual? As in actually having sex with him? What kind of father would EVER think of having sex with his own child? Why did she lie? Why was Lee trying to make people think father was a monster when he was so kind and loving?*

She turned to Kevin, "Why do you think Lee was trying to paint such a horrible picture of my father? My God, she made him sound like a monster."

"I'm not sure, maybe another way of getting back at you. Who knows? What I want to know is where your father took off to for so many years? Where was he during the years that your Aunt Marie raised you?"

"He was away. *Called* away." She answered.

"What does that mean -- 'called' away?" Kevin's frustration peppered his words.

"That's what Aunt Marie always said. Whenever I asked where my dad was she would say, he's been called away. So I've said it ever since."

"What do you think actually happened to him?" Kevin asked.

"I don't know."

"And how did you end up in the hospital?"

"I don't know! I was told that I fell."

"Fell how? You fell so hard that you had to be hospitalized? Where in the world did you fall from?"

"I don't know! I can't remember that far back." Les replied.

"Kevin pulled up his sleeve. "Do you see this mark on my arm?" He revealed an old scar under his elbow that ended about four inches above his wrist.

"I was running with a pair of scissors when I was four years old." He emphasized by holding up four fingers. "I didn't understand the danger of running with scissors in my hand, and I thought my mother was playing when she tried to get the scissors from me. I remember laughing and running from her. The more my mom chased me to get those scissors, the more I ran. When I fell, the scissors sliced my arm. Blood was everywhere. My mom cried worse than me, but she wrapped my arm in a towel and got me to the hospital. I ended up with 23 stitches in my arm at four years old."

He unbuttoned the top buttons of his shirt and pulled his collar down to show his shoulder, "You see this mark? I was playing Zorro with one of my friends; I had the cape and everything. I stood up on a rock and jumped into the air, and when I came down, my feet slid out from up under me, and I fell back on a piece of glass. Hurt like hell. Ten more stitches." He pointed to another scar on his other arm, "This one here. I was at the park trying to be cool. I was on the merry-go-round, and I wanted to show everybody, especially the girls, that I could stay on without actually holding on. I went flying off and skinned my arm all the way to my elbow. I can tell you about cuts and bruises that I've had since I was four years old. I remember them, especially the ones that hurt like hell. I don't understand how *you* can *fall* so hard you needed to be hospitalized and not remember the incident."

"What are you trying to say, Kevin?"

"Sweetheart, I'm bothered by your memory or lack of memory. What could be blocking it? There's no way you could have 'just fallen'. Lee sure never told me about a fall. There has to be more to it, and I think it has something do with your father's mysterious disappearance. Like Alex asked, don't you think it's strange that he was *called away* while you were in the hospital?"

Les nodded her head -- "Yes, I admit it's strange, but what could it be? That's what frightens me. I don't know what it could be!"

The anguish in her voice warned Kevin to back off. "Okay, let's give it a break for right now and get something to eat. We're close to Tom's restaurant. You want to stop in for a bite? I'm famished."

Les nodded.

They pulled into the parking lot and after finding a parking space, Kevin hopped out and went around to open the door for Les. When he helped her out, he lifted her chin and kissed her. "I'm not upset with you, babe, I'm upset about the situation. You understand?" She nodded, and they walked into the restaurant together and were seated right away.

Kevin ordered a glass of Cabernet Sauvignon for himself and ginger ale for Les.

"Is your boss in?" Kevin asked the waiter.

"Yes, he is, Mr. Jenison, I'll let him know you're here."

"Tell him it's the guy who beats him at golf every chance he gets." He winked teasingly at Les.

Les smiled, and the young waiter laughed and disappeared around the corner to Tom's office.

It didn't take long before they heard Tom's laughter. He rounded the corner and greeted Kevin with a handshake and hug. "The guy who beats me at golf, huh? In your dreams. It's good to see you two" He leaned down and gave Les a hug.

Over Tom's shoulder, Les saw Veronica hopping toward them on her crutches.

The two women hugged. Kevin reached over and hugged her too. "What are you doing here?"

"I'm helping Tom with some bookkeeping, and then we were going to have a night cap. Mind if we join you? You just now finishing up at Alex's?"

Tom sat down. "That's right. Your appointment was today! How'd it go?"

"Daunting." Les closed her eyes and shook her head. "Can we *not* go into it right now?"

She nodded 'thank you' at the waiter when he set a glass of ginger ale in front of her. She picked up her glass, closed her eyes, and took a sip. When she finally opened her eyes, she met Veronica's blatant stare. *"What?"*

"I want to know what happened with Alex! I know you don't think I'm gonna sit here and let it blow over. You're gonna have to tell me somethin'." She plopped her chin in her hand and waited.

"This whole thing sounds like the making of an HBO movie! I can't even imagine what the two of you've been going through." Tom added.

Kevin shook his head, "Veronica, you don't even want to know. Hey, you and Les have been friends since you were kids. Did you know her when she was in the hospital after a bad fall?"

"No, but I heard about it. We didn't meet until we started going to the same school." She turned to Les. "Will you tell me what happened with Alex?"

"Wait a minute," Kevin exclaimed, "so you know Aunt Marie?"

"Well, sure I do."

"I've never heard of her until today."

"Well," Veronica shrugged, "I don't *know* her, know her, but Les would talk about her and ask me to call her sometimes."

Les considered Veronica. "I asked you to call her?"

"Sure. Lots of times. You don't remember?"

Before Veronica could answer her, Kevin rushed on, "She talked about her to you, but you never actually met her?"

"Well, no I was never really allowed over Les's house. My mom wouldn't let me go because there were rumors -- you know."

Les looked at Kevin and heaved a sigh. "You're not gonna let this drop. Are you?"

"I'm just trying to solve the mystery. Where's Dad? Where's Aunt Marie?

Veronica took a sip of her drink and picked up the menu. "It's the lawyer in him. So, Les, give up the goods. What happened with Alex today?"

Les took a deep breath and began telling Veronica and Tom about the doctor visit.

After a while, Kevin excused himself and walked toward Tom's office. He unsheathed his cell phone from its case and made a call.

When he returned to the table, Veronica and Les were still in conversation about the appointment.

"Tomorrow he wants to hypnotize me and talk to Lee.

Veronica straightened. "On purpose?"

"How do you feel about that, Kev?" Tom asked.

"If the bitch has to resurface, I feel better that it'll be under controlled circumstances."

Tom's gaze shifted to Les. "How do you feel about it?"

She studied the question, then said, "Alex said there's nothing to worry about as long as we're in his office. I'll just be glad to have all this over with."

Their waiter returned to take their dinner order. Les picked her glass up and took another long sip and closed her eyes to enjoy it. "Oh, and Ronnie, guess what? Alex gave me a letter." She motioned to Kevin and he pulled it out of his inside breast pocket and gave it to her.

"It's a letter from my Dad." Les handed the envelope to Veronica.

"Your Dad?" Veronica fingered it gingerly. "And you haven't opened it?"

"Not yet."

"Why not? You have to be curious. What could he have to say after leaving you all these years?"

"I'm a lot curious," Les admitted, "but I'm afraid too."

"Afraid of what, Les?"

"I don't know. Alex says, I'm afraid of the truth. Maybe he's right."

Veronica looked around the table. "I have an idea!" "Do you remember the year you fell Les?"

"Yes, I do. Why?"

Veronica reached into her purse and pulled out her electronic tablet. "Let's see if we can find *truth*."

"What's that?" Les asked.

"Today's technology. We can find out just about anything we need to know."

"What do you mean?"

"The Internet is a powerful highway to *truth*, Get ready to be impressed."

She turned it on and waited for it to boot up.

"What are you going to do with it?" Les asked.

"Watch and learn," Veronica answered.

Once the tablet was booted up, Veronica typed into the search bar, the year Les fell and her father's name. Immediately two newspaper articles were suggested.

Veronica clicked on one of them. The article provided a clear view of a small picture. She enlarged it. Two police officers were escorting a man away from a house in handcuffs.

Les sucked in a breath. "That's my father!" She exclaimed.

She could also see the paramedics lifting a stretcher into an ambulance.

Les leaned over for a better look "I think -- that's -- I believe that's me." She said pointing to the stretcher.

"What the hell?!" Kevin said as he hopped up from his seat, rushed around the table, and looked over their shoulders. The caption read: *"Father Throws Daughter through Window in Drunken Rage."* He glared at the man in the picture wishing he could peel him off the page and pound his face into the floor.

"He threw me through a window? I -- Why?" Les's eyes filled with tears. "I don't understand. What could I have done that was so bad my father would throw me through a window? I was only five years old! I only remember him being the kindest, dearest man." Les picked up the envelope and turned it over in her hands.

***

Veronica could tell that Kevin was preoccupied through dinner. She wondered if it had anything to do with the phone call he made earlier. After dinner, while Les was gathering her things, Veronica made her way to Kevin's side.

"So, what's up, Kev? You know something. What is it? Who did you call earlier?"

"Alex Whitfield. Shhh, keep your voice down."

"Why, what's happening?" Veronica whispered.

"Veronica, when did Aunt Marie come to live with Les?"

"I don't know, after her father was taken away. Why?"

"Because I don't think there is an Aunt Marie, and neither does Alex."

"What do you mean? Of course, there's an Aunt Marie."

"Did you ever *speak* to her?"

"No, but--"

"I didn't think so. After Les's father went to prison, she was sent to a children's home. It was close to a public school where you met her. Whenever she felt embarrassed or frightened, she'd call for Aunt Marie or have you call her. Right? Then Aunt Marie would come and save the day by taking care of her and making her feel safe, but you never met Aunt Marie. And although you called her a few times, you never actually spoke to her. If there was really an Aunt Marie, think about it, why was Les sent to the children's home instead of Aunt Marie's home? Wouldn't she have been Les's next of kin? Alex and I believe Aunt Marie is another alter that Les created. How is it that Les is your best friend, and you didn't know that she was raised in an orphanage?"

Veronica lowered her gaze.

"You knew, didn't you?"

"Of course, I knew. That was one of our secrets. She asked me not to tell, so I never did. She'd be embarrassed if she knew, you knew about it. How'd you find out? That was a long time ago. It can't have anything to do with what's going on now."

"What are you talking about? It could have everything to do with it. You don't know. Why would you keep quiet about something that important?"

"Okay, okay. Maybe I should have said something, but I thought, if I kept her secrets, she'd be fine."

"How long did it take you to figure out she wasn't?"

Veronica's eyes dimmed. Finally, she said. "The first time I met Lee, but I made a promise."

"You can't help her by keeping her secrets any longer. If you know something – anything, please tell me."

Veronica pulled her gaze away from Kevin's as Les caught up to them. She knew Kevin was right. There were things he needed to know.

"Well, goodnight, Ronnie." Les said reaching out to give her a hug. While the two women embraced, Veronica looked up at Kevin and gave a light nod.

***

Kevin waited for Les to drift off to sleep before lifting his cell to call Veronica.

"Can you talk?" He asked.

"Yeah, I can talk."

"Are you still with Tom?"

"No, he brought me home. He'll be back in the morning to take me to the doctor, and then we're going to look at cars." She laughed nervously, "I can't wait to have my own transportation again. Not that I don't enjoy his company, I just want to come and go as I please, ya know?" She realized she was rambling. "Sorry, Kev, what do you need to know?"

"Anything." He said quietly, "anything you can tell me. You can start with when she went to the orphanage."

"Okay Kev, you're right. Les lived in a Children's Home for a while after her dad went away, but was sent to a group home soon after, which made it possible for her to go to public school. The kids at the school were mean. She was tormented by them. They teased her every chance they got, called her names, home kid, scrub, street rat, all along pushing her around until she cried. The day they made a circle around her and taunted her with the same name-calling, and insults was the day I'd had enough. I went over and broke into that circle. I pulled her away and dared any of 'em to come near her again. From that time on, everywhere I went, I made sure she was with me. There was only one kid who challenged me, and he's probably still nursing his fat lip and black eye today." Veronica laughed, "Les began to trust me, and that's how we became best friends. There were times the teachers would find her cowering in a corner, under the desk, or in a closet. When they tried to coax her out, she'd scream like someone was trying to kill her. Most times I could go to her, wherever she was, and calm her down. It got to the place that the teachers would come get me whenever Les had one of her episodes. That's what *they* called it -- an episode.

One-day, Les got up enough nerve to ask one of the attendants in charge if she could come play at my house. They actually said yes, so she came over, and we had a ball. It didn't take long before they let her spend the night sometimes on the weekend. My mother didn't mind, although she hardly ever called her by her name. To my mom, Les was always 'the little girl'. But they, at the group home, could see an improvement in Les. Her grades and everything were much better, and they said it was because of me. I don't know about that, but what I do know is, Les became the sister I never had, and we were inseparable. The fact that she lived at a group home didn't matter to me. She was my friend."

"Tell me about Aunt Marie?"

"Kevin, if you're really trying to tell me that there's no such person, I'm gonna flip out. I know for a fact I've called her more than a dozen times."

"But did you talk to her?"

"No, but I left messages."

"Did she call you back?"

"*No,* but I would call to tell her that Les needed her to come, or Les needed her to call. I assumed she got the messages because, when I'd see Les again she'd be fine. I had no reason to doubt it."

"I don't know, Ronnie. All of a sudden, *poof,* there's an Aunt Marie, out of nowhere. But until I meet her for myself, I'm gonna think she's a figment of Les's imagination."

"I'm frightened for her."

"Me too."

Kevin's land line phone rang, and he rushed to answer it.

"Hold on, Ronnie."

"Hello." He said into the receiver. "Yes, hi Doc. No, she's asleep. Do you want me to wake her? Okay --" Kevin listened quietly as the doctor continued. Finally, he said, "You mean you knew?" He listened again. "And that's why you gave her the letter? I see, now. Okay, Doc, I'll give her the message."

Kevin hung up and went back to his cell phone.

"That was Alex. He said, he wants to push the fusion back for another week or so until he speaks to Les again. He still wants to see her tomorrow though. I tell ya, Ronnie, I'm really impressed by that guy. I don't think anything gets by him. He's the one who told me about the Children's Home. He does his homework."

Veronica said, "*Paul* Whitfield was good, but I think we're all beginning to see that *Alex* Whitfield is amazing."

"You're right about that, Ronnie."

"So where do we go from here?"

"One thing you said earlier keeps coming back to mind."

"What's that?"

"You said Les was so afraid when she lived at the group home."

"She was! All the time."

"Think about this, if she wanted Aunt Marie called every time she was afraid, and you say, she was afraid *all the time* while she lived there." He got quiet, to collect his thoughts.

"What, Kev?"

"Well, if Aunt Marie is another alter, I would think the attendants at the group home encountered her quite often. What do you think?"

"Woe, I think you're on to something."

"I mean, think about it, she was only a little girl, not much older than Kelly. I can imagine the fear."

Veronica tried to shake off her misgivings, "I feel like I'm betraying her."

"You're helping her get well."

"I only kept the secrets because I didn't want anyone else to hurt her."

"The only one who's gonna hurt her is Lee. And we need all the help we can get to keep that woman buried."

"I trust you with her more than I've ever trusted anyone except Dr. Whitfield. That's why I'm telling you everything now. I'm just saying, I've kept the secrets for so long that it feels awkward opening up and talking to someone about it. Although I feel like I'm betraying her, I know I'm really not. You know what I mean? It's weird, that's all."

"Sure. That's understandable. You're her best friend, and we both love her. But it's okay to talk now. No more secrets. Okay? If you remember anything else, please let me know right away, so I can tell Alex. In the meantime, I think I'm gonna take a ride over to that group home tomorrow and see what I can find out."

"That's a great idea. I'd like to go with you."

"Sure, I'll pick you up after the session with Alex."

"Okay, sounds good, Kev. Hey, don't worry, it's all gonna work out. Okay?"

"Yeah, I know, Ronnie. I love her so much, and I don't want to think about being without her. If Lee resurfaces before Dr. Whitfield can distinguish between her trans-like state and her normal state, we're in trouble. And there's no telling what might happen and that scares me shitless."

"Me too."

"Well, good then. Maybe now you understand how important this is. Please, Ronnie, know that I'm on your side. Okay? Right now, I need to go upstairs and check on her. I'll talk to you later. See you tomorrow."

"I said I was sorry."

He breathed. "I know."

Okay, Bye, Kev."

Kevin hung up and strapped his cell phone back into the case on his belt, then turned to go up the stairs and almost collided with Les.

"Woe, how long have you been standing there?"

"Long enough. What's going on, Kevin?"

"Going on?"

"Kevin, I heard you on the phone. Talk to me."

"Well, Dr. Alex called and said he met with his team, and they all thought he might be moving too fast. So he's not going to do the fusion tomorrow. He wants to back it out for about a week, but he still wants you to keep the appointment at 9:00 though."

"Oh, okay. A week, huh? What do you think about that?"

"I think, as long as we're seeing Dr. Alex it's okay. He knows what he's doing, babe, and he knows what we're up against. I trust him."

"Is that why you were telling Ronnie that you were scared shitless?"

Kevin's shoulders dropped. He was hoping she hadn't heard that part of their conversation.

"Yes, Les" He held up his hands, "Okay, I'm scared -- I'm nervous, but I can handle it. I don't want you to worry about me."

"Okay, I won't worry about you. I don't want you to worry about me either. Can you do that?"

Kevin's shoulders dropped again. "All I'm trying to say is --"

"I know what you're trying to say, Kevin, but it's not going to work. I'm going to worry about you because I love you, so you're wasting your breath. Now, where are we going tomorrow after the session with Alex?"

"What do you mean?"

"I heard you telling Ronnie you'd pick her up after the session. Where are we going?"

Kevin's hand went nervously to the back of his neck, a gesture Les was all too familiar with, since he only rubbed his neck when he was nervous.

"Well, there are things I have to do -- uh, before the wedding and Ronnie's going to help me."

"Oh, that should be fun."

"No, babe, you can't go. The things I have to do are surprises -- for you."

"Surprises?"

"Yes, surprises." Kevin put his arms around Les and pulled her into his chest. "I can't wait to see you walk down the aisle toward me."

Les relaxed in his embrace, she felt safe there. "I know," she whispered, "I can't wait either."

24

At 9:00 in the morning, Les and Kevin were sitting in Alex Whitfield's waiting room. Kevin held Les's hands, they were cold. He knew she was nervous, but he also knew that there was no way he could imagine the extent of her nervousness.

Heather opened the door, "Les Cramer."

Les and Kevin stood up and followed Heather to Alex's office. Dr. Alex Whitfield stood and walked around his desk to shake Kevin's hand and give Les a hug.

"Please, have a seat," He said directing them to the same chairs in front of his desk as before. He went back around his desk and sat down. "Well, I'm sure Kevin told you that we talked."

Les nodded, "Yes."

"It doesn't mean that we're not going to move forward. It only means we're not going to move forward so fast."

"That's what I don't understand," Les remarked. "I thought you said that your father had done most of the work, and I was ready to integrate with Lee? I want to get this over with."

"I'm sure you do, Les, but I came to realize that it's not as simple as we thought. There are other factors that we need to consider here. I believed you were ready according to my father's notes, but I had to step back from looking at my father's diagnosis and evaluate you for myself. As you know, I took my evaluation to my team last night and, like I thought, they agreed with me. See, I don't want to end up putting a band-aid on a wound without cleaning it first. Do you understand what I mean?"

Les nodded, and then chuckled nervously, "So, you think I have a wound that needs to be cleansed?"

"So to speak," Alex answered. "Before we get started, let me ask you. Is there anything you remember or anything that you think you remember about your childhood that you may have forgotten to tell me?"

Kevin knew what Alex was referring to, and he waited to hear Les's answers."

"No, there's nothing else," Les answered.

"Well, let's talk about Aunt Marie. Tell me again how long she lived with you?"

"I don't remember. She was there until I went to college. I believe."

"When did she arrive at your house, Les?"

"Right after Dad was called away."

Kevin sat up in his chair. "Doc, you might as well know that we searched the Internet and found the article about Les's father last night. We saw the picture of him being taken away by the police. He was handcuffed. In the background, we could see paramedics lifting Les into the ambulance. She saw all that last night."

Alex nodded. "What did you think about that, Les?"

"I didn't know what to think. I don't understand why my father would throw me through a window."

"Well, we certainly know this, Les. If your father was a kind, gentle, and loving person, his actions were certainly contradictory to what you believed. Am I right?"

Les nodded, "I suppose you're right?"

Alex was visibly pleased.

"So, maybe your perspective is off about other things concerning your childhood. Have you thought about that?"

"Yes, I've thought about it. Kevin and I had a discussion after we left here yesterday. He showed me some scars that he received when he was a child and remembered how he got them. I thought it was strange that he could remember such early age events, but I couldn't. I want to remember. I just don't."

"That's very important, Les, the fact that you *want* to remember. Yesterday you told me that you remembered being in the hospital, but you didn't know why you were in there. Can you tell me in your own words what happened?"

Les thought for a long while before she spoke, "I remember dreaming about a little girl playing with my dolls. She wanted me to come play too, but I was hiding."

"Do you remember why you were hiding?" Alex asked.

"I was afraid of something. No, I was afraid of *someone.* He was a big man. He came into the room looking for me, but I hid. So he grabbed the little girl instead, and she started screaming. I wanted to help her, but I was so afraid. The man was telling the little girl to shut-up, but she screamed louder. He was hurting her." Les struggled to breathe. "Wait, I...I can't breathe." She gasped for air then turned frantically to Kevin and reached for him, but it was too late; she was gone.

"Ouch! Ouch! I don't want him to touch me like that. He hurts me! Ouch"

Alex's voice was very calm and soothing. He hurried around the desk and knelt in front of Les, being careful not to touch her and close enough for her to feel safe and protected.

"Now, now," Alex said soothingly. "Someone hurt you before but there's no one hurting you here. Can you open your eyes and look at me?"

Les opened her eyes. "I don't know you. Where's Dr. Whitfield." Her voice was childlike and scared.

"Actually, Dr. Whitfield asked me to talk to you. Do you mind?"

She looked around the room. Her eyes were wide and fearful. "I'm not supposed to talk to strangers, only Dr. Whitfield and Ronnie and that's all, only two people." She counted on her fingers, "One, two." And then she held the two fingers in the air.

"I understand that, but do you think I would be here if Dr. Whitfield didn't want me here? He really did say it was okay. Can I ask your name?"

Lifting her eyes to his, she barely spoke above a whisper, "Lisa." She turned to Kevin and her eyes widened, "Okay, but I can't talk to him! Did Dr. Whitfield say I could talk to him?"

Kevin closed his eyes and blinked back tears. He took in a breath and fought hard to keep them from spilling over.

"I'm sure Dr. Whitfield wouldn't mind if you talked to us both."

"Okay, because sometimes I don't want to get in trouble."

"You won't, Lisa. I promise you won't get in any trouble. "How old are you, Lisa?"

"I am four years old." She said proudly.

"Do you know Les?"

"Uh-huh, she's fun to play with. She has pretty dolls and a tea set."

"Oh, so you played with her dolls?"

"Uh-huh, and we drink pretend tea, and we eat pretend cake. She's fun."

"That's nice, Lisa. I'm glad you like her, so do we." Alex continued. "Do you know Lee?"

Lisa's face twisted with sheer panic. She became suddenly terrified looking nervously around the room, and she put her finger to her lips and spoke in a whisper.

"Shh, she'll get mad if she knows I'm here, and she'll make me go back. She always makes me go back. So, I play with Les quietly because I like her toys." She giggled.

"Why does Lee make you go back?" Alex asked.

"Because she hates her, and if I play with her, she gets mad and hurts me. She doesn't want anyone to like her." She sat forward so the doctor could hear her. "She burns me sometimes," Lisa whispered.

"She burns you?"

"Uh-huh sometimes, she burns me, or she cuts me."

"What does she burn you and cut you with, Lisa."

Lisa began to cry, and then she whispered, "I'm not allowed to talk about it. She told me not to."

"Well, I'm here to help you, Lisa. Will you let me help you?"

She looked at Alex. "Uh-huh but I don't think Lee will like you."

"Tell me what Lee would burn you with."

Lisa's eyes widened, and she sat forward again to reveal vital information. "She -- burns me -- with fi ---yure."

Alex responded sympathetically to the childlike response.

"Really? She burns you with fire? That's not a nice thing to do to a person. You also said she cuts you; what does she cut you with?"

"Sometimes she has glass or a sharp thing. Can you make her stop?"

"That's exactly what we plan to do, Lisa, but I'm going to need your help."

"Uh-huh, cause she's mean, and she doesn't like people, and she's a bad person."

"That's right, Lisa. She's not a nice person. Do you remember your father?

"Yes."

"What kind of person was he?"

"He liked to hurt me too." She whispered.

"How did he hurt you?

"He would sometimes hit me. But one time he threw me really hard."

"Did you go to see a doctor?"

"I don't remember that."

"Do you remember being at a home with a lot of children?"

"Uh-huh," her eyes filled with tears that poured out onto her cheeks.

"Why are you crying?"

"Because I'm scared of them. They used bad words to me, and they pushed me and hit me all the time. I wanted to go home, but they wouldn't let me go."

"Why did they say you couldn't go home? Did they tell you?"

"Uh-huh, they said there was no one there to take care of me, but, Aunt Marie was there, and she would take care of me. She would sing to me, and I liked her songs."

Kevin and Alex sat forward.

"So, Aunt Marie came to take care of *you*, not Les?"

"Uh-huh, she came to take care of me." She pointed to herself. "Me!" She pointed to herself again.

"And when she came she'd hold you and sing to you and make everything alright?"

"Uh-huh."

"Does Aunt Marie still come see about you, Lisa?"

"No, Aunt Marie is gone."

"Where did she go? Can we call and talk to her together?"

"I don't know where she is. I think she's gone."

"Okay, Lisa. Tell me about school? Did you go to school?"

"Uh-huh."

"Did you like school?"

"No, I didn't want to be there, they don't play nice there either. Les was scared so I had to come help her, but the kids would say bad words to me there too. They were mean, and I was scared all the time. Aunt Marie had to come get me sometimes. Until Ronnie came."

"Ronnie?" Alex asked.

Her face lit up, and she brushed the tears from her cheeks. "Uh-huh, Ronnie would come and find me, and she would keep me safe all the time."

"Okay, so you liked Ronnie, right?"

"Yep," Ronnie was my best friend. I liked Les too, but I wasn't allowed to be out to play with her. Because Lee would get mad and do bad things." She whispered.

"Would you like to be together with Les, Lisa?"

"Yes!" The little girl squealed excitedly.

"I think we can arrange that, and you'll never have to be scared or be by yourself ever again. Would you like that?"

"Uh-huh, but what about Lee. She might get *really* mad then."

"Yes, but I can make sure Lee never hurts you again."

"You can?"

"Yes, I can, but I want to make sure Aunt Marie knows where you are. Can you call her for me?"

Lisa looked around, "I don't think she's here anymore. I think she's gone."

"Okay, Lisa, it was really nice talking to you. Do you think you'll remember me when you see me again?" Alex smiled.

Lisa nodded her head eagerly and smiled.

"Is it okay if I speak to Les now? I'll see you soon. Okay?"

Lisa closed her eyes.

Alex's gaze lifted from Les to Kevin. "Well, now I know the complete truth."

"I'm glad you do, Doc. I'm sitting here in the dark. Would you mind explaining what the hell just happened?"

"Sure, I'm going to explain it to both of you."

Les moved and shifted in her seat then finally looked up. She saw both men looking at her strangely.

"What? What happened?" she asked uneasily.

"Well, Les, I had a very interesting conversation with your alter."

"Lee! Lee was here? Oh My God!" She looked wildly from Alex to Kevin.

"No, it wasn't Lee."

"But Lee is my alter."

"Lee is *one* of your alters."

"*One*? You mean there's more?"

"Les, do you remember telling me about a dream you had? The little girl who would come and play with you. You thought her name was Lee, but her name is Lisa. She's a little girl about four years old. You created her, and she became your imaginary friend. She loved to play with your dolls, and she loved to have tea with you, but when she came out, she was scared that Lee would find out. Lee would hurt her."

"Hurt her? What do you mean?"

"When you were a little girl, did you ever find cuts or burns that you couldn't explain?"

Les nodded her head in surprise. She never told anyone about that, not even Ronnie.

"Well, we found out today that Lee would burn her or cut her to teach her a lesson. Apparently, that's how Lee kept resurfacing. A circumstance would come up involving your father. It would make you feel vulnerable and alone, threatened or humiliated, whether it was a flashback, a scent or even a letter addressed to you in your father's handwriting. The humiliation would cause Lisa to surface, and although you became strong enough to push Lee back, Lisa was not strong enough to push her back. Lisa was intimidated, afraid, and tormented by Lee, so it was easy for Lee to overpower her and take control. We're talking about a four-year-old girl.

The reason you don't remember being thrown through the window is because it wasn't you. It was Lisa. Lisa went through the window, and Lee rode in the ambulance to the hospital. When you opened your eyes, you were in the hospital, and *your* memory is of all the nice nurses who brought you ice-cream."

Kevin sat forward. "But what about all the time Les lived at the group home. If Lee could overpower Lisa, why didn't she overpower her there?"

Les was shocked but not surprised that Kevin and Alex discovered where she had been raised.

"My guess is that she simply didn't want to. Les would surface during school because she loved school, but when the children made fun of her and called her names, she'd feel intimidated and frightened and she'd disappear, leaving Lisa to protect her. When Lisa would surface, she was a little girl left frightened and alone. So she'd find the nearest table or corner and tried to hide until Aunt Marie or Ronnie would come to her rescue. Lisa was present quite a bit, during Les's stay at the group home. I'm still not sure where Aunt Marie fits into all this, but it'll come out. Maybe during a session when I'm talking to Lee.

Fortunately for you, Les, Lisa thinks highly of you and wants to be with you all the time, which means, she's ready to integrate. Now we can move on to the next part of your treatment. Once you and Lisa integrate, the two of you will become one and Lee will never be able to be in control again."

Alex's words didn't make sense to Les at first, it took a minute for them to sink in and when they finally did, Les's hands went to her mouth and tears streamed down her face.

"You mean I'll be -- normal?" She asked.

"That's right Les." Alex nodded his head to confirm her statement.

Les turned to Kevin then threw her arms around him, and they held on to each other through the remainder of Dr. Whitfield's instructions.

"Now, that doesn't mean this is over." He said, still sitting behind his desk. "Unfortunately during the developmental stage of your life, you were taught to distrust the person who should have made you feel safe. Instead, you had to struggle to survive, and your survival consisted of the only device you knew to use, dissociation. You dissociated by creating alters who managed the trauma you were going through. However, for now on, you'll need to learn how to cope with uncomfortable situations and experiences yourself. What's going to happen if Kevin does something or says something that makes you feel vulnerable? In the past, your vulnerability had an avenue of escape. After we perform the integration, you'll no longer have that avenue. You'll have to be trained to *deal* with your vulnerabilities. You're doing a great job now, but life has many ups and downs, and you're going to need the tools to cope with both. So, by continuing your sessions, we can provide you with those tools. I want you to make the commitment to continue the work. You've got people around you who love you and want the best for you, and you've proven that you can do it."

Les nodded her head wildly, "Of course, I will -- I will! I won't stop until you tell me I'm ready to stop. You have my word!"

Alex stood and walked around the desk toward them with his hand extended to shake Kevin's and hug Les at the same time. "Then let's get busy." He smiled.

"When?" Kevin asked.

"Let me talk to Heather and see where we can sketch out some time as soon as possible. I'll call you this afternoon and let you know."

Alex walked Kevin and Les to the door and watched them leave hand in hand. He smiled. He loved his work.

25

On the way home, Kevin and Les chatted nonstop. They talked about their new discoveries and their expectations for their future. The conversation was light and easy. Unlike their thoughts the last couple of days.

Finally, Les turned and looked at Kevin. She watched his demeanor, how he studied the road and managed to stay on top of the conversation at the same time. He was amazing, and she wanted to tell him, but before she could say the words, Kevin said,

"I love you, you know?"

"She smiled and her heart melted, "I know." She nodded.

"No, I really, *really* love you."

She laughed and nodded again. "I know. I love you too."

He reached out and took her hand, and they rode the rest of the way home in silence.

***

Kevin pulled into Veronica's driveway soon after she had finished her second cup of coffee. He rang the doorbell, then opened the door.

"Ronnie!"

"I'm in the kitchen, Kev."

Kevin walked into the kitchen and leaned against the door frame.

"So, what did Tom say when you told him where we were going?"

"Actually, I didn't tell him. What did Les say when you told her?"

"I didn't tell her either. Let's go!"

Veronica put her cup in the sink and hopped on one leg to pick up her crutches, and then out the door with Kevin. "So, why are we doing this again?"

"Because the truth needs to come out. The whole truth. Do you remember how to get there, if not, I can put it in my GPS?"

"Yep, I remember. And I thought you'd be interested in going to the house where Les used to live. I know where that is too."

"Great – I'd like to go by there."

She studied him. "This has to be hard on you, Kevin."

Kevin laughed as he put the car in reverse to back out of the driveway. "What was hard, was living with Lee for eight years. This is a piece of cake compared to that. At least now I know what I'm up against. You're not going to believe what happened during the session at Alex Whitfield's office."

"What?"

"We came face to face with another of Les's alters."

Veronica turned her face to Kevin then dropped her eyes. "Yeeaah?"

Kevin slammed on the breaks.

"Ronnie, damn it! You knew? How do you expect anyone to help Les if you keep withholding shit? What's wrong with you? You've got to stop this."

"I know, I know. I'm sorry. I wasn't sure if I should say anything because I didn't know if she was still there. I hadn't seen her."

"When were you gonna tell me, Ronnie? My God, we just talked about this. If you keep this up, I'm gonna start thinking you're trying to help Lee for Christ's sake."

"I said I was sorry. Come on, Kev! I'm sorry. I didn't see the point of saying anything. The last time I saw her was years ago.

"Years ago—when?"

"Once when we were in school. We were hanging out with some girls at school during lunch. We thought we were so cool because we were eating lunch with the swim team. One of the girls leaned over and said something to Les, and I saw *Lisa* take over then; she has a little girl voice, and she's scared and shaking. She asked me then to call Aunt Marie, but, before I could call, Lee surfaced and I moved away. I didn't see her again for years. I still called Aunt Marie, but I don't know what happened."

"You called her . . . where?"

"I had her telephone number."

"But I thought you said you never actually spoke to her?"

"You're right, it wasn't until you and I had the conversation about Aunt Marie that I realized I've never spoken to her. I only left messages."

"Is there anything else I need to know, Ronnie?"

"No, Kev, I promise – nothing else."

He cursed under his breath then continued down the driveway. They didn't speak for a while.

Finally, Kevin looked over at Veronica. "What made you stick around, Ronnie? When you found out what you were dealing with, what made you stay? No one would've blamed you for going away and living your own life."

"Les was my friend, like a sister. If I had a real sister and I found out she had cancer or any other type of disease, I would be there with her. I wouldn't abandon her and make her go through it alone."

"But this isn't *just any* disease,' it's DID. She dissociates herself. Sometimes she didn't even know who you were. What was it that made you stick around?"

"She needed me."

"Really?"

"Okay, I guess I needed her too. I knew how she felt, having no one. My life wasn't exactly a bowl of cherries either. I kept to myself most of the time until I met Les. I never wanted anyone to get close enough to find out what I was dealing with. I came from a broken family too. No sisters, no brothers, and a mom who seemed to dissociate herself too. It seemed she was so busy licking her wounds after my father left, blaming herself because he found someone more attractive than her and fell in love. I'd hear her on the phone many nights, pleading for him to come home, and then crying herself to sleep because he wouldn't. I blamed myself for years."

"Blamed yourself? Why?"

"Because I could have told her that she could never compete. I was there the days my father would wait until my mother left for work and had his lover come to the house. I knew they spent a lot of their time in the bedroom and when they finally came out, I'd see them exchange a kiss or two and watch the intimate way they'd touch each other. I may not have been old enough to understand everything, but I knew something wasn't right. By the time mother got home, my father and his lover were sitting at the dining room table playing a friendly game of cards and drinking beer. When I looked at the two, I saw my father and his lover, but what my mom saw was Daddy playing cards with Uncle Benny."

"What?!"

"That's right. I watched her drink herself to death because of it. The only outlet I had as a little girl was when Les would come to play. Somehow we became 'normal' kids, when we were together, although there wasn't anything 'normal' about our lives. She needed me as much as I needed her." Veronica chuckled, "I guess you can say, we became each other's survival kit, and we made a pact that we would always be there for each other."

"Whew! So, your mother passed away. Where's your dad now?"

"I have no idea. When he left, he never looked back. What about you, Kev? When you found out what you were dealing with, why'd you stay?"

"Simple. I love her."

"Right!" Veronica looked at him, folded her arms, and waited. "Truth!"

"That *is* the truth," He laughed. "I will admit, before I knew the situation, I was ready to bail. No one could have made me stay with Lee. But I'd go through the fire for Les. Sure, life would be easier if I didn't have a wife living with DID, but I do. People have a tendency to say they'd go through the fire for someone, but as soon as they're faced with a few burning embers, they kick dirt. I'm not like that. I told Les I was in for the long haul, and I meant it. What concerns me though, is Lee, she's evil! What if she comes back before we have a chance to go through the integration?"

"I know you'd be hurt."

"No, I wouldn't be hurt, I'd be damn mad."

"Me too."

They were quiet while the thought of Lee's resurfacing haunted them.

Kevin broke the silence. "I didn't tell you, but in our last session with Alex, Lisa shed some light on how Lee has been able to take over so easily."

"Really?! What did she say?"

"It's not Les who Lee overpowers, it's Lisa. Through the years, Les became too powerful to allow Lee to surface but, during the times that she's feeling humiliated and scared, Lisa comes to help her. Les couldn't stand for anyone to think she wasn't a tower of strength, so that's why Lisa was there, and then Lee jumped at the opportunity to push Lisa back. Les never felt threatened by Lisa, she didn't even know Lisa was there."

"You know? That makes total sense to me." Veronica said, thinking of the times she'd witness Lee's takeover.

"You never told Les about Lisa. Why?"

"I didn't realize I was dealing with another personality until we were in college. I was familiar with Les, and I knew about Lee, but there were times when Les would suddenly start speaking in a little girls' voice. She was frightened of everything, soon after that Lee would surface, and I'd pull back. I told Dr. Whitfield though. He didn't want me to say anything to Les because he didn't want to add more stress on her. He was going to present Lisa to Les during the fusion, but Lee surfaced before he could perform it.

I use to see Lisa a lot when we were kids. I didn't know her name then. Remember when I told you that the teachers would come and get me to coax Les out of her hiding places? That was Lisa. Lisa was always hiding and afraid. Lee was older—more like a grown up. She wears big hair and red lipstick. I knew when I was talking to Les because Les is strong and funny. She's everything the others are not. College was the last time I saw Lisa. I honestly thought she was gone."

"Well, she's not. She's hidden, but she's there. Do you recall seeing burns or cuts that she couldn't explain?"

Veronica traced her memory back to their school days and the many times she asked Les what happened to her arms or legs, and even her neck. "They were deep cuts. And I remember the burns too."

"Yep, apparently Lee was cutting Lisa or burning her to intimidate and scare her. It worked. That's why you didn't see Lisa anymore. She was afraid that Lee would find out that she had surfaced, and she'd hurt her, so she stayed away. She thought, by staying hidden, she wouldn't get in trouble."

Veronica expelled a breath and shook her head.

"What about Aunt Marie?"

"I'm thinking Aunt Marie is another alternate personality who Lisa created to protect her anytime she felt vulnerable or hurt. Apparently after being hidden for so long, she felt like she didn't need Aunt Marie anymore and Aunt Marie 'left'."

"But Les spoke of Aunt Marie too. So, was Aunt Marie protecting both of them?"

"That's why we're going to the group home. I want some answers."

Veronica nodded and turned to look out the window. They were quiet for the rest of the drive. After they exited the freeway, Veronica directed Kevin through the streets of the old neighborhood and to the group home. He pulled into the driveway and took a long look at the distressed building.

"Do you think people still live here?" Veronica asked.

"There's one way to find out."

Kevin hopped out then went around to help Veronica out of the car.

"I'm good, Kev. I'm getting pretty good with these things." She laughed as she stood and adjusted her crutches.

They walked up the stairs, and then to a door that was splintered by age. They knocked. No answer. Kevin looked around for a doorbell, but there wasn't one available, only a hole where the doorbell used to be.

Veronica looked up at Kevin and shrugged. "Try the door.

Kevin turned the doorknob, and the door creaked open. He stuck his head into a vacant, dark corridor and looked around. The house was old and drafty, and the dim lighting gave it a ghostly atmosphere. When he didn't see anyone, he opened the door wider and stepped in with Veronica right behind him.

"Hello?" He called out.

"Yes," came a frail voice from the other room.

Kevin and Veronica slowly moved in the direction of the voice, the timeworn floor creaked with every step. They cautiously went through a doorway that led to another darken area. The only light shining in the room came from a single tear in the window shade.

"This is the backdrop for a horror movie," Veronica whispered.

"Hello?" Kevin called out again, ignoring Veronica's fearful comment. "My name's Kevin Jenison. This is my friend Veronica Moore. We're here hoping to get some information about someone who used to live here. I hope you can help us."

The elderly woman stayed seated in her chair, a tattered blanket tossed across her legs for warmth. She reached over and flipped on the light switch of a lamp that sat on the table beside her. The sudden brightness caught Veronica off guard, and she flinched then impulsively reached out and hit Kevin's arm.

"Ouch, Ronnie!"

"Sorry."

"Well, come on in," the woman instructed. "Dere's plenty a space to set down in here." She motioned for them to come in and find a seat.

"Thank you," Kevin said moving to a nearby sofa.

Veronica stuck beside Kevin and moved too. They had to remove an armful of clutter from the sofa before sitting.

The woman's face was dark and coarsened by time. Her hands were crooked from arthritis, and they shook as she reached over to retrieve her eyeglasses from the table. When she positioned them on her face, Veronica noticed how the thickness of them made her eyes seem bigger than they were.

"Now I kin see ya." She said smiling. "I usually takes me a nap 'bout dis time, but I reckon it's bein' cut short. Now, what's dat you say brings you dis way? You lookin' fo somebody?"

"Yes, Ma'am, we came hoping to get some information about a child who use to live here," Kevin repeated.

"Chile, der been so many chirrins come through dis old place, I don't think I kin help ya. Dis here place been open fo a long time; full of chirrins! Most of 'em gone now, and dey don't be comin' back. Dis a place dey don't wanna amember. Dey don't come back here. Well, exceptin' Constance, she de onliest one come back ta see bout me." She laughed.

A door slammed, and they could hear a woman's voice.

"Grandma, why's the front door open? You trying to escape again?" A young woman rounded the corner and appeared in the doorway. Her smile quickly disappeared when she saw Kevin and Veronica. She tossed her jacket onto a chair and rushed to the elderly woman. "Grandma, you okay? Who are you people and how'd you get in here?" She asked turning to Kevin and Veronica.

"Gurl, shush up! Dese people here lookin fo some infamation 'bout somebody usta live here. Now, shush up, I'm okay. Stop fussin'." She looked at Kevin and Veronica. "Dis here, Constance, she probly kin help you better 'n me. Now, y'all shoo and let me git my nap afor dem chirrins get here."

Constance kissed her forehead and turned to leave the room. She motioned for Kevin and Veronica to follow her.

"We didn't mean to startle anyone. We're looking for some information." Kevin said as they followed Constance.

"The door was unlocked," Veronica announced, "When no one came to the door, we thought the house was vacant."

Constance entered another room. "What kind of information you lookin' for? Who are you trying to find?"

"Her name is Leslee Cramer. Do you remember her?"

"Leslee -- Leslee -- Cramer." She repeated the name over and over. "No, can't say that I do. There's been so many children who have come and gone from here. I'm not saying that she wasn't here. I'm trying to remember which one she was."

"Hold on, I have a picture." Veronica reached in her purse, drew out her wallet, and flipped through it. "I have it here somewhere." When she found the picture, she handed it to Constance.

Constance studied the picture. "I know this little girl. She was here when I first got here. My mom and dad were killed in a car accident, and there was no one to take care of me, so I was sent here. This little girl was already here then. She was always so sad. Grandma used to try to find ways to make her smile, but she never would. Then one day she asked if she could go visit a friend, and Grandma said yes. I had never seen her smile so much. I remember her because she was odd. You know? Stayed by herself all the time and never let anyone get close. She was guarded. I felt sorry for her sometimes because some of the kids here would go out of their way to tease her and pick on her. Between here and what she went through at school, I'd say the little girl was tormented. She was so little and scared."

"You went to school with her?" Veronica asked.

"Yep, right around the corner."

"I went to the same school. What did you say your name was?"

"Constance. Constance Elliot."

"Connie Elliot?"

"Yeah, that's me."

"I'm Veronica Moore! They use to call me Ronnie."

"They still call her Ronnie." Kevin laughed.

"Oh My God, Ronnie. Yes, I remember you. Why didn't you say something?"

"Well had I known it was you, I would've." Veronica laughed. "This is Kevin, Leslee Cramer's husband. We're here trying to get some information about her."

"Why, is she missing?"

"No, she's not missing," Kevin assured her. "I found out that she was raised here in this group home, and I guess I was going on a whim that there might be other things I could find out. You know, other things I don't know about her."

Veronica said, "Listen Connie. You mentioned that you thought Leslee was odd. Why? What made her different?"

Connie thought for a moment, then said, "She talked to herself constantly. She was the sweetest little girl, but she never had anything to say to any of us. She'd set up her dolls, and a table and chair set and have a tea party with people who weren't there."

"So what's odd about playing make believe?" Veronica asked.

"This was different. She had an imaginary friend who would come every day and play with her." Connie thought again. "Lisa! That was the little girl's name, Lisa. Her *imaginary friend's* name was Leslee. I even tried to play with her, but she totally ignored me. You know kids don't like to be ignored, so I tried to get her attention, and she went ballistic. She claimed I was hurting her, but I barely touched her. Grandma heard her screaming and came running out the door swingin' her skillet. She'd yell, "Who's hurtin' one of my sweets!" I guess, Lisa thought grandma was mad at her, and she went scrambling under the table, and that's where she stayed. She sat there with her eyes closed and her hands over her ears, rocking back and forth, humming." Constance fanned her hand. "She was just odd.

You know how things get around. When the kids heard what happened, they teased her. They'd tell her that Leslee was outside, and she'd run outside and she wouldn't be there. Then they'd say Leslee's under the bed, and she'd scramble to look under the bed, and of course she wouldn't find her there either. Before long, word traveled to the kids at school, and they teased her too. My thought was, if there was an imaginary friend, didn't she know that she wouldn't be there. Why would she go looking for her and make a fool of herself?"

"Because Lisa was a little girl who didn't understand that *she* was, in fact, the imaginary friend." Kevin shook his head, and his heart sank for the little girl who must have felt so alone during that time.

Veronica reached out and rubbed Kevin's shoulder to console him.

He stood, "I guess we're not finding out any more than we already knew, Ronnie."

Connie stood too, "I'm sorry I wasn't more help to you."

"Are you sure there's nothing more you can tell us?" Kevin asked.

Connie thought for a minute more then shook her head. "That's all I know. I came back here when I heard they were trying to close this place down. Grandma would have been put in a home, and I couldn't bear that. She took care of so many of us. Somebody had to step up and take care of her now. It's a no brainer, but nobody came, but me."

"She said she wanted to take her nap before the children got here. Are there still children here?" Veronica asked.

Connie chuckled. "In her mind, there are."

"Oh, I see. And you call her grandma?" Veronica asked, moving toward the room where the elderly woman was. She tried to get another glimpse of her by peering through the darkness, wondering if she had drifted back off to sleep, or if she was waiting for them to come back to say their good-byes.

"Yes, I call her Grandma. It's my way of letting her know she's family to me." Connie said. "I'm sure she's gone back to sleep by now."

They walked through the dim corridor to the front door.

Kevin faced Connie, "I'm sorry for wasting your time. I thought for sure I'd --" He shook his head in disappointment. "I thought we'd find something that would've helped us. It was nice to meet you, Connie. Thanks for your time."

Veronica nodded, "Yeah, Connie it was so good to see you again. And please tell grandma we said good-bye."

"I will. It's too bad you didn't bring Leslee with you. I think it would have done them both some good, ya know?"

"I don't think so," Kevin answered. "For some reason, Les is under the impression she was raised by her Aunt Marie. I'm not sure if this would have done her good or caused more harm."

"But she *was* raised by Aunt Marie."

Kevin and Veronica stopped and turned to Connie.

"What?"

"She *was* raised by Aunt Marie." Connie gestured toward the room. "That's Aunt Marie!"

Veronica moved back toward the room. "That's Aunt Marie?" She asked.

"That's what all the kids called her, Aunt Marie. Me too. But when I came back, I didn't want to be considered 'one of the orphans who came back', so I started calling her Grandma."

Kevin looked at Veronica and gave a chuckle of relief. "That's Aunt Marie."

Veronica nodded wildly understanding Kevin's relief. Her eyes filled with tears, and she reached out and pulled Connie into a bear hug. "You have no idea."

Connie laughed, "What did I say?"

"The right thing, Connie. You said the right thing." Kevin laughed and reached out to hug her too. He opened the door, and the two hurried to the car. Kevin put Veronica's crutches in the back seat and got behind the wheel. They waved one last time, backed out of the driveway, and drove off with information that eased both of their minds. They were glad they had come.

Veronica directed Kevin to Les's old house. When they pulled up, Kevin got out and walked around it. He could tell the house had been vacant for a long time, its gray paint was cracked and peeling, and weeds had taken over the yard.

"I wonder how long it's been since anyone's lived here?" He moved over to stand in front of a huge picture window. "This must be it." He said quietly. Then he shifted his weight to move back and look at the sidewalk where Les probably laid until the paramedics picked her up. His hand went nervously to the back of his neck as he visualized the whole ordeal.

"She was only a little girl." He said.

Veronica moved to him and rubbed his back. She understood what he was feeling.

"I feel like I'm glued to this spot," Kevin said.

"Listen, Kev, she survived it. It's over. Her new life began when you recognized who she was and made the decision to stay with her despite the disorder. Our being here is proof that we care."

"It's not over, Ronnie, and it won't be over until our next session with Alex. You know what I thought about today?"

"What?"

"There's been so many twists and turns in this thing, what if we go through with the integration and find that *Lee* is actually the host personality and *Les* is an alter? Have you thought about that?"

Veronica's head shot up, and it felt as though the wind had been knocked out of her. "That couldn't happen. Could it?" She whispered.

"I hope not, Ronnie. It was only a thought. Let's go home. I want to hit the freeway before dark."

Kevin was finally able to pull himself away, and they returned to the car and left.

The drive home was much easier than driving there. Both Kevin and Veronica felt at ease even in their conversation. But still in the back of their minds, the thought tugged; *What if Les is the alter? Could it be? Was it possible?* And, if it was possible, not only would Veronica lose her friend for good, but Kevin would lose the woman he loved too.

Kevin glanced over and saw Veronica deep in thought. "What?"

"Sorry, I was thinking about what you said back there."

"Which time?" Kevin laughed.

"What if Les is the alter and Lee is the host."

"Oh, that."

"What if it turns out to be true?"

"Then we'll cross that bridge then, not now, Ronnie."

"I don't want to lose my friend--"

"-- And I don't want to lose this sweet wife of mine. All I know is that I'd rather see her well and not have her in my life, than sick with this disorder and wonder when Lee's going to resurface. I guess either way I could lose her. Let's put it to rest for the night. Okay?"

Veronica nodded but knew it would be on her mind the rest of the evening. It was 8:00 when Kevin pulled into Veronica's driveway. Kevin leaned over and gave her a hug.

"You need help with those things?" he asked, as Veronica reached in the back for her crutches.

"No, I've got it. I'm an old pro now." She laughed.

"Thanks for going with me."

"Thanks for letting me go. See ya, Kev." She got out of the car and hopped to the front door.

Kevin waited until she was safely inside before pulling off, and then he was alone with his thoughts.

He was relieved to know Aunt Marie existed, and he pulled his cell phone from the case and called Alex to share the news. He got his voice mail and left a message.

"Hi, Doc, this is Kevin. I wanted you to know we found Aunt Marie. Give me a call as soon as you get this message."

Kevin hung up and returned the phone to its case and drove the rest of the way home in silence. It wasn't until he pulled into his driveway that his cell phone rang. He knew it was Alex, and he answered and shared the whole story with him.

"Wow, that solves a big piece of the puzzle, Kevin. Now I know how to proceed. All I needed was the link to Aunt Marie. I think it's safe to move on to the next phase."

"Which is what, Doc?"

"Integration."

"When?"

"Whenever you think she's ready."

Kevin swallowed hard. "Hey Doc, Listen. I need you to be honest with me. Is there any chance that I might lose her?"

"What do you mean, Kevin?"

"I mean, what if you're wrong, and Lee is actually the host, and Les is one of the alter personalities?"

"Hmph, I thought this question would have come earlier. But, I'll tell you this. I've done my homework, Kevin. I don't believe that's something to worry about. I will tell you though, I do have one concern."

"What's that?"

"Well, I haven't been invited to the wedding."

Kevin exhaled, and then laughed, "There's no question about it, Doc, of course you're invited. I'll give you all the information when I see you."

Alex was laughing too. To tell you the truth, I think we should meet this week. What do you think, Kev?"

"I'm on your schedule, Doc, whatever you say."

"How about Friday?"

"That's the day after tomorrow."

"Too soon?"

"No, I just pulled up into the driveway when you called. I'll talk to Les when I get in the house. I'm sure she'll agree with me, and we'll see you on Friday. Thanks, Doc."

"No, thank you, Kevin. You've helped me more than you know."

"Talk to you later, Doc." Kevin hung up, then hopped out of his car, and walked into the house.

Les was with Keith and Kelly in the living room. They were on the floor with a coloring book and crayons. Les looked up at Kevin when he walked in.

"Hey, babe, so how'd it go?"

"Fine." He reached down and playfully patted the children on their heads and motioned for Les to join him.

Les pulled herself up and walked out of earshot of the children.

"I spoke to Alex. He wants to see us on Friday. I told him we'd be there, is that a good time for you?"

"Sure." She shrugged, "What's up? Is he going ahead with the fusion?"

"Those are the plans."

"Good, I'm ready to get this over with. Did he say whether we needed to bring anything with us?"

"Only one thing."

"Yeah, what?"

"His invitation to the wedding."

Les laughed and reached up and pulled Kevin's face down for a long kiss.

Keith and Kelly looked at the two and giggled.

.

26

On Friday morning, Kevin and Les were sitting in the waiting room of Dr. Alex Whitfield's office.

Alex came to the door and had them follow him to a room. This room was different than the room they were in on their other visits. It looked more like a library than an office. He led Les to a chaise lounge and asked her if she wanted to lie down or would she be more comfortable in a chair. Les chose to lie back on the chaise. She got comfortable. Kevin found a huge cozy chair in the back of the room. He wanted to be as far away from Lee Cramer's field of vision as possible. He knew it would be disastrous if she saw him, and he didn't want anything to jeopardize what the doctor was trying to do.

Alex explained the procedure to Les and let her know what was going to happen during the session. Les wore a ghost of a smile but nodded to let him know she understood. Alex then turned to Kevin to reiterate the need for complete silence.

"It's highly unusual to have someone, other than another doctor, sit in on a session like this, Kevin. If you don't feel like you'll be able to stay quiet, please say something and leave now."

"No, I'm good. I want to stay."

"Also, it's very important for Les to get as relaxed as she can during the session. If I find that she's not able to relax because of you being present, I'm going to have to ask you to step out. Is that understood?"

Kevin nodded.

"I'm scared, Alex" Les admitted quietly.

Alex studied Les and nodded, "I'm sure you're a little frightened because of the unknown, but let me assure you that everything is under control. You need to trust me, Les. Do you trust me?"

"Yes, I do. I trust you," she answered.

"Then let's get started. Are you comfortable?"

Les nodded her head.

"Good, I need you to close your eyes, and try to relax." He said.

Les closed her eyes, took a deep breath then released it. She relaxed her shoulders and prepared herself to follow his instructions.

Alex's voice was soothing as he spoke. "Les, I want you to breathe with me. He inhaled through his nose and exhaled through his mouth and repeated the process. Les followed his directions. He guided her through a method of relaxation that made her feel like she was floating on air, and she sank deeper and deeper into the relaxation. There was nothing else in the room, just her breathing in and breathing out and floating carelessly, listening to Alex Whitfield's soothing voice. He counted backward from ten to one, and as he said each number, Les went deeper into the relaxation. When he saw that she was completely relaxed, he suggested that she continue to breathe in and out and listen *only* to the sound of his voice.

"Les, there is nothing here that can frighten you. You are strong and courageous. You are confident and safe. You can face adversity with confidence. You are not fearful. Do you understand? If you understand, let me know by giving me a slight nod of your head."

She nodded.

"Very good, you're doing great, Les. Now, because you are safe here, I need you to imagine sitting in a huge comfortable chair. You are in a place where it's safe, and the chair allows you to view everything around you."

Alex waited. "Good Les, just continue to breathe in and out as you sit in the chair. Look around you. There is nothing there that frightens you. You know you're safe."

Les breathed in and out. She nods again.

"Now I'm going to count from ten to one, Les, and with each number, you will feel more and more confident and more and more certain that truth will be revealed today. A truth that will make you self-reliant. Do you understand?

Les nods.

"To accomplish this, I need to speak with Lee. Lee is not going to be in control here, so there is no reason for you to feel anxious or worried. You have no reason to be alarmed at all. Do you understand?"

Les nods again.

"Now, while you are in your comfortable chair, in your safe place, you will be able to hear everything that Lee and I talk about. It will not frighten you because you know you're safe. Do you understand?"

Les nods.

Alex paused. "Lee," He called, "Lee Cramer. Can you wake up and come forward to talk to me?"

Les moves around then repositions herself.

"Lee, are you there?"

Lee, takes a deep breath, "Yes, I'm here." Her voice was raspier than Les's voice.

Kevin closed his eyes and bit down hard to clench his teeth. Hearing her voice brought back unpleasant memories, and it made him cringe. He couldn't understand how he didn't know the difference between the two voices, Lee's voice was cold and withdrawn, so different than the warmth of Les's.

"Lee, do you know who I am?"

Lee nodded. "You're Dr. Whitfield."

"That's right, Lee, I'm Dr. Whitfield. Now, we've done these types of sessions before, haven't we?"

Lee nodded.

"So you know the type of questions I ask; am I right?"

She nodded again.

I would like you to think back to when you were five years old?

"I have never been five years old, Dr. Whitfield. How do you suppose a five-year-old knows to do such grown-up things? Daddy's not interested in little girls. He wants me."

"I see. Can you tell me how old you are, Lee?"

"A lady never tells her age but when I get dressed up and put on my lipstick everyone knows I'm older. Daddy liked my red lips, and he said I looked just like Mommy when I put my hair up. He loved it."

"Okay, I understand now. So, let's think back to when Les was five years old, it's bedtime. You are lying in bed. Is your father there?"

"No, but I can hear him coming down the hall."

"Is it unusual to hear your father come down the hall, Lee?"

"No, he does it every night. I listen for him, and I put on my lipstick, pin up my hair, and wait."

"Is he in your bedroom now?"

"Yes."

"Why is he in your bedroom?"

"He comes to my bed, picks me up, and carries me to his bed."

"Where is Les when this happens?"

"She disappears—goes away. I'm the only one who can take care of Daddy now. Les wasn't old enough to know what Daddy wanted, but I was. She said Daddy hurt her. He never hurt me."

"What do you mean, Lee? What does your father do when he carried you to his bed?"

"He tells me how beautiful I am and he kisses my red lips. Then he shows me how to touch him to make him feel good. He tells me he's going to teach me how to be his good girl.

"What does your father show you, Lee?"

"He showed me his penis and takes off my clothes. He puts his penis inside me."

"And this goes on every night?"

Lee nodded.

"So your father has sex with you?"

"Yes, I know exactly what he wants. I knew how to be his good girl, until he went away, and he went away because of her."

"Okay, Lee, let's move forward. Do you remember when Les was taken away in the ambulance?"

"Yes." Lee's face turned dark, and she frowned. "That was the day the other one came."

"Okay, but right now let's talk about you."

She shifted.

"Why did they take her to the hospital?"

"She wouldn't let me out! Daddy wanted me, and she wouldn't go away. I tried to make her go into the darkness, but *she kept pushing me back, she wouldn't go away.* Daddy was getting so angry. He tried to get Les to touch him, but she wouldn't. All she had to do was touch him. She kept screaming and screaming until Daddy couldn't take it anymore. I heard the glass break, and I heard her body when she hit the ground." Lee giggled, "Blood was everywhere. I was hoping she was dead."

"Do you realize, if Les dies, you die too?"

Lee shrugged, "Yes, so?"

"Lee, have you ever tried to kill Les?"

"Many times, especially after that."

"What did you mean when you said, "That was the day the other one came?"

"The other one -- the little girl. She came to stay that day. Usually, I could scare her away, but not this time. I'd try to catch her when she'd come out, but she'd hide."

"Tell me more about her."

"What's there to tell? She's a little brat. Always whining. Wahhhh wahhhh wahhhh. This hurts, that hurts. Don't touch me! Ouch, ouch! I can't stand that little bitch." Lee spat

"So of course you tried to get rid of her, right?"

"Yeah. Until I realized how useful she could be."

"Useful?"

"Yes, useful."

Can you tell me about the last time you tried to kill Les?"

Lee smiled. "I planned it for years, and I used people she knew."

"What do you mean you used people she knew?"

"Kevin thought I was her for an inordinate length of time, and I made him hate her as much as I did. He couldn't wait to get rid of her. I bought a tent, and I was going to take her bratty kids out somewhere secluded and leave them there and make sure no one found them -- alive."

"I don't understand how's that harming Les."

"I was going to go disappear and leave her to take the blame for everything. No one would believe her about me -- *no one.* There'd be a long, drawn-out trial. And in the end, the courts would have no choice, but to send her to prison for life. That would've killed her."

"So what happened to your plan?"

"That two-faced friend of mine told Kevin."

"Friend?"

"Yeah, Brenda. She told him everything. She's so lovesick over him. She's pathetic! And she'll do anything to have him back. Anything! So I used her too."

"How exactly did you use Brenda?"

Lee laughed. "Brenda and I go back a long way. How do you think she got Les's telephone number? I even told her what to say to Les that would cause her to go over the edge, and she actually did it. Exactly the way I said. She's so easy to manipulate."

"So, because Brenda told Kevin, your plan actually failed?"

""Oh no. My plan may have *changed,* but it didn't fail. The outcome will still be the same. You'll see." Lee laughed.

"And Lisa?"

"What about Lisa? I have nothing to say about her."

"Well, then we'll move on. You mentioned wanting to hurt the children. Tell me about that, Lee?

She shrugged. "What about it?"

"You didn't care how you were affecting them?"

"No. Especially that little girl. I hate that little bitch. Wahhh – wahhhh -- wahhhh." I can't stand her. She reminds me of Lisa."

"Lee, did you hurt the little girl?"

Lee chuckled, "Every-chance –I -got."

Knowing her comment would infuriate Kevin, Alex turned slightly to make sure Kevin was still seated and thought it was best to move on before his fury became unbearable for him.

"Do you know any of Les's friends?'

"She doesn't have any friends!"

"Then you don't know Veronica?"

"No, I don't know who that is. I only know Brenda. If it hadn't been for her, I would never have been able to push through. Les refuses to handle the humiliation. That's why she has me and Lisa. She stopped trusting me a long time ago so Lisa would come forward and scramble under a table somewhere to keep Les from feeling embarrassment. She'd whimper and cry until I'd come forward. At first, she thought I was coming to help her, and she'd give up her space willingly. Then later, when she realized what I was doing, she became more guarded."

"What do you mean, more guarded?" Dr. Whitfield asked.

"She was cautious -- more careful. If she felt me coming forward, she'd rush off, and that would bring Les back before I could get my footing, and then Les wouldn't let me through. I hated her. I'd get her back though." Lee laughed. "I always got her back."

"Yes, we know about the burns and the cutting. That was your doing, huh?"

"Oh yes." She laughed again.

"So you're saying, when Les would feel humiliated, Lisa would come forward to take the humiliation for her, and you could overpower Lisa. That's how you did it? Why you say Lisa was useful? And you stayed out for ten years? But, Lisa was *out* most of the time during your stay at the group home. Why didn't you overpower her during that time?"

"I didn't want to. We should never have been there in the first place. It was their fault that we were there, so I let them deal with it. I had my own strategy. It was simple. Once Les went to sleep, I was going to push her so far into the darkness that she couldn't come forward unless I conceded. And I wasn't going to concede until I was sure my plan was going to work."

"You're plan to destroy Les?"

"Everyone. My plan to destroy everyone."

"What was it that Brenda did to make Les so weak that Lisa had to come forward?"

"Oh My God! Don't you get it? Brenda referred to Les as a *dumpster*. She said Kevin was known to go play in the dumpster every now and then, but always found his way back to her. I couldn't have planned it better. She told Les that Kevin was only using her for sex, just like her father." Lee laughed.

"So you're saying that Brenda lied, which made Les vulnerable, causing Lisa to come forward, and then you? Did that happen often?"

"Often enough and I'd wait for the opportunity. Other than that, Les had gotten too strong and knew how to push me back. If it hadn't been for Brenda, I would never have been able to accomplish anything."

"Lee, today Lisa and Les are joining forces against you. You can no longer hurt either one of them.

Lisa, you can come out of your safe place and, Les, you can receive Lisa as a part of you. She's your childhood. Lisa remembers every humiliation, every disgrace, and every shameful moment, and she will continue to protect you, but as a part of you. Will you receive her?"

Les stayed seated in her chair but noticed a little girl peeking out of the shadows in the distance. Les nodded and then smiled. Lisa knew it was safe, so she came out and ran to Les and Les embraced her.

"Now I'd like to speak to Lee and only Lee. I want you to understand that there is no way you will ever be in control again. I need you to know that, from your own admission, the only way you could come forward is when Lisa was in control. Now that Les and Lisa are together you will never be able to overpower Lisa again because Lisa and Les are one. Do you understand what I'm saying?"

Lee nodded.

"You have only one choice, and that is to integrate along with Les and Lisa. Are you willing to do that?"

Lee chuckled. "Sure. It's just a matter of time anyway."

"A matter of time?"

"Yes, when Kevin has her arrested, she'll still die." Lee chuckled. "It's a matter of time."

"Oh, that's right. Your plan was foolproof, and Kevin will soon give Les what she deserves."

"Exactly!"

"Thank you, Lee. Les, you can come out of your safe place now. Lee will continue to be with you, but only as an integrated part of you. She cannot harm you or have any control over you. You're no longer worried about her pushing you back into the darkness because you've proven to be more powerful. You no longer need someone to help you handle fear because you are unafraid. I'm going to count backward from five to one, and when I say *one*, you will open your eyes. You'll remember everything Lee said, and it will not hinder you, it will enlighten you. When you open your eyes, it will feel as if a huge burden has been lifted from your shoulders. You will take a deep breath and know that everything is alright with the world, 5-4-3-2-1."

Les opened her eyes, took a deep breath, and smiled.

"How do you feel?" Alex asked.

"I feel – really -- light. I feel good!"

"Do you remember what was said here?"

Les thought for a minute, "Yes, Alex, I remember everything."

"And how do you feel about what you know now?"

"I feel enlightened. I don't feel like I have missing pieces or that I'm in the dark about anything."

"Kevin, you can come up now?"

Kevin stood and walked to Les's side. He put his arm around her and spoke for the first time since the session started.

"You were great, Sweetheart. I was so proud of you." He told her.

"Now there are going to have to be some follow-up visits, Les," Alex instructed. "You were given a lot of information today so you'll need guidance on how to channel it all, but we'll start setting those appointments next week. I understand there's a wedding to plan for?"

"Dr. Alex Whitfield, how can I ever thank you?" Les asked.

"I'm the one who needs to thank you, Les. You allowed me to bring closure to one of my father's cases and for that I'm grateful."

27

Brenda chose a pale yellow dress and accented it with silver accessories, she felt this particular color of yellow looked good against her chocolate complexion. She pulled her new Prada bag from the top shelf in her closet then stood in front of the full-length mirror. She was pleased with her appearance "Yes," she thought, *"Kevin would be very pleased too."* She turned from one side to the other and nodded. She brushed her long black hair back away from her face to give herself a classier appearance. She liked how it looked so she used the hairspray hoping it would stay in place for the entire afternoon. Kevin liked long hair, so she took the time and spent the money at the salon to get it done. She was satisfied and dabbed a little cologne behind her ears before leaving her bedroom.

The overcast was unusual for this time of year in Arizona. The light drizzle and the gray sky would normally have put her in a dreary mood, but she didn't have time to think about that now. Her only thought was to get to Kevin and finally begin their lives together. Too much time passed already. She laughed. The *gall of Lee to show up at Kevin's party. Who does that? It was a divorce party! I mean -- hello?*

There was no doubt in her mind that she had given Kevin enough time to call the police and have Lee arrested. She wished she could have seen the look on Lee's face when they slapped the handcuffs on her and took her away. Putting her in the back of the police car had to have been the ultimate satisfaction for him. Once again, Brenda chuckled at the thought.

She already decided. She was going to Kevin's house to tell him what a wonderful time she had at the party. With all those people there, he probably didn't even notice when she left. He was doing such a good job at pretending to be the doting husband. Brenda thought. Beneath that cool demeanor, Kevin must have been furious when Lee walked into the room. She should have stayed around to see what happened! But she allowed her anger to get the best of her. She really must work on calming her temper at times like that.

Brenda grabbed her purse from the counter and left. Pulling out of the garage, she realized the rain had gone from a dull drizzle to a steady shower. She turned on her wipers, adjusted the mirrors, and then drove off. *This was perfect. Because of the rain, Kevin would surely ask me to step inside.*

She had gone over and over in her mind what she was going to say when Kevin opened the door. *"Hi, Kev!" I thought I'd drop by to see how you were doing. Had a great time at the party."* She couldn't wait!

When she got closer to Kevin's house, her heart began to race. She was excited. She checked her breath then reached into the console for the case of breath mints and popped one into her mouth. At the next traffic light, she pulled the visor down and looked into the mirror to check her makeup. She used her pinky finger to smooth and blend the creamy red color on her lips, and then moved the visor back into place. The drive only took twenty minutes.

Finally, she pulled in front of Kevin's house. She cleared her throat and hopped out of the car then rehearsed her lines all the way to the door, "Hi Kev-- no – no -- no, Heyyy Kev! I thought I'd drop by to see how you're doing. Great party the other night."

She rang the doorbell. She could hear a dog barking, and then voices telling him to keep quiet. He didn't.

The door opened. Riley darted out, but Brenda's attention was on the little girl who opened it. *What was her name again?* "Hi Sweetie, is your daddy here?" The little dog ran around the yard, and then trotted into the nearby flower garden.

"Yes, he's here. Daaddddyyyy! Some lady's at the door for you!" Kelly yelled. "Daaddddyyyyyyyy!" Kelly yelled again. She called for the dog, "Riley, come boy!" Riley came running back toward the door, his tail wagging and so happy to see the stranger that he hopped up to greet her. His paws smeared Brenda's dress with the fresh mud from the garden. Appalled and shocked Brenda jerked around, causing her hair to fall into her face. "The little girl stepped back wide eyed, "Daaaaddddyyyyy!"

"Here I come," Kevin said rushing down the stairs.

Then Brenda heard a lady's voice, "Kel, don't hold the door open like that."

"But Mommy, there's a lady at the door for Daddy."

Les hurried to the doorway, "A lady?" she asked. "Yes, hello?"

Kevin and Les reached the door at the same time. Riley was still barking, but no one moved.

Brenda couldn't believe her eyes. She looked from Kevin to Les and then back to Kevin.

"Brenda?" Kevin asked not sure why she would be at his door. "What are you doing here?" He sent Kelly into the other room.

"I-- thought, I mean, I -- I." The words wouldn't come. She looked at Les and shouted, "What the hell are you doing here?"

"So," Les said ignoring Brenda's question, "this is Brenda?" She looked at Kevin and waited for him to answer.

"You know exactly who I am, you bi---!"

"Hold on!" Kevin bellowed. "You don't come to my house and think you're gonna talk to my wife any kind of way. What's wrong with you? What do you want, Brenda?"

"I was under the impression that *she* was gone. I thought we would - - we could -- because *she* said -- uh, I mean, we agreed -- no, we didn't agree --but she said." Brenda was stammering over her words so badly, Kevin didn't know what she was trying to say. All the while, she was getting drenched by the rain.

"Listen, Brenda," Kevin started, "I know everything -- EVERYTHING! Every lie you told, I know about. You can't think I'd want anything to do with you after all you've done. Come on! This," he pulled Les to him, "This is my wife. She will *always* be my wife. And I need you to know that even if we part in *death*, you *still* won't have a snowball's chance in hell. Do you understand that? Now get away from my door."

"But Kevin! You don't know what all she's done. Ask her about the bruises on Kelly-- and -- and the tent in the garage." Brenda stepped back, and the heel of her shoe sank deep into the earth between the cracks of the sidewalk and when she tried to pull it free, she heard it break. When she picked her foot up, she saw the heel of her shoe was still embedded deep in the ground.

"Kevin," Les said, "I need to say something to Brenda."

"Brenda, I don't know if you just got caught up in Lee's web of lies or what, but --"

Brenda shrieked, "What do you mean, *caught up*? You *are* Lee. You're the one who's lying!"

"No, I know this is hard for you to understand, but I'm not Lee. That's not who I am."

Brenda looked from Kevin to Les. "What kind of game are you two playing?" She yelled.

"What I'm trying to say to you Brenda is, it's over! There's no reason for you to come around bothering me or Kevin anymore. Now, if you don't understand that, let me put it in a way that may be easier for you to comprehend. If you ever come to my door again, I – will – kick – your – ass!"

Veronica hopped on her crutches from behind Les, "And I'll be around to help her." She said.

Brenda huffed at the gall of them speaking to her in that manner. She turned and limped awkwardly to her car.

When her car sped off, Kevin turned to Les and Veronica and smiled "I'm scared of you two." He said.

"What do you mean, you're scared of us?" Veronica asked, "You're the one talking about her not having a snowball's chance in hell." They laughed, and Kevin closed the door.

28

Les sat at the vanity and gazed intently at her image in the mirror. She could hear the commotion of everything going on in the house, but her attention was right here, staring at herself –her image-- in the mirror. Actively searching closely, her own eyes, thoroughly investigating who was actually present at the moment. It was only *her*. No more wondering when it could happen or why, or even what occurred when it was happening. She felt whole. "This," she said quietly, "is how it feels to be whole." She smiled and inhaled deeply. She glanced at the clock on the dresser. The makeup artist will be there soon – a wedding gift from Veronica. She turned back to the mirror, swooped her hair off her neck and began pinning it into the style that she wanted. The excitement of the day was escalating.

Veronica had arrived early in the afternoon and chose to get dressed in one of the bedrooms down the hall from Les. Crutch placed under each arm, she hopped into the room to say hello and give a final okay on the up-doo.

"I like it," she said, "Are you excited?"

"Excited is not the word, Ronnie, I am elated, overjoyed, and walking on cloud nine, but at the same time, I'm so nervous. Why is that?" She laughed, shaking her hands in front of her to calm her nerves.

"Where's Kevin?"

"You didn't see him downstairs when you came in?" Les asked in a panic.

"Girlfriend, will you calm down! He was probably out back with Timothy, giving last minute instructions. Now, calm down!" Veronica instructed, "Les, it's beautiful downstairs," She said in an exaggerated tone.

"Is it? I knew it would be. I can't wait to see it. Timothy is such a good designer."

Veronica looked admiringly at the wedding dress hanging on the door. "Girl, you are going to knock 'em dead in this dress."

"Where's Tom? Did he come with you?"

"Uh-huh," she said, still looking at the details of the dress. "He's downstairs with Kevin."

"So what's up with you two?" Les asked.

"Oh nothing," Veronica said in a sing-song voice, then looked at Les and smiled.

"Ronnie, what's going on?"

"Well, I know he likes me." She said teasingly.

"Okay?"

"Umm, I know he likes me a lot." She stated.

"Ronnie! Come on. Tell me!"

"Nope, we'll talk later. Today is your day, and we have plenty of time after the wedding to talk about me and Tom."

"He proposed, didn't he?!"

"We'll talk later." Veronica smiled.

"He did propose!" Les screeched. "I can tell. It's written all over your face."

"Come on, Les. This is your day. We'll talk later!"

"Oh, okay," Les pouted, "but don't forget. We'll have coffee and talk about it." Les thought for a minute, "You know, Ronnie, When I was at Alex Whitfield's, he asked Lee if she knew you, and she said she had no idea who you were."

"Uh-huh, Girl, that was so difficult. Dr. Paul Whitfield told me to move away from you as quickly as possible every time you went to sleep because I could be the one to help you piece things together when you woke up. But, if Lee knew you and I were friends, she would duck and dodge me to keep me from seeing what she was up to. Her not knowing who I was helped me to help you. Does that make sense?" Veronica asked.

"If it hadn't been for you most of my life --" Les shook her head slowly. "I don't know where I'd be right now. You actually saved me, Ronnie. You were there every step of the way, and I'll never be able to repay you for that. I mean, think about it! What would have happened to me?"

"You would've fallen flat on your butt," Veronica teased, "Now, girlfriend, that part of your life is over. This is an exciting day, and you're not gonna get me cryin' and what not. I refuse to! I'm happy!" She put on a big smile as a lone tear streamed down her face. The two women hugged and wiped away tears as Kelly wandered into the room.

"Mommy, do I get to wear my beautiful dress today?" Kelly asked. She giggled and hopped up on her mom and dad's bed, something she was never allowed to do before.

"You sure do, Kel, did you get the basket of rose petals?"

"Uh huh, and Keith got something from Daddy, and he put it in his pocket."

Veronica hurried to the little girl, "Kel, did you see the cake downstairs?"

"Yes, it's a big cake, with people on it."

"Can you run downstairs and tell Daddy that Mommy's almost ready?" Veronica asked.

"Yep," She ran across the room, and then out the door.

"What was that about?" Les asked.

"What?"

It was obvious Veronica was trying to keep Kelly quiet about something. Les looked at the clock and smiled. "Only four hours!"

"So how's Kelly been doing?" Veronica asked.

"I'm not sure, Ronnie. Sometimes I think she's doing okay and other times she slips back to the little girl who doesn't want me to touch her. One minute she's a happy four-year-old-and the next minute she's crying in a corner." Les said

"What do you make of it?" Veronica asked.

"I don't know what to make of it. I wonder if sometimes she remembers the way Lee used to beat her, and then looks at me and gets confused."

Veronica shook her head. "Hopefully, she'll grow out of it."

"We'll see. I'm going to talk to Alex. I'd like him to see her." Les answered.

"You don't think --?"

"No, but I don't want to take any chances either." Les dismissed the thought. "We'll talk about it later."

"Okay, I'm going to get dressed, and I know you can't wait to put on that beautiful dress." She gathered her crutches and moved toward the door with as much dignity as she could gather then turned to give one last smile, and she was gone.

Les sat at the vanity, and took a deep breath, then glanced at her watch. It was almost time for the make-up artist to come, and then she could put on her dress.

Her wedding dress was breathtaking. A Strapless, white satin fitted gown with exquisitely embroidered beading on the bodice and around the waist, coming to a 'V' in the front. And then the same embroidery around the bottom near the hem. She stared at the dress hanging from the closet door. It was all like a dream. And she knew the day was going to speed by and become a haze of memories captured in still-framed photographs to remind her that it was real and that it happened.

She opened the drawer of the vanity, and immediately her smile faded and everything stopped. Laying in the drawer was a long white envelope with the words: To Leslee Cramer written in her father's handwriting. The eerie feeling made the hairs on the back of her neck stand up. She suddenly remembered coming home from the restaurant and shoving the letter in the drawer hoping never to look at it again. She slowly reached into the drawer and picked the envelope up. She laid it on the top of the vanity and stared at it, touched it, and then turned it over and traced along the seam where the letter had been sealed.

"What could you have to say to me?" She whispered.

She turned the letter around again. She was startled at how easy it was for anger to creep up and cast a shadow on her happiness. She spoke to the letter as if her father was standing with it.

"*You*, who violated the trust a little girl had for her father. Do you even care that you almost destroyed my life? What – is it that you *need* to say to me?!" She shouted as her tears spilled over onto her cheeks. "You send me a letter?!"

Les stood and walked violently away from the vanity only to turn and storm back.

"Because of your destructive actions, I was left with nothing, but fear, anger, and confusion, and you took away the only chance I had to have a father I could love and respect." She shook her head in disbelief and shouted again, "What is it that you *need* to say to me?!"

Kevin heard Les's shouting and darted up the stairs two at a time to get to her, his heart beating uncontrollably. Veronica hopped clumsily from her room, holding on to the wall for balance. The two exchanged perplexed looks and before long Tom joined them. He was confused and bothered by the unexpected jolt as well.

Veronica's first thought was to rush in and protect her friend from whatever foe reared its head, but Kevin stopped her. He peeked into the room and saw the letter on the vanity and knew this was the day Alex Whitfield said would eventually come. This was the one final unpleasant incident Les was going to have to face on her own. He closed the door quietly and allowed Les the privacy she needed.

After sending the others away, he stood outside the bedroom door and waited.

Les picked up the envelope and trailed the edges of it with her finger. She turned it around and slowly opened the envelope. Inside were two pages. She began to read:

My Dearest Daughter, Leslee,

I've wanted to write this letter for a long time. I just didn't know where to start. I need you to know that I am sick to my soul because of what I did to you. I have been told that I am dying, and so I might not get the chance to see you in person to tell you what needs to be said. I hope this letter will suffice when you begin to ask; Why?

When I met your mother, my life exploded with the wonderment of being in love. I wanted to please her and make her happy for the rest of her life, and I did. Then she got pregnant with you. It was miraculous, we had made a baby together. I remember the playful arguments we had about whether you were going to be a boy or a girl. She won, you were such a perfect baby girl. Life was great. It was wonderful!

She was so excited to go into town to buy clothes and diapers for you. She wanted to show you off to her friends, so she bundled you up and took you with her. You were gone the whole day. When it started getting late, I began to worry. My worry turned to terror when the police officers knocked at my door and told me that the car had been hit and knocked into a ravine. They took me to the hospital where you and your mother were. I ran into the emergency room and passed the desk, searching frantically for the woman I loved. When I found her, she was laying there, staring up at me -- it wasn't long before I realized she wasn't looking at me at all, there was no life left in her eyes, she was gone. Just as quickly as she had come into my life, she was gone. I sat by her bed and cried for hours.

I don't know how long I sat there, but when I got up to leave, the nurses stopped me and came around the corner with you in their arms. How could that be? How could you be alive and the woman I love was lying dead in the other room? But there you were, vibrant and healthy. They handed me the diaper bag and not one bottle inside it was broken. Nothing was out of place, but my wife was dead. I got angry. I didn't want a baby, I wanted my wife!

I went home and didn't stop drinking. I finished the first bottle of rum, and then I started on another, and then another. I never wanted to be sober again. I remember stumbling around, in my drunken stupor, to care for you-- feeding you, diapering you.

However, it all changed when you were four years old. I was having a bad day of memories, and I was trying to drown them with alcohol. You came in wanting to comfort your daddy, and I wanted my wife. So, I used you to replace her. You were so willing to love me, but not like that. I took you and all your innocence. I could hear you crying in your bedroom that night, and I went in to comfort you, but instead, I picked you up and took you to my bed.

In my sick mind, I justified what I was doing to you by saying you owed me. If it hadn't been for you, my wife would still be here. You must have been left to take her place, and it went on like that for about a year and then one day, you stood up to me and said NO. I was furious and wanted to scare you. When I lifted you up, all the anger of losing my wife and the shame of what I was doing to my daughter combined, and I threw you with all my strength. The sound of the window breaking-- glass shattering -- and the sound of your little body hitting the pavement outside brought me to myself, and I called the police and told them what I did. I thought you were dead, and I was so ashamed!

I prayed for the death penalty, but they only gave me 25 years. However, God is merciful, and I will die soon. Knowing I will no longer be haunted every day by the memory of my actions, makes me welcome death. My only regret is that I wasn't the kind of father my daughter could be proud of and for that, I hope you can find it in your heart to forgive me. I pray that, if you ever have the opportunity to love a child that you love her with all your heart and use the time you have with her to provide memories that make her life worth living.

I love you,
Daddy

Her tears flowed freely. Les put the letter down and sat staring at it.

Kevin leaned against the door to listen then cracked the door and peeked in. He tapped to get Les's attention, but after seeing the letter face down on the vanity, he opened the door wider and walked in. Les heard the sound of footsteps and looked up. When she saw Kevin, she ran to him and buried her face in his chest and cried. She cried for the little girl who suffered the loss of her innocence and replaced it with shame. She cried for the man who groped for comfort only to uncover the hollowed emptiness of grief, and she cried for the life that had been shattered by ruthless distrust and cruelty.

She handed the letter to Kevin, he read it and understood. He took Les into his arms and embraced her. He leaned down and kissed her hair and her face. He tilted her face to kiss her mouth, then he held her closely, whispering how much he loved her.

Les knew it was true. All that he was saying to her was true. She reached up and took his face in her hands until she knew she had his full attention. She smiled, nodded wildly, and simply said, "I know."

29

The makeup artist was superb. Les found herself staring in the mirror, turning her face from side to side.

"Exquisite!" she said aloud.

Veronica looked at her and smiled, "You look absolutely beautiful!"

"I know." Les teased.

They both laughed.

Veronica placed a crutch under both arms and turned to Les, "You ready to do this?" She asked, handing Les her bouquet.

Les thought for a minute and took a deep breath.

"Just about," she said. She turned to the vanity, picked up the letter from her father, folded it tightly, then stuffed it into the center of her bouquet, "Now, I'm ready."

A strange new feeling swept over Les as she walked out of the room and down the stairs. A feeling that not only tugged but also warmed her heart at the same time. When she stepped outside and looked around at the many friends who gathered to witness the exchanging of vows between, she and Kevin, she realized, the strange new feeling was none other than forgiveness.

The backyard was turned into a beautiful garden wedding scene. The trees and the summer flowers were the perfect background to a perfect day. Veronica paced herself and moved down the aisle with as much grace as she could muster up in her condition, but to Les, she looked beautiful.

Timothy Josephs had to stand back and smile listening to Kelly ask, "Mommy, do I go now? Do I go?"

"Yes, Kel, go now," Les whispered, and Kelly walked the aisle and dropped rose petals on each side of the runner. When she got to the end, she turned around and motioned for her Mom to come. The guest chuckled quietly at the spontaneous gesture.

Les stepped to the beginning of the runner which initiated the playing of the wedding march, and Les began her walk into the next chapter of her life. Half-way down the aisle Kevin turned and walked up to meet her, he cocked his head to the side, took her hand and linked it in his arm then together they approached the altar.

Keith stood with Tom off to the side. And when it was time to exchange rings, Les slipped a gold band on Kevin's finger. Kevin turned to Keith and winked. Keith stepped forward and with a grin that showed all the empty spaces in his mouth, he handed his Dad the diamond ring they had carefully chosen for the occasion. Les cried as he placed the ring on her finger.

***

With all the guest gone, Veronica and Les sat in the living room enjoying the peace and quiet. It was difficult to think that a few hours earlier the room was full of people laughing and music scaling the walls toward the ceiling. Both women had their heads resting on the back of the sofa with their eyes closed.

"Oh my God, I'm tired. I've never seen you dance so much in my life. You danced so much *my* feet hurt." Veronica groaned, lifting her cast from the floor.

Les laughed. "I know."

Veronica turned her head to look at Les, "Everything was so beautiful though -- Just beautiful. You, the decorations, the food. -- *everything!*"

Les nodded, "It was beautiful, wasn't it?"

"Let me look at that ring, girlfriend!" Veronica demanded. She sat up and reached out for Les's hand.

Without lifting her head, Les moved her hand to show Veronica her ring.

Veronica examined the ring closely, "It's gorgeous. You really had no idea he got this for you?" She asked suspiciously.

"Nope, had no idea." Les sat up and looked at Veronica. "Okay, Missy, it's your turn. Spill it! Did Tom propose to you?

Veronica smiled and gave a slow nod. "Yes, he proposed. This is your day though, and I didn't want my news to overshadow the excitement of it. That's why I didn't want to tell you upstairs."

"I understand, but nothing could have overshadowed this day, Ronnie. It was perfect! I'm so excited for you. When? Did you set a date?"

"I'm not sure when. We're still talking about it. Tom wants a big ceremony, and I want a quiet, intimate one with only our closest friends there. I wanted to make sure you were okay first."

"Me?! Les shrieked, "Ronnie, don't worry about me. I'm fine. Alex Whitfield is amazing."

"I told you." Veronica teased. "It was good to see him here today. It looked like he had a good time. I heard him, Kevin, and Tom talking about going to play golf next weekend."

"Oh good."

Veronica turned to Les. "So, you read the letter?"

Les, lifted her head, picked up her bouquet and pulled the folded paper out of it then handed it to Veronica.

Veronica took the paper and opened it. She sat forward and began to read.

Les didn't speak.

After Veronica had finished reading the letter, she looked up at Les with tears in her eyes.

"Oh, Les!" Veronica whispered.

"I know," Les said quietly and slowly shook her head. "If he wasn't my father, and I hadn't gone through everything I went through, I think I would feel sorry for him."

"So you put the letter in your bouquet, why?"

Les thought for a minute before answering, "He never seemed real to me, Ronnie. All my memories of him were blurred and disconnected. It wasn't until my sessions with Dr. Whitfield that I realized I had lived so long with misconceptions of who he really was. I know that he's my father and that he did some horrible things to me that altered my behavior and my life. But after reading his letter, it made me aware of the many years he lived saturated in unforgiveness and it eventually killed him. I don't want that life for me, Ronnie. Today, my father became a *real* person to me. He's not only my father, but he's a man who went through a tragedy and lost himself in the process. Here he was, standing in front of me asking for my forgiveness in the only way he could before he took his last breath. The best way I could show him and God that I had truly forgiven him, was to include him in the most important day of my life." Les admitted quietly. "In a sense, my father walked with me down the aisle."

Veronica looked at Les and shook her head, "I've always thought that you deserved so much better than what you were handed. And I realize, sitting here listening to you, I'm looking at an original oyster's pearl, ya know?" She smiled.

Les laughed, "What do you mean oyster's pearl?" she asked Veronica.

"Yes, Kevin said, walking into the room with Tom following him. He walked to Les and pulled her up from the sofa and into his arms.

"Well, a pearl is made from an irritant, a grain of sand or a parasite, that gets into the mouth of an oyster. The oyster films over the irritant with something called nacre. For years the oyster films over this irritant until one day, when the oyster is opened, instead of finding the irritant that caused so much discomfort and pain, there sits a beautiful pearl. You've allowed the irritants in your life to make you the woman you are today." Veronica nodded and then confirmed. "You, Les Jenison, are an original oyster's pearl."

"I like that!" Les admitted.

"Me too." Kevin said. He reached into his breast pocket and pulled out a jewelry box. "When Veronica told me about the oyster's pearl the other day, I couldn't get it out of my mind so, when I went to the jewelry store to pick up your ring, I picked this up too." He opened the box and revealed a necklace, an exquisite single pearl surrounded by a cluster of diamonds.

He draped the dainty chain around her neck and fastened it in the back. "This, my Love, is what you are. An exquisite oyster's pearl."

Les reached up slowly and touched the necklace and then turned to Kevin. She leaned up and kissed him gently on the mouth while he wiped her tears. "I love you," she said.

He smiled at her and winked. "I know." He said proudly.

***

Les could hear Kelly crying long before she reached the room where they were. Her dress was covered with mud.

"What's wrong, Kel?" Les asked reaching out to her. "Oh, Kelly, look at your beautiful dress." What did you do?

"I didn't do it!" she cried. "She wouldn't stop. I told her to stop, but she wouldn't."

"It's okay, Kel, tell me who did this to you--who wouldn't stop? Kelly, who did this to you?"

"It was her!" She cried, pointing out the window, "Katlin! She said all she wanted to do was play with me, and then she took mud and rubbed it all over my dress. I told her to stop, and she wouldn't. She doesn't play nice."

Les gave Kevin a quick glance and rushed across the room to the window. There was no one there. She knelt in front of Kelly and smoothed her hair back from her face, then wiped her tears. "Kelly, look at me," she said quietly. "Kelly, I need you to tell me how long you've been playing with Katlin?"

Kelly immediately stopped crying and threw Les's hands off and away from her then she went totally rigid. Les was familiar with that feeling. Kelly's eyes were empty of life as she stared into thin air. Les was familiar with that stare. She shook Kelly and called her name, but she finally had to admit that the little girl she was desperately searching for was gone. This person was *not* Kelly.

The Oyster's Pearl

I find, the irritations of my life,
made me who I've become.
and I've learned that wisdom is a gift.
God has given some.
I've acquired knowledge of the simple things,
and understanding of the hard.
And I've inhaled the scent of unbelief.
ONLY, when I've dropped my guard.
It seems my heart is wearing scars.
Most hidden - - some cut deep.
Yet I know that, where I've sown.
is where I'll also reap.
I'm at the age where, what goes around,
Now stares me in the face,
and, my running to keep up with time,
is slowing down a pace.
In many ways, I know,
looking back on things I've done,
it's not so much what I've gone through.
as it's what I've overcome.
So. . . the oyster takes the sand of life,
the irritations of the world
and, as years pass and time matures,
we become the oyster's pearl.
© By Adele Hewett Veal

CPSIA information can be obtained
at www.ICGtesting.com
Printed in the USA
FSOW01n0921030417
32646FS